SAVIN

By Kim Jones

This book is licensed for your personal enjoyment only. This book may not be re-sold or given away to other people. If you would like to share this book with another person, please purchase an additional copy for each recipient. If you're reading this book and did not purchase it, or it was not purchased for your use only, then please return it to the author and purchase your own copy. Thank you for respecting the hard work of this author.

This is a work of fiction. Names, characters, businesses, organizations, places, events and incidents are either the product of the author's imagination or are used fictitiously. Any resemblance to actual persons, living or dead, events, or locales is entirely coincidental.

Table of Contents

DEDICATION
To my grandmother, for always believing in me.

Everything good in me, I got from you in some way; you wonderfully kind woman-my grandmother-Gloria Mae.

Chapter 1

Sitting alone in a bar, throwing back shots of Jack was not how I pictured my Saturday night. I had managed to wedge myself into a corner of the patio bar where I was shielded by the drop door that led to the bartender's area. My intentions were to get drunk, then make myself available to the first guy who could show me a good time with no strings attached. I was in a three-month slump and was ready to come out of hiding.

My ego had recently been crushed by my previous boyfriend whom, I thought was in love with me -- not that the feeling was mutual, but I thought it ensured his devotion to only me. He was perfect -- great body, good job, fast car – and he was a machine in the bedroom. Come to find out, I was not the only woman under his spell. Catching that skanky bitch from Arby's in his bed, wearing nothing but a smile informed me of everything that I needed to know. I was replaceable.

Being replaced by a five when you are nothing short of a ten can do some major damage to a girl like me. I'm used to getting what I want.

Being five foot four with a body most people only dream of, can get you a lot when it comes to men. Not to mention my long, silky brown locks, my perfect teeth, and a smile that would make the devil himself bow down.

But all of the charm, looks, and money were not enough for Jeff. No, he had to go fuck it up with a fast food worker who drove a Honda.

So for the past three months, I have been sulking, crying, feeling sorry for myself, and praying that a damsel-in-distress moment would come along so Jeff would feel the need to come running to protect and take care of me. It didn't happen. This was the real world, and Jeff was a prick, and I had stooped low enough to come to The Country Tavern to get laid by some lucky bastard.

The urge to pee hit me, and I was grateful for the change of scenery as I motioned to the bartender that I would be back and I came out of my pseudo-hiding spot. The bar had filled up, and the shots had definitely caught up to me. I put on my seductive face and made my way to the restrooms inside the bar. Passing the pool tables and the main bar, I scanned the crowd to look for any potentials, but none of these faces could compare to Jeff's. Scolding myself, I went into the bathroom and did my business.

On my way out, I paused and looked in the mirror at the lovely creature standing before me. "You can do this Dallas," I told myself. I straightened my black Dior minidress, pushed my long soft curls to the front of my shoulders so they fell over my breasts, and flashed myself a smile before sauntering out of the bathroom to accomplish my goal.

I headed back to the patio bar only to find my corner taken by a bunch of bikers. *Great. Just fucking great.* I pushed my way past them, ignoring the lewd comments, and asked the bartender for a Jack and Sprite. He gave me a small apologetic smile. "This one is on me gorgeous," he said as he passed over my drink.

"Thanks," I replied with as much enthusiasm as I could muster. Turning to face the crowd, I realized my chances of getting laid were slim to none if I continued to be surrounded by intimidating bikers, so I strolled over to the opposite side of the bar.

"Hello ma'am."

I turned to see the face of an attractive male sporting a cowboy hat and Wranglers that did amazing things for his package. "Well hello yourself," I replied with my best fuck me smile.

"I must say that you have to be the prettiest thing I've seen in here all night," he said with a southern drawl that had me smiling even wider.

"I was wondering if anyone would notice, or if I was just going to have to drink alone tonight." I could tell he was taking in the sight of my perky D cups as he took my drink, sat it on the bar, and grabbed my hand to lead me onto the dance floor. Dancing with a cowboy does something to a girl. Maybe it's the way they hold you, or the way you feel respected and appreciated. Whatever that feeling is that you get, I didn't have it. This apparently was not a real cowboy. He was offbeat, drunk off his ass, and had hands that wandered over everything except for my waist.

"Whoa, cowboy," I said as we both nearly tripped over several stray bar stools. *What the fuck was up with this guy?*

"What's the matter baby? You don't like my dancing?" He was laughing at someone over my shoulder. I turned to see a group of guys motioning for him to slap my ass and acting like a bunch of drunken frat boys, which they probably were.

Now, there are several things that really piss me off, but at the top of the list is being the butt of a joke. Who the fuck did they think they were? I pushed the prick posing as a cowboy harshly – he didn't even budge.

"Hang on baby, the song ain't even over," he said, moving his hand over my ass.

"Oh, it's over. Get your hands off of me." Angrily, I pushed him again, only to be rewarded with an ass slap. That did it. "Get your fucking hands off of me!" I yelled, pushing his shoulders as hard as I could.

Three things happened next. One: I was flat on my ass, seeing stars as my head bounced off the wooden deck. Two: The massive creature that landed on top of me was being dragged out the side door, along with his shithead friends, by guys in leather vests with reapers on the back. Three: I was looking into the bluest eyes that I had ever seen, and they belonged to a face that instantly made my panties wet. "You okay, babe?" asked a voice should belong to a fucking movie star. I closed my eyes, trying to ease the pounding in my head and gather my thoughts. *What the fuck happened? Who is this beautiful creature leaning over me? Had my damsel in distress moment finally arrived? Was my dress over my waist, showing my goodies to everyone in the bar?*

Strong arms grabbed me and hauled me to my feet. Without even opening my eyes, I knew by the feel of his shoulders he had the sexiest arms that had ever held me. I opened my eyes and held back a gasp. He was perfect. His hair was dirty blonde and cut short. His chest was strong and big. The white thermal he wore under a leather vest, defined his muscles all the way down to his waist. His jeans were slightly torn giving me a view of his leg that let me know this guy worked out -- hard. My gaze slowly moved back up his body, stopping momentarily on his crotch, making me have thoughts of him in my mouth. My eyes finally made it to his face. That face. Strong jaw-line, light blonde stubble, lips that screamed "kiss me," and eyes that were the color of the ocean.

"You like what you see?" he asked while adjusting my dress and keeping a firm hold on my waist. His hands on my body had me clenching my legs together trying to find a release for my aching center. *He asked me a question. What the hell was it again?*

"I'm fine." I replied all breathy like some fucking virgin teenager getting ready to screw the high school quarter back. *Get your shit together, Dallas.*

His face held a smirk as his eyes laughed at me -- taunting me. He was sex in leather, and I didn't care if the way I looked at him made me look like a complete fool, or if he was getting pleasure out of me looking at him like I could take him right here in the bar.

"Well I can see that, but how is your head feeling?" he asked still smirking at me. *Arrogant asshole*. I managed to find my voice and inner bitch. Fueled by too much alcohol, a shitty night, and the fact that I would be going home alone -- again -- *un*-fucked. I responded, "It's fine. Thanks for your help, but I believe I can manage from now on without the help of you and your goon squad." I looked around to see a few guys standing guard behind him, but the rest had disappeared.

Thankfully, the crowd had gotten over the drama and was back to drinking and having a good time; ignoring us completely.

Surprising me, he laughed. *Damn he has a great laugh*. "I'm glad you are feeling better. My goon squad and I will be at the bar if you need anything. Don't worry, your boyfriend still has a few teeth left and I'm sure tomorrow morning he will be calling to beg for your forgiveness."

"He's *not* my boyfriend." *Why was I getting so defensive?*

"Could have fooled me, or do you normally let strangers fondle you in public? If so, maybe me and my goon squad, as you call them, can get in on the action." He was laughing at me. This sexy beast towering over me was making an ass out of me.

"For your information, I did not allow him to do anything. I asked him to stop several times. If I had plans to get fondled tonight by someone, he would definitely not live up to my standards." *Liar.*

"So, do I live up to your standards? Miss...?"

"Dallas, my name is Dallas, and no, you do not. Biker trash isn't on my to-do list tonight."

"Dallas, what an interesting name you have. And I could have sworn the way you were looking at me all "fuck me" like, that I was most definitely on your "to-do" list, as you say."

Shit. I was at a loss for words. Probably because his hands were still securely on each side of my waist and the throbbing between my legs had only intensified over the past few minutes. Instead of coming back with a comment that would leave him shocked and wanting more, I did something that I never do. I walked away. Well, I tried to walk away. I removed his hands, which let go of me easily causing disappointment to my groin area, and turned around to see the floor coming up to my face before those big strong arms were around me again.

"Slow down babe. I think you might have a mild concussion."

That's all it took. I was putty in his arms. I had prayed for a damsel-in-distress moment, and God had given it to me. It wasn't Jeff, but it was something so much better. Who cares that he rode a motorcycle, and was probably working as a mechanic while out on parole? I came here for something and I was going to get it, and if this biker bad boy wanted to give it to me I would gladly take it and regret it tomorrow.

The pounding in my head was loud. And hurt -- a lot. Mixed with the laughter and loud music, it was too much.

"I think I need some fresh air," I said barely audible. Somehow, my knight in shining leather heard me, and led me out the same door he had tossed the guys out of only minutes before. I silently prayed they were gone. No such luck.

"There's that fucking bitch!" I looked up to find us surrounded by all six of them. The cowboy was leaning on the tailgate of a truck holding a shirt soaked in blood to his mouth. Panic filled me, and I started to shudder.

"Don't worry babe, having a goon squad has its perks," he said smiling without a hint of worry on his face. "How about you sit here?" he said calmly, leading me back inside to a chair behind the karaoke stage. "I'll be right back. Don't move." He winked to the red headed girl running karaoke and she gave him a knowing nod. *What the hell was that about?* I watched him walk back outside and found myself worrying over a man whose name I didn't even know.

"Would you like a drink?" the tall red headed girl asked. She wore a bright yellow t-shirt with Queen of Karaoke inscribed on the front. Her hair was long and straight and she had big brown eyes lined in black eye liner. I couldn't help but wonder if her long lashes were real or not. I started to ask her when she spoke. "I'm Red, how about I get you some water and aspirin. It will probably help that headache that I'm sure you have. You took a nasty fall."

"Thanks that would be great." I couldn't keep my hands from shaking. I kept glancing at the door hoping he would walk back through it, unharmed.

"Here ya go." Red handed me the two pills and a cup of ice water. "Luke is a really great guy. If you break his heart, I'll fuck you up," she said matter-of-fact. And I believed her. She didn't look like the type you would want to piss off or the type that would tell you a lie just because it sounded good.

"I don't even know his name." Red looked at me with an impassive face and lifted the microphone, never taking her eyes off of me.

"And next up we have Jud. Bring your sexy ass up here and sing me a song, big daddy." She put the mic down still staring at me. This bitch was starting to freak me out. "I don't know where this is going or if it's anything, but I swore the next bitch that broke his heart would eat through a straw for a week. You look like the heartbreaking kind. I've watched you in here all night. I know you came looking for something and I hope you get it. If Luke is the one to give it to you then you are one lucky girl. But, just remember, you fuck him over - I'm gonna fuck you up." She gave me a smile with no warmth in it and handed the mic to Jud with a wink.

"You're wrong," I said. "Look, I just came to have a good time. I didn't ask for any of this. I appreciate Luke's help, but look where it has gotten him."

She smiled and patted my shoulder, "Don't worry about him, he will be just fine." As if on cue the side door opened and relief rushed over me as I made eye contact with Luke. He was still perfect - nothing out of place.

"Thanks, Red. Tomorrow night?" he asked as he grabbed my hand to pull me up.

"Wouldn't miss it," she said with a smile and a look that made me think they had a history together.

"Come on, babe. Let's get you somewhere a little quieter." Luke opened the door and led me out into the fresh air.

The guys were gone. No sign of the goon squad either. Had they just disappeared into thin air? Knowing I should stop this charade now and head home, I turned to tell Luke I was leaving when he suddenly picked me up, and carried me across the parking lot. I didn't protest. I could feel his muscles flexing against my side. The smell of him, even clouded by cigarette smoke, was so intoxicating I found myself leaning into him and inhaling his scent. He smiled down at me but didn't say anything. Thank God. I was already blushing from being caught. One smart ass remark would have been enough to ruin my night. *Hadn't I embarrassed myself enough?*

We came upon a white Ford F-250, and he opened the passenger side door and sat me inside. I noticed he did not even put me down to open the door. Was it because he didn't want to let go of me? Not that it mattered- this was just a one night stand. He took off his leather vest that was covered in patches, and climbed into the driver seat.

"So, are you gonna tell me your name, or should I just call you whatever I want?" I asked trying to strike up a conversation. This guy didn't talk a lot. I liked that.

"You already know my name." *How did he know that?* "I know that because I left you with Red, and knowing Red she gave you the third degree. Surely, she also said my name," he said smiling adoringly.

"She seems nice enough. You speak fondly of her. Is she your girlfriend?" I held my breath waiting for his answer. Again, he surprised me by laughing.

"I wish. Although, I would never let her go if I had her. She is married. Happily, she claims. She has been my best friend for a long time. She is my confidante -- my rock, the one who takes care of me when I'm down."

"While you are out taking care of other women in need," I said with a small smile playing on my lips. He didn't answer. Instead, he reached over and lifted the console separating the two of us.

"We have about a thirty minute drive ahead of us. You're welcome to lay your head in my lap and take a nap. I don't think you're supposed to sleep with a concussion, but I don't see what staying awake will do for you."

I wanted to scream at him. I wanted to tell him to kiss my ass. I was *not* laying my head in his lap. I wanted to tell him that I had not agreed to go anywhere with him, and to take me back to my car. But surprising myself for the second time tonight, I did something I never do. I trusted this complete stranger to take care of me. My head was pounding, so his offer was more than appealing. I scooted across the seat and laid my head in his lap.

Closing my eyes, I tried to make sense of what I was doing but nothing made sense, so I stopped trying. I felt his hand brush the hair off the front of my face and run down my arm and back up again. It felt so good to be touched after so long. Even if it was for just one night, I was going to enjoy every moment of it. I drifted off to sleep, and for the first time in three months, Jeff's face was not the one that I dreamed of.

CHAPTER 2

"Wake up, darling." The endearment caused butterflies to form in my stomach even before I opened my eyes. "I'm gonna carry you inside, okay?"

I was sure I could walk but not really wanting to-I nodded my head and sat up trying to pull down my dress that had ridden up my hips. Clearly not doing a very good job of covering myself, Luke laughed softly reaching his hands up my legs to pull my dress back down. It felt so much better when he did it anyway.

"There, now you're all covered up and I can't see you," he said smiling at me and making my heart of stone melt. He scooped me into his arms and led me inside what I assumed was his house. We entered through the kitchen and he sat me on the counter. "Don't move and don't fall. I'll be right back." He said with a smirk before disappearing from the room.

I looked around the small kitchen and noticed that even though it was not very large in size, it was nicely decorated and clean. Granite countertops, stainless steel appliances, and deep mahogany hard wood floors scattered with rugs made it feel like a home. I could hear Luke throughout the house. I was just about to hop down and go find him when he came through the door.

"Oh no, you don't," he said walking up to me causing my mouth to go dry. He really was beautiful. "If you fell and hurt yourself, you would mess up my plans, and I have something great in store for you."

I once had this friend named Leigh Ann and every time she saw a good looking guy she would say, "Oh! He makes my liver quiver!" Well, my liver was quivering. "What kind of plans?" I asked trying to sound flirty and failing miserably.

"Well, I know you are tired. You have had a rough night so I thought I would run you a bath and let you sleep in my comfortable king sized bed."

"Well, what are you waiting for?" I asked attempting to mirror his smirk.

He stepped in between my legs causing my dress to ride up. Before I could protest, he had my legs wrapped around his waist and was holding me by my bare ass, carrying me to the bathroom. Not letting me go and not taking his eyes off mine, he leaned down and turned on the water. Breaking the silence he asked, "Do you need a minute?" Setting me on the toilet, the urge hit me and I nodded silently, cursing my bladder for being the reason he had to let me go. He adjusted the water then turned and walked out.

Relieving myself, I stood up and glanced in the mirror. *Holy- shit.* I looked like hammered hell. My eyes were puffy and bloodshot. My hair was a tangled mess, and although the pain had dulled, standing on my own caused me to get a little dizzy, so I held onto the counter.

"It's a common side effect when you hit your head," Luke said, gazing at me from the door. I turned to notice he had taken off his shirt. For some reason, the pain in my head immediately subsided. If Luke looked good in clothes, he looked amazing without them. Tattoos covered his arms from his shoulders to his wrists and his chest was perfectly sculpted and tanned. His abs were flawless and his jeans hung low on his waist showing off the V that formed at his lower abdomen.

"Never seen a half-naked man?" he asked slightly amused at my expression.

"Not like you," was all I could manage to say, and it was the truth. Luke was the epitome of sexy. My eyes were glued to the panty dropping smile on his lips.

"Let me help you," He said taking a step towards me.

"I can do it." I said suddenly feeling a little self-conscious about myself. I was usually so confident, but I was intimidated by him and that made me uneasy.

"Dallas, I promise not to take advantage of you or make you feel uncomfortable. You have had a bad night. I just want to help. I'm afraid if I leave you, you might fall." *How sweet he was. I liked sweet biker boy. Hadn't he been sweet to me all night?*

"Okay," I said quickly before I could change my mind. I would never see him again anyway. He walked over to me and wrapped his hands around my waist and once more lifted me onto the counter. I was beginning to enjoy the way he carried and lifted me as if I weighed nothing. He knelt down in front of me, grabbing my Jimmy Choo's and pulling them off one at a time.

"I have a thing for heels," he said smiling up at me. I momentarily stopped breathing as his hands rubbed my feet that I didn't even know were sore until a soft moan escaped my lips, letting him know how good it felt. He continued massaging each of my feet while on his knees in front of me. The sight of him, bad boy biker, kneeling in front of me rubbing my feet made me tingle with excitement. Far too soon he stopped and stood, bringing his face inches from mine.

Breathing a little heavier now he said, "Raise your arms." I hardly recognized his voice. Knowing I had an effect on him almost sent me over the edge. I slid my dress up over my hips then raised my arms above my head. The heated look in his eyes let me know that he wanted me just as bad as I wanted him. He grabbed the end of my dress and pulled it over my head slowly, never taking those ocean blue eyes off of mine. He folded my dress and sat it on the counter beside me, then grabbing my waist helped to steady me as I stood in front of him.

"Do you know how beautiful you are Dallas?"

"Yes," I breathed like an idiot. *Why had I said that?* Yeah I was sure of myself but now was not the time to be such a bitch. He rewarded me with laughter instead of calling me a self-centered bitch, which made me smile.

"I thought you did. This is the first time I have seen you really smile tonight. I must say that you, Dallas, have the most amazing smile I have ever seen. You look like Christmas morning."

Wow. Had anyone ever said anything like that to me before? No. And for some reason coming from him it meant so much more. This guy, this un-believably sexy guy, thinks *my* smile looks like Christmas morning. I smiled even wider. My all – American- girl smile that had been my key to success, my ticket to drive any man crazy, and the only thing that mattered to me was that *he* liked it.

Shaking his head, as if he was trying to clear his head, he returned to the task at hand. Here I was, standing in his bathroom only inches from him in my lacy black bra and matching thong, and all I wanted was for him to strip me and fuck me right here on this bathroom floor. He looped his thumbs under the thin lace of my panties and slowly slid them down my legs, and like a perfect gentlemen, held his hand up to me to hold while I stepped out of them. Standing, he threw my soaked panties on top of my dress and reached around behind me to unclasp my bra. I could smell the faint scent of his cologne as he leaned over me causing my face to be level with his chest. *Why did he have to smell so fucking good?* He took my bra and laid it with my other clothes and I noticed that ever since I had become naked, he had not once let his eyes leave mine.

Was he afraid to look at me? Answering my unspoken question he said, "I promised not to make you feel uncomfortable, and I won't. I have seen many beautiful women, but you, Miss Dallas, are perfect and I'll be damned if I let my eyes wander over something I can't have- at least not tonight." The sincerity of his gaze had me hanging my mouth open like an idiot. *Why not tonight? There would not be a tomorrow. Would there?*

"What's wrong with tonight?" I asked, kicking myself for opening my big fat mouth. I could really ruin a moment.

"How about you get a bath?" Without another word, he leaned over, shut off the water, and helped me step in. I let out a sigh as I sank down in the hot water. It was perfect. The bathtub was actually a Jacuzzi tub. The small pillow at the back fit perfectly under my head as I stretched my legs out and let the jets massage my body. The water was perfumed with pomegranate and the sides of the tub were lined with many different shampoos and body washes.

"It's nice to see someone enjoying that tub." His voice broke through my cloudy thoughts. *How had I forgotten he was even there?* "I hardly ever have time to use it. Let me know when you are finished and I'll help you get out." With that, he left. *How strange. I thought he would join me.*

Too tired to think, I washed my hair, wincing when my fingers found the sore spot on the back of my head. I took the wash cloth that was folded neatly on the side of the tub and washed my body, noticing for the first time my bruised ass and elbows. The excitement of the night had kept me from noticing, but as the adrenaline was wearing off, I was becoming aware of the pain my body was in. I didn't realize how bad of a fall I had taken. I leaned back into the water letting the sound of the jets soothe me.

"You are gonna be mighty wrinkly if you sleep in that bathtub all night."

I jumped at the sound of Luke's voice. "I must have fallen asleep," I replied, shivering from the water that was now cool.

He chuckled, "Here I warmed you a towel in the dryer. I figured you would be cold by now, but I didn't want to disturb you." *Was this guy for real?*

"Thanks." I seemed to be saying that a lot tonight. He grabbed my hand to help me up and pain shot all the way down to my toes. My head was throbbing and my ass felt like someone had beaten me with a crowbar.

"Steady babe. Are you okay?" he asked with concern on his face.

"It if I put any weight on my left leg," I said holding onto his hands for balance. "I think I bruised my tail bone when I fell." Without any further question, he scooped me into his arms, soaking wet, and carried me into the bedroom. Setting me on the bed, he quickly went back to the bathroom to retrieve the towels. He covered me with one towel and gently began patting my hair dry with the other.

I'm a strong person. I can tolerate pain and I hate to show any sign of weakness. I had already allowed this man to carry me everywhere, undress me, put me in the bathtub, and wait on me hand and foot. I'm not sure why I decided to break down at that moment. Maybe it was the enormity of everything that had happened today. Maybe it was the loneliness I had felt for so long. Maybe it was the sexual craving that I had earlier that had now turned into a yearning for intimacy. Whatever it was caused me to start crying, which soon turned into sobbing.

"Shh, Baby. It's okay. Look at me." I raised my head to find him eye level with me with concern etched all over his face. "You are safe. I am not gonna let anyone hurt you or anything happen to you. I'm gonna dry you off now, put you in some of my clothes and put you to bed. You will feel better once you have had some decent sleep."

Deciding not to correct him by letting him know it was not my safety I feared for, and that I had handled guys like the cowboy prick before, I just nodded. Through my tears, I could just make out his face. I could tell that it pleased him to do something for me and have control of the situation. That was fine by me. I had been strong for too long and if I was gonna fall apart, at least it would be at the hands of a stranger that I wouldn't have to see again.

Luke dried my hair as gently as possible and then dried the front of my body. He helped me to stand on my one good leg and never letting his arm leave my waist, he dried my back and then my butt, pausing to skim his fingers over what I assumed was now a bruise. He softly ran the towel between my legs, drying me as quickly as possible, then moving on to my legs and feet. He took a black t-shirt that was on the bed and slid it over my head paying careful attention not to let it touch me.

Still holding me by the waist, he slid the covers back and helped me to sit. Holding out the two little brown pills in his hand, he handed me a glass of water. I took the pills and drank the whole glass.

"That's better," he smiled at me making my heart clench. Most of my tears had subsided and I was beginning to feel better. He leaned down and kissed my forehead. "I'll be in the next room if you need me." I couldn't help the disappointed look that crossed my face or the fact that hearing those words caused more tears to fall.

Suddenly looking panicked, he placed both hands on the side of my face. "I'm sorry, babe. I didn't mean to upset you. It's just that you have had a long day and I thought you might want to be alone. I'll stay. Lie down and let me hold you." Before he could change his mind, I put my legs under the covers, wincing as I slid down under them. "I'm gonna grab some sweats. I'll be right back."

He walked out of the room and I was immediately lonely. I wanted to call out to him to come back but caught myself. *No need to make a bigger ass of yourself, Dallas*. He returned less than a minute later wearing a pair of black sweats. He should really be a model for Calvin Klein. He turned the light off and slid in behind me, wrapping his arm around my waist and pulling my back towards him. My shuddering stopped the minute he kissed my hair and whispered in my ear. "I'm sorry about what happened today. I can't tell you what will happen in the future, but tonight, you can rest easy. As long as you are in my arms I will not let anyone hurt you."

He slid his hand under my shirt and splayed it across my stomach. The rubbing of his thumb back and forth across my skin, his promised words in my ear, and his strong arms holding me tight was enough to set my mind at ease. I closed my eyes and drifted but not before hearing him whisper in my ear, "Sleep *my* beautiful girl." *His*?

I woke the next morning to find myself alone. It took a minute to figure out where I was. Outside the window I could hear talking and laughing but the closed blinds didn't allow me to see who was there. Looking around the room, I noticed it was just as nicely decorated and clean as the kitchen. The king sized bed was centered in front of a large plasma T.V., mounted above an oak dresser. There were nightstands on each side of the bed with matching lamps and a chaise lounge in the corner that was covered in throws, making the room look cozy and warm.

I got out of the bed feeling energized and alert. The pain in my head was barely noticeable, and the pain in my leg was completely gone. I went to the bathroom, freshened up, pulled my hair back, and then started rummaging through the drawers to find something to put on. I managed to find a pair of grey sweats and socks, which would have to suffice since I only had heels. Voices from the kitchen reminded me that I was not alone and I was going to have to face Mr. Beautiful, looking like a train wreck. I tried my best to smile and seem at ease as I walked towards the kitchen. I had not expected to see a room full of women when I walked in.

"Well, I'll be damned. The princess can walk on her own." My eyes settled on a leggy blonde who held a glass of soda in one hand and an unlit cigarette in the other. She wore a bright orange t-shirt that said "Do Me" in bold letters with black leggings and boots. Her face was pretty, with big blue eyes and lips covered in red gloss. Her bobbed hair was slightly teased and laid perfectly with not a strand out of place. I recognized Red from the bar, propped up against the counter with a huge smile plastered on her face. The other two women, who could have been twins, were staring holes through me like I had offended them just by walking in the room. You could tell by just looking at all of them that they belonged on the back of a motorcycle. They appeared rough around the edges, but classy in their own way.

"Let's go smoke," the blonde said letting herself out the kitchen door that led to the carport. The twins followed, leaving me standing like a fool, watching them go.

"Honey, that bitch is gonna rip you apart unless you grow some balls," Red said smiling over at me.

"Good Morning, Red. It's nice to see you too." Her head fell back and she laughed so hard I couldn't help but laugh too, not really knowing what was so funny.

"Luke will be in shortly. Make yourself at home," she said then disappeared out the kitchen door to join the others. I was left standing in the kitchen alone once again. I fixed a glass of orange juice and tried to recap all that had happened since last night.

Here I was, in the house of a complete stranger, being laughed at by what appeared to be an ex. *Who did she think she was? He invited* me *over here. He slept with* me *last night. It was* me *who he had given his undivided attention to, and I would be damned before some bitch said something to try and make me feel like shit about it.*

I wanted to see Luke. I wanted him to hold me like he held me last night. I didn't want this to be a one night stand and I knew it, but first I was going to have to put that bitch in her place. I placed my glass on the counter and opened the door, prepared to brawl if need be when I looked up into the eyes of Luke.

"Leaving already?" he asked flashing me his winning smile. It took my breath away. I stood speechless, staring at him in his ripped faded jeans and black T-shirt. *How had I slept in bed with this man and not taken advantage of him?* He was the sexiest man that I had ever seen. His arms bulged from his shirt and his smell was so intoxicating, I swayed at the scent of him.

"I'm fine," I replied breathlessly.

"That I'm aware of gorgeous, but where are you going?" he asked smiling.

I took a deep breath and gathered my wits. I didn't want to mention that my plans were to put Blondie in her place so I just smiled and said, "I was actually coming to find you. Did I leave my clutch in your truck?"

"No, you must have left it at the bar. Red brought it in with her. It's on the table. Hungry?"

"Starving," I replied stepping back and letting him in. "I have to go to town in a few. Maybe we can grab something to eat?"

"I'd love that," I said a little too quickly.

He smiled, "I just have to grab a few things. I'll meet you at the truck." He turned, walking toward a part of the house I had yet to explore. I went back to the bathroom to gather my things, stopping long enough to make the bed, and headed back out to the garage. I had forgotten about the bitch crew, but was quickly reminded when I stepped into what appeared to be a gossip circle where I was the topic of conversation.

"Dallas!" Red said, smiling brightly as always at me. "I'm sorry I didn't introduce you earlier. This is Maddie," she said pointing to the blonde I was growing to hate, "and Monica and Jennifer."

"How nice to meet y'all. Sorry we got off to a bad start. I'm Dallas, the princess bitch that was cared for and pampered by Luke last night." I said looking directly at Maddie who looked like she had been slapped in the face. Red busted out laughing, and before Maddie had a chance to retaliate Luke walked out saying his goodbyes. Perfect timing.

"Well ladies, as always, I hate to leave great company, but I must get going. Make yourselves at home." He walked over to Red, planting a peck on her lips and giving hugs to the others. Seeing him kiss Red did nothing to me, but when Maddie wrapped her arms around his waist and buried her face in his neck, I almost lost it. She shot me a "go fuck yourself" look, but made sure to shield it from Luke. He grabbed my hand after hugging everyone goodbye and led me to the truck. Opening the door for me, he made sure I was in and settled before walking around to get in, giving me just enough time to flip Maddie the finger before he came into eye range. Feeling satisfied, and much like a Jr. High drama queen, I smiled with contentment as we pulled from the driveway and headed out.

Chapter 3

The front of Luke's house appeared to be a lot larger on the outside than what it was on the inside. It was beautiful, made of wood that gave it a log cabin look. The yard was landscaped perfectly and I could see what I thought was a shop in the back. The driveway was concrete, but the road we pulled out on was dirt and lined with large pines all the way down as far as I could see. Where his house stood, about a half- acre, was the only area that was not covered in trees.

"This place is amazing," I said, mostly to myself.

"Thank you. I have two hundred acres of seclusion right by myself. I built it myself too, from the ground up. I even cut and cleared the timber with a little help from some heavy machinery," he said with a sense of pride in his voice that I couldn't help but admire.

"You should be very proud. That's a great accomplishment."

"Enough about me, tell me a little about you," he said to me, wearing that sexy smile and looking me over like it was the first time he noticed what I was wearing.

"I borrowed some of your clothes, I hope you don't mind," I said, feeling a little embarrassed.

"They look much better on you than they do on me."
We had finally reached the end of the road and he pulled onto the highway heading north.

"So, where are we exactly?" I asked, once again avoiding the subject of me.

"South of Hattiesburg, just on the Forrest County line."

"Have you lived here all your life?" I asked, trying to keep the conversation away from me. He let out a light laugh.

"I know what you're doing Dallas and it's not going to work. Tell me about the woman who is responsible for this smile on my face." He said, pointing at the face that I had become so infatuated with.

"There's really not a lot to tell," I said, turning to look out the window. I didn't like feeling exposed. I didn't want to open up and get too close to this man when I had no idea how long this, whatever this was, was going to last.

"I don't believe you. Tell me. I would really like to know you better." The sincerity in his voice and face instantly put me at ease.

"I was born in Atlanta, Georgia to Herman and Kay Knox. My father was a real estate investor and my mother ran a clothing boutique downtown." I smiled to myself, remembering how graceful she looked sashaying from one customer to the next. "She would always let me sit in a chair facing the dressing room, applauding the ladies that came out in an elegant evening gown or cocktail dress. She had such a way with fashion. My dad always wanted her to take it further. He even offered to open up her very own exclusive line, but she said her happiness was right there, in that little boutique she had dreamed of having since she was a child. I can still see my dad walking in there, sweeping her off her feet and kissing her like they were sixteen again. I don't think love like that exists anymore," I said, my eyes glossing over at the memories. The aching I felt in my chest was heavy. It had never ceased. Even after all these years the pain was still there.

"What happened to them?" Luke asked, breaking me from my thoughts.

"My mother was closing late one night. There was a charity ball that weekend and most of the locals shopped there, so she had been pretty busy all evening. I was in Panama City with some of my girlfriends for spring break, so she was alone. A group of men were later seen leaving the store on foot. She had been shot and killed. The police wrote it off as a robbery, but my father knew better. Most of her customers used a charge account and only a small amount of money was taken. After that, my father spent weeks trying to solve the mystery. He kept saying that it was an inside job. I never knew what that meant and I never asked because he had distanced himself completely from me. Six months later, he was found dead in his office. The autopsy revealed it was the result of a brain aneurism, but I think it was a broken heart."

Luke reached over, grabbing my hand and bringing it to his lips. He didn't say anything; he just held my hand and let me cry. I had never opened up to anyone like this before. I knew in that moment, that I felt something for this man.

"After that I moved to Mississippi to live with my grandmother in Collins. I left everything; my friends, my life, my hopes and dreams. I was seventeen and I had nothing. My grandmother did the best that she could to raise me, but at nineteen, I lost her too. So, I got my shit together, went to college, got a degree in business, and took after my father investing in real estate. That's it. Now you know more about me than anyone I've ever met," I said, my tears subsided and my impassive face back intact.

"I want to know everything about you. I have somewhere I have to be tonight but I would love it if you would join me," he said, looking at me in that way that melted my heart.

"I'd love to, but you have to feed me first," I said smiling at him.

He laughed, picked my hand up and kissed my fingers once again, "For you, Miss Dallas, anything."

We pulled up outside of a run-down building just off the highway. The outside was painted blue with Christmas lights strung from one end to the other, even though it was September. Beer signs covered the front, helping to hide the wear and tear of the structure. A huge sign stretched across the top giving the place the name, Donnelley's.

"Don't judge the quality by the outside. This place has the best steak around," Luke stated, pulling the truck up to the front door.

"I don't have any shoes," I said, even though by the looks of this place they were not rendered necessary. I was hoping my lack of proper attire would be enough to convince him of a drive thru rather than the outlandish place he had brought me too.

"Do you really think that I would take you out looking the way you do in public? I ordered out," he said winking at me and letting me know that he was joking. I sighed in relief, which must have been obvious because he laughed as he got out of the truck and walked inside giving me a view of his great ass.

Bored, I turned the volume up on the radio and found it was tuned to a country station. Funny, I placed him in the hard rock genre, definitely not country. And not only was it country, but it was classic country. I often listened to that myself. Merle Haggard was singing about the good times being over and I sang along with him word for word. My concert came to an end when Luke appeared carrying a large brown sack that smelled so good it had my mouth watering.

"I hope you don't mind, but I just ordered you what I always get. I promise that you won't be disappointed."

I had not realized until that moment how hungry I was. It took a tremendous amount of will power to keep me from digging in like a savage.

"Well, it smells wonderful," I said with a smile.

"So, where do you live babe? I figured we could take this picnic to your place. Unless you have a boyfriend you're hiding there," he said without looking at me.

"The only man in my life goes by the name of Neo. He's a seven year old black lab who loves me unconditionally, no matter what," I replied. "And to answer your other question, I live on the Flemming Plantation. It's off of highway ninety-eight."

"Are you serious?" he asked, looking at me like I had lost my mind.

"Yes, I'm serious and don't go telling me that I'm crazy." I knew what it must look like. After the massacre in 1993 where all four family members were brutally murdered by the wife's secret lover, the plantation was put on the market, but never sold. A small real-estate company bought the plantation in hopes of selling it off piece by piece. They were only able to sell the acreage that surrounded it leaving the ten gated acres along with the house and barn, where the family was found dead, to be overgrown and neglected. I bought out the company about two years ago and have since restored the magnificent house to its former glory.

"I wasn't going to say you were crazy. It just surprised me that you would own something with such a tragic history," he said, still looking at me like I had lost my mind.

"Well, I think it's a lovely place and when I purchased the company, the house came as a bonus. When I went to look at it, I couldn't help but feel like it was a part of me. If it makes you feel any better, I only learned of the tragedy after I decided to keep the house," I said defensively.

"I'm sorry if I offended you. If it's a part of you then I'm sure it's amazing," he said, smiling and knocking down my protective walls once again.

"I'd really like to get my car first, and then you can just follow me out there."

"You don't need your car," he said with finality in his tone that let me know the subject was not negotiable.

"Yes, I do," I replied. Not wanting him to think he had complete control over me, although I knew he did.

"No, you don't. I'll get someone to bring it to your house later. You already agreed to be with me this evening anyway."

"I don't want someone that I don't know driving my car and coming to my house," I said, getting more than a little aggravated at his proposition.

"Do you not trust me, babe?" he asked, giving me a daring look. "Well, I really don't even know you," I snapped back at him. *Where had that come from?*

"Well, we'll just have to work on that, now won't we?" he said, never letting his eyes leave the road.

I didn't argue. I had agreed to join him this evening and just the thought of not seeing him caused my heart to ache. So, if that meant giving a complete stranger access to my car and home, then it was a risk I was willing to take, because I did trust him. I just didn't want him to know how much. Not yet, anyway.

We drove the rest of the way in complete silence. Luke never asked for directions. He knew exactly where we were going, which wasn't uncommon considering the history of the place. We pulled up to the gate and I gave him the key code to let us in. Not wanting to ruin the rest of our evening, I turned to face him.

"I'm sorry I snapped at you. I'm just use to always being in control. I do trust you," I admitted.

"It's cool, babe. I'm sorry, too. I just assume responsibility and control over everything. It's my nature. I'll try to be a little more lenient in the future," he said with a heartwarming smile that made my chest swell. "Wow, this place looks amazing," he said looking out at the property.

Most of the property had been cleared of any trees giving a full view from just inside the gate. The left side looked like an open field which ran all the way to the tree line adjoining the neighbor's property. The massive black wrought iron gate stood tall all along the edge of the field. The grass was a lush green color and cut short. The right side, where the paved driveway curved around, was landscaped with seasonal flowers and shrubs. A stone garden patio equipped with a fire pit, swing and small fountain sat near the fence. It was slightly hidden from view by crape myrtle trees giving it a secret garden feel. The house loomed big before us. The red brick was slightly faded and the weathered shutters gave it an old look. We pulled under the open carport at the back of the house and Luke's eyebrows shot up at the sight of the old Ford pickup truck parked next to us.

"To haul things with," I said. He still looked at me quizzically, not fully convinced. "Seed, mulch, fertilizer, the dog... Did you think I would put that stuff in my *car*?"

"You just don't appear to be the type that would do all this on your own," he said, almost like a question. I could tell he was trying not to offend me.

I laughed. "Yeah? Well you don't seem much like the hard core biker type either. I'm not even fully convinced you are a biker. Don't they usually ride motorcycles?"

"True," he replied, laughing with me, but not elaborating further. We got out and were immediately greeted by Neo.

"Hey, big boy!" I said, patting his head and allowing him to jump all over me. He soon left me to go sniff out Luke. Traitor. I got my things out of the truck, digging the keys out of my clutch to unlock the door. As soon as I walked in, I closed my eyes and inhaled the scent of the room. It was covered wall to wall in old books. It had originally been a library and when I bought the house, I couldn't change it. The only piece of furniture was an old couch that sat in the corner and swallowed you when you sat on it. The overstuffed cushions were a tan color and homemade quilts and pillows were piled high all over it.

"I spend a lot of time in here," I said to Luke when he made his way inside. Neo had gotten bored with him too and was now inside exploring. I was sure that I would find him asleep on the couch by the time we made it to the living room. "Most of the books were already here when I moved in. I added a couple hundred more from my own collection," I said, not being able to contain the smile that formed on my face every time I looked at it.

"I can see this room makes you happy," Luke said with a low voice that caused me to turn and look at him. Before I knew what was happening, I was in his arms. One of his hands held the back of my neck, while the other lifted my chin. We were so close that I could feel his heart beating through his shirt. Then his lips were on mine. His tongue invaded my mouth, kissing me roughly. The taste of him was overwhelming. The smell of him was intoxicating. I fell limp in his arms allowing my hands to slowly explore all over his chest and arms. He deepened the kiss, stroking his tongue over and over mine. *Man, this guy knows how to kiss.* My nipples betrayed me by hardening through my shirt and the sheer pleasure I got from them rubbing against his chest made me moan into his mouth making him kiss me harder. I could feel him hardening through his worn jeans, and at that moment all I wanted was him. He must not have wanted the same thing. He pulled away from my body, but still held my face as he planted sweet tender kisses on my mouth.

"Let's eat," he announced. Leaning down, he grabbed the bag of food and headed toward the kitchen leaving me standing there breathless. I walked into the kitchen to find him staring up at my collection of champagne flute sets above the cabinets. "Celebrating something?" he asked with a tone in his voice I couldn't recognize. *Jealousy, maybe?*

"The New Year. It's a tradition. Every New Year's Eve, I set my alarm clock to wake up just in time to have a glass of champagne to ring in the New Year," I said, feeling stupid for sharing the fact that I was such a loser that I sat at home on New Year's Eve alone.

"But there are two in each set you have," he said, matter-of-fact.

"You ever tried buying a set of one?" I asked getting defensive once again. *What did it matter to him anyway?*

"So let me get this straight," he said setting the food out on the bar while I got some plates out of the cabinet. "You have stayed at home every year for the past six years, alone, and drank champagne at approximately midnight to ring in the New Year?"

"Correct," I replied while rummaging through the fridge in an attempt to find something to drink.

"Hmmm, ok," he replied tersely.

I decided to drop the subject and not over think his comment. *What the hell was wrong with me?* Since when did I want to avoid confrontation? The thought was disturbing, but I pushed it back, afraid that if I thought too much on it, I would be scared of the conclusion.

"How about we eat and then I'll take you on the grand tour," I said hoping to deter him from the subject.

"Sounds great," he said, taking a seat at the bar.

I grabbed the plates, silverware and two bottles of water before joining him. The food was delicious. The steak was cooked to perfection and the still warm, loaded baked potato was everything a carb should be. We ate in silence- probably both trying to figure out what in the hell we were doing, and how we had gotten ourselves where we are now. It seemed we didn't have a lot to talk about. Mostly because he knew everything about me and I knew nothing about him. I knew what it was like to be hounded for information you didn't want to freely give, and I was not going to put him in that position. I figured if and when he wanted me to know something about him, he would tell me.

Right now I was content with knowing that he was sexy as hell, could kiss better than any man I knew, and wanted to spend another day with me. I stole a glance at him while he drained the last of his water and noted how his throat moved when he swallowed. Shit, he was even sexy when he ate. I was suddenly not hungry anymore for food. All I wanted was him to bend me over, right here on this bar, and fuck me.

"What are you thinking about?" he asked, ruining my day dream and bringing me back to the real world.

"You ready for that tour?" I asked, blushing in response. He smiled at me, showing off his perfect teeth and making my mouth water.

"Absolutely."

Chapter 4

Even though I lived here and saw it every day, I couldn't help my excitement as I grabbed his hand and led him to the back of the house starting with the guest bedroom that was once the room of the children that lived there.

"I left this room just as it was. Not to make it a shrine or anything, but I felt the family would have appreciated it. It belonged to the children, Jessie and Katie. From the stories that I have been told, the children who were only a year apart, were inseparable. They were only seven and eight years old when they died." The melancholy in my voice must have been obvious.

"Well, I think you did the right thing," Luke said giving my hand a sympathetic squeeze. I realized at that moment that I had not let him go since we left the kitchen. We spent a minute, standing in silence just looking at the room. The two twin canopy beds were separated by a single table with a lamp. A pair of matching dressers sat on the wall facing the beds. A blue painted toy box sat next to a small desk and chair with drawing paper and pens.

"I hate the colors of the walls," I said breaking us both from our reverie. "I think it's too dark.

Maybe I'll repaint it a lighter blue one day." Not wanting to dampen the mood, I pulled him out of the room and across the hall to my bedroom. "And this," I said opening my door and dancing into my bedroom. "Is where the magic happens." It had taken me months to finish this room.

The house was older so all the walls were covered in brown paneling. I stripped it all out, replacing it with sheetrock and painting it a deep mauve. It had sliding glass patio doors leading out to the pool. The bed was a custom made, California King Size, mahogany hard wood sleigh bed with a four-inch memory foam that gave you the impression of sleeping on clouds.

There was no artwork on the walls because in the two years that I had lived here, I had never been able to make up my mind on exactly what it was that I wanted. "And the bathroom here has the most amazing shower..." I trailed off. Luke was staring at me with a dubious look on his face. "What?" I asked, totally confused.

"Magic?" he asked me, in a way that made me feel like there was no right answer.

"What are you talking about?" I asked, noticing for the first time the darkness in his eyes.

"You said this was where the magic happens. I thought you weren't in a relationship," he said piercing me with his darkened stare.

"I'm not, Luke. I was just joking. I guess it was a figure of speech?" I said not even convincing myself.

"Do you make a habit out of bringing strangers to your house, only to ridicule them by leading them on, and then suggesting that you make 'magic' happen in a bedroom that you sleep in every night?"

Whoa... What the hell had happened to him? "No, Luke I didn't mean it that way."

"Well, just what in the hell did you mean, Dallas?" he snapped at me, causing my head to jerk back like I had just been slapped. "Look, it's been fun but I'm not into playing your game. I won't share and I won't be taunted by you and stories of your ex-lovers while in this god-forsaken house," he said, raising his voice staring at me like I had two heads. What the hell was happening? He had done a complete one-eighty in less than a minute.

"Look, I don't know what your problem is, but you're scaring me," I admitted.

In two steps he was in front of me, grabbing my face and kissing me hard. It happened so fast that I didn't even have time to step away from him, not that I wanted to. I returned his kiss with just as much determination. Kissing him made me lose my mind, and this time I was not going to let him get away. I grabbed his neck, pulling him further in and deepening the kiss. When he pulled away, we were both breathing heavily. My lips were bruised and hurting, but I wanted more. I grabbed his neck, once again bringing him to my mouth. The moan that escaped my lips must have sent him over the edge, because the next thing that I knew he had scooped me up in his arms and was tossing me onto the bed.

"Does it turn you on when people scare you, Dallas?" he asked, with a murderous look in his eyes. My panties became soaked at the sight of him. Danger did turn me on. It drove me crazy, and he had figured it out.

"No," I lied.

"I think it does. I think you like it when I become jealous and take control. Is that what you want, Dallas? Control?" he said in a deep raspy tone that made me let out a sound I didn't recognize. "Answer the question, Dallas."

"No, I want you," I said, in a whiny voice full of yearning. I was sitting on my ass, leaning back on my elbows with my knees bent, allowed me to see him from his thighs up. I found myself opening and closing my legs constantly, and shuddering from the small relief it gave me.

"Be still," he said sternly, making me afraid to breathe. In one swift movement his shirt was off and he was undoing his belt. My mouth went dry when I saw him without his shirt. His body was amazing and the way his muscles bulged, I would have sworn that he had just got through bench pressing a Camry, if he had not been with me all day. Slowly, he slid his belt off. For a minute, I thought he was going to spank me with it, making my legs involuntarily come together again to find some relief. "You just can't sit still, can you?" He asked in that dark raspy voice.

"I'm sorry," I replied, my voice coming out too high pitched.

"Does this turn you on, Dallas?" he asked, holding up the belt in his left hand. I was scared to say anything, so I stared at him, closing my legs together once again hoping that would be answer enough. "Get up," he said with so much authority in his voice that I was sure there would be a wet spot where I had been sitting. I scrambled off the bed and stood before him. He threw the belt into a chair by the bed and with more grace than I thought was possible, he climbed onto the bed, crossed his ankles, and put his arms behind his head. "Since you can't sit still, I thought maybe you could put those moves to good use."

I started to shed my clothes and climb on top of him, but before I could, he reached over and grabbed the remote off of the end table and powered up the Bose stereo that sat on my dresser.

"Dance for me," he said with a hint of challenge in his voice. The opening notes of *My Ruca* by Sublime filled the room. Without question, I clambered onto the bed silently thanking the dance gods for the endless classes that I had taken in high school and the fact that I had only two articles of clothing on, other than my socks. I stood over him, straddling his legs, allowing my body to move in sequence with the bass as the song started. My body swayed as I turned my back to him and slowly pulled my shirt over my head, never losing rhythm. I let my hair down, shaking the soft curls from side to side. I pulled my long hair to the front of my shoulders, just covering my nipples, but leaving the bottom part of my breasts visible. I turned to face him wearing nothing but his sweatpants. When I looked down, I could see him biting his lip and staring at my chest. The look that he gave me fueled my confidence. I looped my fingers into the waistband of the sweats, dropping them to my ankles, making perfect timing with a break in the song.

Dropping to my knees, I leaned over and started kissing my way up his chest, grinding my ass to the beat of the bass. I could feel his thickness through his pants every time my pussy slid over him. He lifted my chin so that I was staring into his eyes, then gathered my hair to one side of my head completely revealing my breasts, and pulled it to lower my mouth to his. Kissing me slowly but passionately, his hips started to flex, moving in rhythm with me. I could feel the dampness of his jeans from my juices, causing the fabric to roughen, intensifying the contact.

I started to grind harder, forgetting the song completely, just looking for some kind of release. He sat up quickly and flipped me onto my back. Removing the sweats from around my ankles and my socks, he started kissing the inside of my thighs. It felt so good, my back arched off the bed. He took his time kissing his way up to my wet center, and when I thought for sure that I would die; he ran his tongue between my lips making small circles on my clit. I came loudly, moaning and shuddering. It had been too long since a man had given me an orgasm, and never one this intense.

Once my moaning ceased, he kissed his way up my stomach, making tiny nips with his teeth. He stopped to suck on my sensitive nipples before invading my mouth once again. I could taste my sweet juices on his lips making me want him even more. I looked down and realized that he was naked, lying on top of me. *When did he take off his clothes?* Assuming it was during the peak of my orgasm, I decided to not ruin the moment by asking.

Luke sat back on his heels; stroking his massive cock that I knew was going to rip me to pieces. He looked so good on his knees in front of me, completely naked and stroking himself. I could feel my body responding. I was dripping wet and my nipples were so hard that they hurt.

"Fuck me. Please." The yearning I had for his cock had me saying things that I had never said. I was internally begging this man to fuck me, beat me, use me as a slave -- I would have done anything to have him inside me at that moment.

"Get on your knees." My breath hitched in my throat at the sound of his deep voice and the direction of his order. Not needing to be told twice, I got on all fours bringing me face to face with him. I could see the veins bulging in his neck and hear his ragged breath. "Turn around," he said, once again in that authoritative voice. I turned around sitting up on my knees, bringing my back to his stomach. He grabbed my hip with his hand firmly -- his palm pressing into the side of my ass. I sucked the air in between my teeth, not from enjoyment, but from pain. I had forgotten about the bruises and soreness until this point. Apparently, Luke did too and mistaking my intake of breath for pleasure instead of agony, he ground harder.

"Ah! Ah!" I cried, arching my back and pulling slightly away from him. His hand immediately released me and then I could feel his thumb rubbing over the top part of my ass. He let out an exasperated sigh and collapsed on his back beside me, putting his arm over his face.

"What the fuck am I doing?" he asked with all the hot bedroom talk completely out of his voice.

"Yes, what the fuck are you doing?" I asked him, still on my knees and completely confused.

"This is wrong. This isn't me and it's not you, either. I am no better than that sorry bastard that I beat the shit out of last night," he said, still talking with his arm over his eyes and sounding completely defeated.

"Okay, I'm confused. I *want* this. I *begged* for this. What's the problem?"

"The problem is I have done things wrong for so long, and with you, I want to do them right."

"Are you fucking kidding me?" I practically screamed. I jumped off the bed and stomped into the bathroom. "Here I am, allowing you to see me naked, twice," I said sticking my head out of the bathroom to make sure he was listening. He was now sitting up in the bed with a pillow covering up his package. "Then..." I continued while stomping around the bathroom, "I let you sleep with me, but only after you drove me to an undisclosed location. Then I wake this morning to be confronted with Blondie the Bitch, pour my heart and soul out to you, bring you to my house, give you the code to the gate, do a fucking strip tease for you, and you can't even fuck me?" I was panting by the time I turned the shower on and stepped in. "And now you are on some guilt trip about celibacy. Let me guess, you want to wait twenty dates? Well, this is not the 'forty year old fucking virgin'," I screamed at the showerhead.

Suddenly, the curtain was snatched open and Luke was standing there in all his glory. "You're cute when you're mad. First of all...," he said holding a finger up silencing me when I started to snap on his ass again. "I don't feel guilty about anything. I just like you, a lot, and I want things to be different with us. Secondly, I'm sorry about last night and today. I know things are moving fast. That's another reason that I want to slow down a little. And third, that was the best lap dance that I have ever had in my life. Were you once a stripper?"

I playfully slapped at him while he laughed at me, my fury gone, replaced with only mild disappointment. He wrapped his arms around me and kissed me tenderly.

"Well, will you at least join me for a shower?" I asked while poking my lip out.

"Babe, nothing could stop me from getting in here with you," he replied stepping into the shower.

"Oh yeah?" I reached around cutting off the hot water causing us both to shriek and lose some of that sexual tension that was building between us once again.

Chapter 5

A cold shower was just what we both needed. We managed to keep our distance from one another, barely making eye contact. I stepped out of the shower, dried off quickly, and made my way into the walk-in closet -- shutting the door behind me to give Luke some privacy.

My closet was like stepping into another room. It was every woman's dream - one hundred square feet of the latest fashion designs from around the globe. The room was solid white. The shelves ran from the floor to the ceiling. Both sides were open and covered in everything from jeans to evening gowns. The back wall housed over seventy pair of shoes, all set in their own cubicles. A large vanity covered in the finest of perfumes and lotions and lined in studio lights sat in the middle of the room. Built in drawers full of endless lingerie, bras, and panties stood on opposite sides of the wall of shoes.

I selected a black strapless bra with matching panties, a red strapless sundress, and then grabbed a gold pair of sandals to complete the outfit. I dressed in front of the mirror I had custom made to fit perfectly on the back of the door. My toned body had a golden brown tint to it, as a result of spending endless hours lounging naked by the pool. I sat in front of the vanity applying some black mascara and red lip gloss to my plump lips.

The girl looking back at me in the mirror seemed to be the happiest that I had seen her in a long time. I had a glow about me and my big hazel eyes seemed full of life. I towel dried my hair, ran my fingers through it and then piled it on top of my head in a messy bun. I was sure it would be dry within the hour. Satisfied with my appearance, I walked out of the closet in search of Luke.

I found Luke in the living room, admiring the mirrors that covered the wall. They were framed in antique wood and made the space seem much larger than it actually was.

"They were my mother's," I said, standing beside him staring at our reflection in the mirror. "She had them custom made from wood that she found from an old barn."

"You look lovely," Luke said, turning to me and planting a sweet kiss on my lips. "But, that outfit is not going to work." I looked back at him, only inches from his face, searching his eyes for a sign of humor and hoping that he was only kidding. "I'm serious. Go change into some jeans. We're going out on the bike. My goon squad may get a little excited seeing your dress over your head," he said, smiling down at me.

The thought of riding on a motorcycle with him sent a chill of excitement through me. I bit my lip trying to hide my smile, and was rewarded with a smile from him that spread all the way across his face, making his eyes crinkle at the corners. I reached up, planting a peck on his lips.

"I'll be right back," I said, turning to leave and practically skipping back to my room. I stepped into my closet, selecting a pair of dark wash designer skinny jeans and a long black three quarter length shirt that was cut low in the front and belted with a rhinestone belt. I chose a pair of low heeled black boots that covered my calves and headed back to the bathroom to dry my hair.

Less than fifteen minutes later, I walked back into living room just as Luke was walking out of the kitchen. He stopped in his tracks when he saw me. I noticed that the dishes from earlier had been washed and the bar was cleaned off. His eyes roamed over my body from my face down to my boots. I had decided to leave my hair down and added dark eye shadow and black liner to my eyes giving them a smoky look.

"You are so fucking sexy," Luke said, sauntering over to me. I couldn't take my eyes off of his face. The stubble around his mouth and chin reminded me of what his face felt like between my legs. I could feel the sexual chemistry forming between us once again. "Why now, at thirty-two years old am I just meeting you?" he asked, still looking at me like he could eat me, which at the time sounded pretty damn good. "I mean, I feel like I have known you all of my life. I have always felt like I was missing something in the world, running a step behind, but with you I just feel... whole."

Hearing a confession like this from him had me thinking I had already fallen in love with this man that I had known for less than twenty four hours. I almost said it. I almost told him I loved him and I didn't even know his last name. My thoughts were interrupted by the ringing of his cell phone.

"I need to get this. Get your stuff. I'll meet you at the truck," he said, giving me a wink and heading towards the library.

I grabbed my clutch and emptied the contents on the table. My cell phone fell out showing I had absolutely no missed calls or messages. It made me sad to know that the only person I spoke to regularly was my assistant, Lindsey. She was the closest thing I had to a friend, although we never talked outside of work. I slipped my credit card, along with a little cash and my license into the back pocket of my jeans and sat my phone back on the table. I walked to the laundry room, making sure Neo had plenty of food and water, and that the dog door was accessible.

"Dallas!" I heard Luke yell.

"I'm in here," I yelled back to him, filling Neo's bowl with food.

"Sorry to rush, but you about ready?" Luke asked, coming to grab the large bag out of my hand.

"Yep, all set," I said, leading us out of the laundry room and back into the kitchen.

"Don't you need your phone?" he asked, holding my cell phone in his hand.

"Nah, I only use it during the week anyway," I said nonchalantly.

"Well, what if someone calls?" Luke asked, seeming amused at my lack of need for such a popular piece of technology.

"They won't." I couldn't hide the disappointment in my voice as I busied myself in the kitchen avoiding eye contact.

"Dallas," Luke said, walking up behind me and turning me to face him. "I never want you to go anywhere without your phone, ever. This is very important, do you understand?" I nodded my head, still keeping my eyes from his. "I'm putting my number in your phone and I'm going to call myself so I have yours." Less than a minute later I heard his phone ringing in his pocket. "There, now I can talk to you anytime I want," he said smiling down at me.

Warmth flooded my body when he reached his hand up to move the hair off my face. He leaned down, kissing my head then grabbed my hand and we headed out.

As we headed out the drive and back towards Luke's, I couldn't resist the temptation of asking him to tell me something about him, even though I had promised not to pry. I decided to keep the conversation light in hopes that he would open up on his own just as I had. "Have you been riding bikes for long?" I asked, turning to him and admiring his profile.

"Ever since I was old enough to climb on one," he responded smiling. "My grandfather was the founding president of the Devil's Renegades Motorcycle Club. He passed away less than two years ago and since, I have taken over the gavel."

"Gavel?" I asked, fully intrigued.

"The presidency. When he stepped down about 6 months before he passed, we voted that the Vice President be awarded the position. The VP refused and nominated me. Everyone was in agreement, so I was given the presidency and the opportunity to carry on my grandfather's legacy."

"I bet he is very proud of you," I said, smiling reassuringly.

"I don't know about that. Times have changed. My Pops was pretty old school. I don't think he would agree with some of the decisions that I make," he said to me in a voice not much more than a whisper.

"What about your mom and dad?" I asked trying to change the subject because I could tell he was becoming uncomfortable.

"Let's just say my dad did not follow in my Pops' footsteps and wasn't really happy about me doing it either," he said, laughing a little and lightening the atmosphere. "My mom is great. A true southern belle is what some would call her. You remind me of her," he said turning to look at me.

I laughed, "You are kidding, right? Honey, I'm far from a southern belle. They're charming, classy and refined and I am none of those things." Most people would think so by my appearance on the outside and I could even convince some, mostly my clients, that I was a real lady. I was not. I had been broken and hurt and had a past that would make some of the worst kinds of people look like saints.

"I think you are all of those things," Luke said, with no trace of humor on his face. I just smiled in response. It was hard to argue with him when he was being so sincere, and honestly, I didn't want him to know the real me. I wanted him to believe I was all the things he thought I was.

"So, tell me about tonight," I said, that same chill returning that I had earlier when I thought of being on his bike.

"Our club is hosting a benefit for a local boy who has brain cancer. We are going to a couple bars around town gathering the donations that were taken for him and then we are going to his house to visit with him."

"Wow, that's very charitable of you," I said, blown away by what he had just told me. I was not expecting that answer at all. I had stereotyped him, believing we would be intimidating people around town while delivering illegal drugs to the back of a warehouse.

"I try to do my part," was all he said. The look on his face looked like that of guilt. I wondered if his show of charity was only a decoy, while he did the things I was silently accusing him of. "I should probably let you know that I will have some minor business to attend to while I am there, so I'm gonna have to leave you with the girls."

I knew it. "Is that okay?" he asked nervously. *It most definitely was not okay. I would much rather be in the comfort of my own home, hiding away in my big bed and away from the scrutiny and callousness that I was sure to endure by hanging out with the trashy bitches that he considered friends.*

"That's fine," I responded tersely. I was not going to give these bitches the satisfaction of not having me there. I would handle it, one way or another. Plus, Red would be there and she wasn't that bad.

"I promise I'll make it up to you," he responded. "They're really not that bad once you get to know them."

I didn't respond. I just stared at him, my face completely impassive, but on the inside I was burning with rage. Hearing that I would have to be around those women tonight sent me straight into bitch mode. They had the home field advantage, but I had the sweet satisfaction of knowing I had Luke. That in itself was worth fighting for.

"Carmical," he suddenly said.

"Pardon?" I asked confused.

"My last name is Carmical, Lucas Lorn Carmical. Some people may refer to me tonight as LLC and I didn't want you to be in the dark when you heard it. Maddie will use anything she can to make you feel unimportant. Please don't over think anything she says, she is just jealous."

"You think pretty highly of yourself," I said, not really meaning for it to sound as demeaning as it did.

He laughed. "No babe, it ain't me she is after. It's this," he said pointing to the leather vest lying on the seat between us. "It's a power trip for her. She thinks that if she can't be the President's Ol' Lady, no one else should be either."

"Ol' Lady?" I asked, confused once again.

"We'll get to that. Just remember, tonight you are with me and no one else. I don't want you associating with any other men. Understood?" The seriousness in his tone made me feel uneasy, but it quickly vanished when he added, "I couldn't stand the thought of anyone else's hands or eyes on you."

I understood jealousy. I wanted to tell him the same went for him, but my phone rang, interrupting us. I was surprised that someone was calling me on a Sunday. No one ever called me. I dug the phone out of my pocket, seeing my assistant Lindsey's name displayed on the screen.

"Yeah," I answered, a little aggravated that she had called, messing up my conversation.

"Hi, Dallas! I'm so sorry to bother you, but my mother Is coming into town tomorrow and I was wondering if I could come in a little late so I could pick her up at the airport," she rambled, talking fast, probably in hopes that I would say yes if she said it quickly. Why did people do that?

"What time will you be in?" I asked, getting pissed that she would call on such short notice when she knew we had a closing tomorrow.

"By noon," she responded, already sounding defeated. Good. She had just made my job a little easier.

"That's ridiculous, Lindsey. Just send a car to get her. We have a deal to close in the morning. The clients will be there at nine."

"Actually, Mrs. Holifield called today to re-schedule for twelve."

How convenient. "Well, go ahead but you better be back by twelve. I don't want to have to deal with that bitch on my own."

"O-okay, I will. Thank you so much," she stuttered. I didn't even say goodbye. I just hung up the phone. So much for enjoying my morning. I would have to be at the office early tomorrow, all because she didn't have her priorities straight.

"What was that about?" Luke asked, pulling me from my thoughts.

"My assistant. She wants the morning off," I responded boringly.

"From what I could hear, sounds like you didn't want to give it to her. Does she call in often?" he asked interested. I thought for a minute. In the two years that she had worked for me, she had never asked for a day off. Nothing outside of her two week vacation and holiday time, anyway.

"No, this is highly unusual for her. I guess she will start to. Now that I have given her an inch, I'm sure she will take a mile."

"That's not fair Dallas. I'm sure she had good reason to take off to call you on a Sunday and ask. Why are you so hard on her?" he asked, making me feel like shit.

"I'm not hard on her," I responded, my defenses going up. "I pay her very well to do her job. I'm more than fair and I never ask her to do anything that I have not done. What's the big deal about picking someone up from the airport anyway?" I asked, mostly to myself. I realized then how little I knew about Lindsey. I didn't even know her mother lived out of town.

"Give her a break. I'm sure she deserves it. Everyone does every now and then," Luke stated, making me feel even guiltier.

"Do you mind stopping somewhere? I am in desperate need of some caffeine," I said, dropping the subject completely.

"No problem," he said, turning into a service station just off the highway.

"You need anything?" I asked, opening my door to get out.

"No, I'm good," he responded with a mischievous smile. What was that about? I walked inside, browsing at items that I did not need. I selected a candy bar and a soda and made my way to the cashier. I looked outside to see Luke looking down at what I assumed was his phone. He was so breathtakingly gorgeous, even from a distance.

"Thanks," the cashier said handing me my change. I smiled in response and headed back to the truck.

"Lindsey texted," Luke said as soon as I sat in the truck.

"I'll text her back later," I responded with absolutely no intention of doing so.

"I already did," Luke said, pulling back onto the highway. I jerked my head around towards him.

"You did what?" I asked, trying to remain calm but failing to do so.

"I messaged her back. I told her to just take the whole day off tomorrow."

"Why would you do that?" I asked calmly, too calmly.

"Because we are making each other better people, Dallas. I want to be a better person when I am with you and I can tell you do, too. I want you to act towards her the way you act around me. I bet she's never seen the playful and fun Dallas that I know," he stated, making eye contact with me as much as possible without running us off the road.

He had me. This sexy man knew that he couldn't do or say anything that would keep me mad at him, and without knowing it, he had used this new found knowledge to benefit someone other than himself. I wanted to be mad, but I couldn't. He was right, and as much as I hated saying that anyone other than me was right; I couldn't help but smile. He had won me over with his good looks and his charm. Now he was making me feel better about helping someone, even though I had not done anything.

"You're welcome," Luke said, grabbing my hand and pulling me across the seat next to him. I snuggled into his side and let out a sigh of contentment. "Sometimes those who are fortunate tend to overlook those who are not. I promise by doing this you will benefit more than you ever thought possible. Trust me, I know from experience," he said, sliding his arm around my waist, pulling me closer and kissing my head.

"So, you were once a crude self-centered bitch, too?" I asked. He threw his head back and laughed. "I guess you could say that. I took out my own misery on others. It never ends well."

I glanced down at my phone, reading the message of thanks from Lindsey. I wasn't real happy about what had happened, but I knew in my cold heart that it was the right thing to do and just acknowledging that was a big accomplishment for someone like me. I opened my candy bar and took a huge bite, letting the chocolate soothe my worries and chased it with a large drink of soda. I continued in my own selfish thoughts, ignoring the world completely, consuming the entire thing in only four bites.

"I like chocolate, too," Luke said, interrupting my thoughts.

"I'm sorry, did you want some?" I asked innocently, staring up at him with pure satisfaction on my face.

"I guess not," Luke said, seeming hurt. I rubbed my tongue across my lips moaning to myself.

"It was so delicious, too," I said, closing my eyes and dramatizing the moment.

"You'll pay for that," Luke said giving me his dark bedroom stare.

"Looking forward to it, LLC."

Chapter 6

We pulled into Luke's driveway around two-thirty. I took notice that everyone else seemed to have left and that it was just the two of us. Luke grabbed my hand and led me through the house into a room that I had never been in before. The entire room was covered in brick and the floor was concrete. The walls were decked out in black and white pictures of motorcycles. The ceiling was painted into an American flag and there were French doors that led outside. Parked in the middle of the room was a huge motorcycle that took my breath away. I had never seen one so beautiful. It was solid black and covered in chrome. The gas tank had orange flames outlined in white that ran all the way to the leather seat. The saddle bags were hard plastic and had a chrome bar that ran all the way around them. Road King was inscribed on the front fender.

"You like it?" Luke asked, staring at me with a huge grin on his face.

"I love it," I replied enthusiastically. I was surprised at myself for having such strong feelings toward a motorcycle. I had never taken notice of one before, but then again, I had never fallen for a motorcycle man either.

"Wait 'till you ride it," Luke said with a grin. I could tell that this was something that he loved. His whole demeanor seemed to change in the presence of this beautiful machine. "Here," Luke said handing me a helmet that looked like it was custom made just for me. "I hate 'em but it's the law."

I silently thanked the great state of Mississippi for enforcing such a law and put my helmet on as Luke pushed the bike out through the door.

"That lid never looked so good," Luke said grabbing his own helmet off a large chrome tool box that I just noticed was there.

"Lid?" I asked, completely confused. He patted my helmet with a wink. I was going to have to purchase a motorcycle lingo for dummies book in the near future.

"Ready?" he asked, taking my hand and leading me out the door.

"As I'll ever be," I replied nervously. My breathing quickened and I realized that I had really not thought this whole motorcycle riding through.

"Hey," Luke said wrapping his arm around my waist. "You'll love it. Don't be nervous. I won't let anything happen." He grabbed my chin and lifted my face to his before leaning down and giving me a kiss that erased every doubt that I had. He climbed on and cranked the bike, causing the vibrations to carry through the concrete and all the way up my body. A thrill of excitement surged through me as I stepped onto the foot pegs, slung my leg over and settled on the back seat. It was much more comfortable than I thought possible and the back rest gave me a little more sense of security as I settled back, placing my hands on Luke's shoulders, not real sure where to put them.

"You don't have to hold on so tight babe, you're not going anywhere," Luke yelled, turning to me laughing. I realized my knuckles were white from grabbing him so hard and I immediately let go. "Just move with the bike, it will come naturally." I took a deep breath, trying to relax. The vibrations were so intense I could almost feel the sensation through my pants. Luke pulled the bike onto the dirt road. The bike leaned to the left, then right and my automatic reaction was to bail off the side, but I realized that it was over before I could react and my body had not moved an inch. I knew he was trying to help me get the feel of it, but I wasn't going to lie. *I was scared shitless.*

By the time we got to the highway, I was afraid that I wasn't going to make it. Luke must have felt my uneasiness because he didn't pull onto the highway. Instead, he pulled the bike over and got off. He came beside me, opening the saddle bag and pulled out an iPod with ear buds.

"Here, this will help calm you down a little," he said, selecting a playlist and handing me the ear buds. I put them in and was surprised to hear Coal War blaring through the small speakers. Once again, he kissed me sweetly, giving me a wink, and then climbed back on and pulled out onto the highway.

I closed my eyes, smiling to myself and let the lyrics take me away. When I opened them, I felt like a new person. The wind blowing through my hair and the music in my ears made me feel so free. The air was warm and inviting. I lifted my hand up letting the air pass between my fingers. I felt like I could ride forever. The iPod shuffled to the next song which just so happened to be one of my favorites. Hearing the song brought back memories of one of my best childhood friends, Kandice. Just like so many others, life had taken her from me way too soon. Kandice loved music. She was such a free spirit and I envied her ability to be so carefree. A hippie at heart, she was able to quote any song from The Beatles to Lynyrd Skynyrd. I laughed through my tears at the memory of us on our road trip to Texas, singing at the top of our lungs. We replayed the song over and over until we knew every word.

Listening to the Black Crowes sing "Josephine" changed me in that moment. Life had dealt me a shitty hand, but I had an ace in the hole. Luke. He was my saving grace. It just took me until now to realize it.

I wrapped my arms around Luke. Leaning forward, I placed my chin on his shoulder and whispered in his ear, "Thank you." I knew there was no way he knew what I was talking about. Perhaps he thought it was the iPod, or the ride, or the wakeup call he gave me when he texted Lindsey, but he responded when he reached back and ran his hand down my thigh and landed it on my knee, where he held on while I rested my head on his shoulder until we came into town.

Our first stop was at 59 Hangout, which was an old run down bar off of Highway 59. On the left and right sides of the white block building were old junk cars that had grass growing up around them. A wooden fence separated the building from two trailers that were overgrown with vines and brush. The large green door that led into the building was the only sign of color. We pulled in alongside about fifty other bikes, parking towards the front. Before Luke had time to even cut the bike off, we were surrounded by people. I recognized some of the men's faces that shook Luke's hand from the bar the other night. Most of them gave Luke a big hug, slapping him on the back, seeming genuinely glad to see him. I noticed that none of them made any attempt to speak to me until Luke introduced me.

"This is Dallas. Dallas, these are my brothers; Tiny, War and Regg," he said waving his hand in their direction. I slid my helmet off, doing my best to smooth my hair and shook each of their hands. Tiny was a large man, every bit of 6'5" with long, stringy hair and kind eyes. I noticed the patches on his vest were similar to the ones Luke wore. War was a man of short stature with a no-nonsense look on his face that made me think his bite was just as bad as his bark. He made me nervous, causing me to quickly dart my eyes to Regg.

"Hello, beautiful!" Regg said to me smiling, and then pulled me into a bear hug. He had a boyish face with big brown eyes. His hair was a very light blonde and his goatee was the only thing making him look a day older than fifteen. He was shorter than Luke but not by much and his husky size reminded me of a big ol' teddy bear. I returned his hug and not being able to help it, landed a kiss on his red cheek.

"Damn girl, you gonna make me take you home with me?" Regg responded laughing. I liked him immediately. He seemed so full of love and life.

"Red will beat the hell outta you, boy," Tiny said while playfully punching Regg in the arm.

"Okay, okay, that's enough," Luke said breaking us apart and running his arm around my waist, claiming his territory.

"Red inside?" Luke asked, looking at Regg. "Yeah, that crazy bitch is in there. She is giving hell to a prospect at the bar." He replied, shaking his head.

"That figures. Come on, babe." Luke led me towards the door, stopping several times to shake hands and hug people, but never introducing me. I wondered why, but just passed it off as him being in a hurry. I just stood there and smiled, although they never acknowledged my presence.

When we walked in, it took a moment for my eyes to adjust. The bar was so dark that I couldn't even make out Luke's face standing beside me. Never slowing, Luke led me through the entry and to the bar where he ordered two beers. I looked around, my eyes starting to adjust, and noticed that a line of men, all wearing leather vests, were lined up to say hello to Luke.

Once again, they never looked my way and Luke never bothered to introduce me. I couldn't help the feeling of unimportance that passed over me. I was used to being the center of attention wherever I went. In the Luke's presence, it seemed as if I didn't even exist. I turned my back to Luke and looked around the bar. There was a stage in the far left corner of the bar that was set up for a band. The entire floor was a concrete slab, except for the make-shift dance floor that was covered in wood colored linoleum. Floor to ceiling mirrors covered the back wall of the dance floor. Christmas lights were the main source of lighting and were strung up all around the bar. Mismatched tables and chairs were scattered throughout the bar and all of them were occupied.

"Hey, you!" I looked across the bar to see Red coming towards me. She was dressed in tight black jeans and a white t-shirt with an orange bandana wrapped around her head. A black leather vest full of patches and black boots completed her outfit. She looked absolutely gorgeous. Her smile was wide, making her eyes sparkle and I couldn't help smiling back at her. "I had no idea you were coming!" she said, walking up and wrapping her arms around me. I returned her hug enthusiastically, feeling better by just seeing her face.

"Here I am!" I said smiling.

"Well, come on and let me get you a beer," Red said, grabbing my arm and leading me to the other side of the bar. From the angle we were now at, I could see Luke looking like a damn celebrity -- shaking hands, hugging necks, and kissing women on the cheek. I tried not to let it bother me, but I just couldn't help it. Why was he acting like I wasn't even there?

"Two Millers, Cas," Red called to the hot bartender who looked like she belonged in a fashion magazine and not behind this dusty old bar. I wondered why someone who looked like her would want to work in a place like this. Then I noticed the overflowing tip jars and I knew. She probably made more money in a weekend here than she would if she worked a whole month in some clothing store.

"Thanks," I said as she handed me my beer.

"No problem," she replied with a wink.

"Sorry Cas, this one is taken," Red said, wrapping her arm possessively around my waist. Cas just gave a slight shrug then turned to help another demanding customer.

"She likes you. This means that when the guys start bringing in whiskey and feeding it to her, she is gonna come looking for you. You can thank me later," Red said, pulling out a barstool and gesturing for me to have a seat. We sat down, facing Luke from across the bar. I lifted my beer as a toast to Red and we clanked bottles.

"So, are ya wondering how he does it?" Red asked with her eyes following Luke.

"Does what? Pretends that I don't exist?" I blurted out.

Red laughed. "Honey, you should feel very special. You are the envy of every girl in here. Luke has not brought a woman around for some time. For your pretty little ass to even have the opportunity to grace his bitch seat is more than most women, who have known Luke for years, get."

"Then why doesn't he introduce me?" I asked, sounding like a petulant child.

Red turned to face me. "What the hell do you want exactly, hmm? For him to give you his un-divided attention at all times? For him to turn his back on what he has worked so hard for, just to make sure you feel appreciated and comfortable? Do you want to know why he hasn't introduced you? Because you are nothing. This is a CDC world you are living in, honey, and the sooner you figure it out, the better off you will be. Stop being so fucking selfish for once in your life and know your place."

I was shocked at the outburst. She had not said it with any type of animosity, just very matter- of-fact. "CDC?" I asked of yet another biker reference that I had never heard before.

"Cunts Don't Count. It's not derogatory or demeaning; it's just how it is. See, this is a man's world. We are only here for decoration and moral support. You will always come second. It's kinda hard to deal with at first, especially for someone like you, who is used to getting everything she wants. But, it has a way of growing on you," she said, pulling a cigarette out and lighting it.

"Why would you want to surround yourself with people who consider you a nobody?" I asked, truly intrigued by what she had just shared with me.

"You see that man right there?" she asked, pointing to Regg. "He is the reason that I do this. I love him and this family. I am appreciated, loved and respected. As long as I know my place and stay out of club business, I will always be welcome and have a family here."

"Okay, I am confused. If you don't matter, why are you here?"

"I never said that I didn't matter. Stop trying to think of it as a bad thing. There is not a man in here that would do anything to disrespect you. You can have a good time, be protected, and genuinely loved by everyone here. But, these men are not here to see you. They are here for Luke because he asked them to come. He doesn't introduce you because you are not of importance right now. If you had a title, it would be hang-around, unless you and Luke have become an item in the last twenty-four hours. If and when you become official, chances are, even then, he won't be rolling the red carpet out for you. When you walked through that door with him, everyone in the room knew who you were. And that is property of the Devil's Renegades' President, LLC."

I sat on the stool with my mouth slightly open, trying to take in all that she had just told me. Was this the kind of life that I want? Did I really want to play second fiddle to a bunch of greasy bikers? What the hell was wrong with me? *The kind of life that I wanted?* Hell, I just met the guy. I had so many more questions that I wanted to ask but the band was taking the stage and Red's attention had quickly turned to them. I suddenly wanted nothing more than to leave from this place. I didn't belong here and I knew it. It was apparent that Luke didn't want me here either; if he did he would be here beside me. *Wouldn't he?* I looked across the bar to see him chatting with a pretty blonde. Judging by his facial expressions and the sexy smile on his face, I knew that he was flirting. I watched him as he put his arm around her shoulders and whispered something in her ear, causing her to throw her head back in laughter.

Naturally, being the woman that I am, I assumed that whatever joke was told was on my behalf. My suspicions were confirmed when our eyes met and she gave me a wink. Some would probably consider it just a friendly gesture, but I knew that face. It was the same one that I had used when I knew I had one up on someone. She was letting me know that she was stepping on my territory and was enjoying every minute of it.

"Hey!" Red said, eyeing me warily. "Stop it."

"Stop, what?" I asked, confused at her demand.

"You are looking for a reason to be jealous. That's his sister." My whole body sagged with relief. *His sister, it was his fucking sister and I was two seconds from making a scene.*

"Oh," was all I could manage to say. I had assumed that Luke was an only child. Now, looking at the two, I don't know why I had not seen it before. They did favor each other.

"Well, not technically," Red said from beside me. My head turned in her direction and I managed to pull my eyes away from the siblings to stare at her.

"What? So, they're not brother and sister?" I asked completely confused. *Just how many beers had Red drank since she had been here?*

"Okay, that's Creek's Ol' Lady. Creek is Luke's riding brother, so that makes BeBe, Luke's sister," Red said, looking like she was trying to choose her words carefully so she didn't get them confused.

"Damn it, Red, just say what the hell you mean. I don't know motorcycle slang. Is that his fucking sister or not?" I said a bit too harshly.

"Hey, chill out, man. It's been a while since I have had a conversation with someone outside this life." I just stared at her expectantly. I could tell that the drinks had obviously caught up with her. She seemed somewhat spaced out. "They are not blood kin if that's what you are asking," she said smiling, obviously enjoying my aggravation.

"Fuck it," I said, grabbing my beer. "I'm going outside." I went to stand up when someone touched my shoulder.

"Dallas?" said a man's voice from beside me. I turned to see my very first love staring back at me.

"Sam?" Sam Ervin. The All-American quarterback turned surfer boy was smiling at me. His big green eyes were creased at the corners from smiling his megawatt smile. I had loved Sam since the tenth grade, although the feeling was never mutual. Partly because he never knew that I had a crush on him. When I moved to Collins from Atlanta, he was the first person to speak to me in class. Through our junior and senior years of high school, I managed to keep my secret hidden. My fear of rejection was greater than the opportunity of truth. Looking at him now, I felt nothing. I had stopped feeling for him a long time ago, but it sure was nice to see a familiar face, and his was a nice one to look at.

"What are you doing here?" he asked me. Letting his eyes travel over my body. I had matured a lot since the twelfth grade, and he was taking notice. Sam had matured a lot also. His blonde curly hair was still wild and untamed, but his skin was sun kissed, and his shirt bulged from his muscles. I noticed that we seemed to be the only two in the building who looked as if they didn't belong.

"Maybe I should ask you the same question," I responded.

"My little brother is playing in the band. Skill-Saw is what they are calling themselves. I guess joints like this are their only takers," he said laughing. His laugh was contagious as I joined in with him. I happened to look across the bar and saw Luke glaring at me. His face was that of stone, but his eyes were full of fire. He shook his head from side to side as if telling me "no" about something. I quickly averted my eyes, looking at anything but him.

"That your new boyfriend?" Sam asked, nodding his head towards Luke, but never taking his eyes off of me.

"No, just a friend," I said, looking down at my beer. I tried focusing all of my attention on removing the label from the bottle.

"You could have fooled me. The way he looks at you is the way a man looks at a woman who belongs to him," Sam said. I looked up to see him staring at me intently.

"Well, I may be considered his property, but I most definitely do not belong to him," I said defiantly.

"Ah, gotta love the biker world," Sam said, taking a long pull from the bottle of water he was holding.

"And just what do you know about the biker world?" I asked. I knew that Sam had walked out on a full athletic scholarship to a four year university to move to Hawaii and become a surfer, but I had no idea he had any knowledge of this life.

"I watch a lot of T.V.," he said grinning at me like we were fifteen again. I smiled at him. He had always been so easy to talk to.

My frustration lifted somewhat, until a deep voice spoke into my ear, "Let's go." Before I could jerk my head around, to see who it was, Luke had me by my arm pulling me from my spot at the bar. I had not even recognized his voice. I could feel the tension radiating through his body. I half expected Sam to come to my rescue, but was somewhat relieved and yet slightly disappointed when I turned to see him still sitting at the bar as if nothing had happened. Luke pulled me through the door, never letting go of my arm. I had to practically run to keep up with him. Excitement coursed through my veins at the feel of his touch. I didn't care if the touch was forceful or not, it felt so good to be this close to him, too good.

"Get inside," Luke barked to the two guys out front. Without hesitation, they went inside. I found myself shoved up against the front of the building. Luke's hands were on either side of my head on the wall, casing me in. "What the fuck are you doing?" he asked in a surprisingly calm voice. I couldn't speak. His eyes glared deep into mine looking for an answer. "Answer me," he snapped, no longer in a calm manner.

"I don't know," I replied, not sure what was a right answer. I'm not sure why, but just like at my house the sound of his rough, dominating voice had me wanting to take him right there.

"You don't know? You trying to make an ass out of me, Dallas? You are here with me and only me. I will not tolerate you hanging all over another man in my presence. Do you understand?"

"I wasn't hanging on..." Luke slapped the wall beside my head, cutting me off mid-sentence and making me jump.

"Yes, or no?" he growled. I could tell that this was *not* the Luke that I had seen in the bedroom. That Luke was domineering, but in a sexual way. This one looked like he could rip me to pieces with his bare hands.

I swallowed the lump that had formed in my throat and replied with a simple, barely audible, "Yes." Without another word, Luke walked back inside, leaving me alone. Not sure what to do, I turned and started walking down the road.

Chapter 7

I could not face the humiliation of going back inside. Even though no one said anything, I knew everyone in the building had watched the scene unfold. I knew I could not walk down the interstate, so I grabbed my cell from my back pocket and dialed the only person I knew in Hattiesburg that would come get me. Lindsey's phone rang only once when she picked up with her normal cheery greeting.

"Hey, Dallas! What can I do for you?"

Somehow, I found my voice and was surprised to find it working without a hint of despair. "I need you to come pick me up from Blackwell Grocery off of Evelyn Gandy Parkway."

"Um, okay. Just so happens, I am in Petal. I should be there in about ten minutes. Is everything okay?" I ended the call without answering her and placed my phone back in my pocket. I would have to concoct some story to tell Lindsey as to why I was sitting on the curb at a run-down grocery store, on a Sunday afternoon. If she knew what really happened, she may take that as a sign of weakness and that was the last thing I wanted.

As promised, Lindsey's shiny white car pulled into the parking lot less than ten minutes later. "I don't want to talk about it. I just want to go home," I said, never looking her in the eye. I had slouched down in my seat, staring out the window, silently hoping that she would just let it be. I knew that she would. She was not the type to pry or ask too many questions. I suddenly remembered that Luke had the code to get in the gate at my house. "Do you mind if I come to your house for a little while?" I blurted to Lindsey without thinking.

"Of course not," she responded. I felt like a complete fool, an idiot. It was degrading, lowering myself to ask for assistance from someone who made less in a month than I did in a day. Here I was, CEO of one of the largest real estate companies in the south, calling on a girl with an associate's degree from a junior college to assist me with my personal life. She was sure to take this as a sign of distress and lack of confidence, which would lead to her leaking my story to a group of middle class workers at a Thursday night Bunco party. She would eventually lose respect for me in the office, causing me to let her go and hire a new assistant. By that time, she will have gone to the media hoping to get some sort of attention by letting everyone in on the secret life of the most eligible millionaire bachelorette, Dallas Knox. My private life would be aired like dirty laundry for the entire world to see.

I would eventually lose clients causing my business to fold and once I dipped into my savings and CD's, my interest would go down, and by the time I was forty I would be broke and without a job living in a trailer with thirty-five cats. The thought was so revolting; I started to tell Lindsey to just take me home. I would rather face the wrath of Luke and his goon squad than be known for the woman who once had it all, but lost it after her assistant sold her out. I wanted to say those things, but I couldn't. I needed Lindsey. I needed a friend and of all the people I had come in contact with over the years, it was her that I was closest to. I wanted someone I could confide in and share all my secrets with. It was a little overwhelming at times being me and trying to keep an all business persona when deep down all I wanted was to be just like everyone else.

Luke had turned into a complete failure and my melancholy mood that his actions had put me in made me feel extremely vulnerable. It was time to let go of the past and try to become a new person. A better person. I looked over at Lindsey as if seeing her for the first time. Her long hair was so dark that it was almost black and her tanned skin was flawless. She didn't wear a hint of makeup, and didn't need to. She seemed innocent, yet full of life. She wore khaki shorts and a plain white shirt. Even sitting down, I could tell that it complimented her curvy figure. It was a requirement of mine for her to dress in business attire for work. I even gave her a bonus when she started, just so she could look the way I expected her to.

Seeing her now, dressed down in casual clothes with no makeup on, I almost felt as if we were friends, maybe coming back from a movie or a shopping trip together. My heart smiled at the thought, but my body responded by rolling my eyes at such a silly daydream. I was twenty-six years old and acting like I was ten again. Next thing I knew, we would be skipping along together with our hair in pigtails singing Mary, Mary, Quite Contrary.

"Well, this is awkward," Lindsey said, pulling me from the comfort of my own thoughts and back to the situation at hand.

"Yeah, I guess it is. Sorry to inconvenience you," I said looking down at my feet embarrassed. *This was a first*.

"Not this," she said, motioning with her finger between the two of us. "This." I looked up to see her pointing out the windshield. It seemed that we had a front row seat to an all-out dog orgy happening in the middle of the driveway before us. I had not even realized the car had stopped, or that we had turned into a driveway that I assumed led to her house. Lindsey jumped out of the car, shooing the dogs out of the way. I laughed at the sight of her, kicking the air around the dogs, hoping to scare them out of their sexual craze. After about two minutes of swearing and kicking and shooing, the dogs broke up and decided to take their business elsewhere, but not before shooting Lindsey a look that had her giving them the finger in retaliation, which just made me laugh harder.

"Fucking dogs. You would think that they could find somewhere else to fornicate, other than my driveway," Lindsey mumbled, mostly to herself, when she got back in the car.

"Who do they belong to?" I asked, still laughing.

"Me. I got them from a Wal-Mart parking lot salesman for ten dollars. They are just mutts but they let me know when someone is coming over. There is a bitch in heat somewhere, so that's all they have been studying for the past few days. Just like a damn man." I laughed. Lindsey was funny, although I knew she was not trying to be.

"Well, welcome to my Ponderosa," Lindsey said, putting the car in park and getting out.

Lindsey's house was a small wooden framed cottage that was painted a light blue. A white picket fence went around the front of the house and opened into a small garden. We walked up the steps onto the porch that housed two white rocking chairs. The porch went down the side of the house and across the front. The railing was white and looked freshly painted. I had always imagined Lindsey living in an apartment somewhere, so it was surprising to see how much pride she took in the small cottage. Now that I had seen it, I could not imagine her living anywhere else. She opened the front door, which I noted was not locked and led me inside the living room. "Make yourself at home," she said, throwing her purse on a turquoise couch and walking out of the room.

The walls were covered in canvas paintings, each with an LI inscribed on the bottom. Lindsey was quite the artist. There were pictures of various insects, animals, trees, flowers and even a couple of portraits of some woman. The old hardwood floors were covered in worn rugs and all of the furniture looked distressed, but it made the room look airy and bright. There was no television in the room, but an easel with a half-finished canvas painting stood in the corner next to a shelf full of paints and brushes. I looked through the doorway that Lindsey went through and could see all the way to the kitchen.

With my curiosity getting the best of me, I walked through a door that led to a large bedroom that stretched the width of the house. There was a large four post bed. It was white and looked like it had once been a canopy bed, but was now draped in a mossy green net that was blowing in the breeze coming from the open windows in the room. It looked like something out of a dream. Large, white, overstuffed pillows were piled high on the matching white down comforter and I could see a slight dip in the middle of the bed letting me know that the mattresses were old and worn. Just like the living room, the walls here were also covered in paintings, but all of streams, rivers, woods and cottages similar to the one she lived in. An old dresser covered in perfumes and framed pictures sat across from the bed.

"I'm kind of a do-it-yourselfer," Lindsey announced from the doorway.

"I think it's amazing," I said truthfully.

"When I started working for you, I lucked up and found this place for rent really cheap. The outside was overgrown and the inside was covered in dust, but the structure was good, and the owner told me I could paint the furniture if I wanted. I have been here over two years and I have never paid full price for my rent. He always finds a way to knock something off, because I have fixed or updated something," she said smiling.

"Have you thought about buying it?" I asked.

"Maybe. Wanna see the rest?" she asked turning and leading me out of the room and into another. I knew she was avoiding the topic, but I didn't mind. I was pretty discreet myself. *Something else we had in common.* "This is my guest bedroom, but I use it as an office. Whoever lived here before must have too, because I didn't have to buy anything but a new desk chair," she said, spinning the chair around and taking a seat. The desk was painted a bright yellow, but didn't look gaudy or tacky in the least. It went well with the room that was painted an off white color with only a few large paintings of flowers on the walls. A small sofa sat in front of a large stone fireplace and the walls around it were lined with books.

"I love to read. During the winter, I spend almost all of my time in here reading," Lindsey said, abandoning her seat to run her fingers along the books on the shelf, just as I had done many of times in my own library.

"I do, too," I said, liking the fact that my employee and potential friend loved reading as much as I did. We walked into the kitchen, which just like the desk, was painted a bright yellow. The cabinets were white, as were the appliances, and the small breakfast area had a white wooden table for two. There were so many windows that there wasn't very much room for paintings, but Lindsey had still managed to squeeze in a few here and there.

"Would you like something to drink?" Lindsey asked. "I have water and milk."

"Water would be great. Thank you," I said, taking a seat at the breakfast table. Lindsey handed me a bottle of water and sat across from me.

"So, you gonna tell me what's going on?" Lindsey asked. I had never seen her relaxed. Nor, had I ever heard her speak so bluntly. *I liked it*. I had an overwhelming urge to tell her everything. So, I did. From the first moment I saw Luke, to the moment I walked away from the bar. I lay the last twenty-four hours of my life out on the table, like an open book. Lindsey sat quietly, listening intently to everything I had to say. When I was finished, I felt as if a huge weight had been lifted off of my shoulders. I sat there a minute, delighting in the fact that I had just opened up to someone, even though the last one I had trusted, only hours ago, had already betrayed me. I was ready to hear Lindsey's feedback, her advice. I wanted her to get mad and volunteer to drive me back to the bar so that we could team up and beat the shit out of Luke. Maybe even vandalize his motorcycle. I looked at her expectantly, ready for the wrath.

"So, who gave me the day off, you or Luke?" Lindsey asked her face wrinkled up in confusion. *I was speechless. Dallas Knox, one of so many words, was speechless once again.* "Just kidding," Lindsey said, laughing and looking very pleased with herself. I laughed along with her, although I didn't find the comment as humorous as she did. "Well, it sounds to me like you have it bad for this incredibly hot guy," she said, laughter subsiding.

"I had it bad. Not anymore. I am totally over him. I could care less if I never see his face again," I said, nodding my head in agreement with myself.

"Liar," Lindsey retorted. Before I could respond, she was speaking. "You like him. And I'm not fully convinced that you aren't in love with him. Either way, this guy has had a major effect on you. Trust me, it's a good effect. No offense," she said, holding her hands up as if to surrender. "Now, your problem is that- Wait, can I speak bluntly and like, not lose my job?" she asked.

I motioned to her with my hand, "By all means, you have the floor." I knew to prepare myself for the bitter truth of what a bitch I was. I had heard it before, but it would do me some good to hear it again.

"Good. Anyways, your problem is that you live in a bubble. In your bubble, everything has to be perfect and just as Dallas sees it. That's fine when you are at work, running a multi-million dollar company. But, when you step into the real world, you have to learn to stand out of the spotlight a little. You follow me?" Lindsey asked.

"I follow you, but I don't live in a bubble, Lindsey. I just simply know what I want and what I deserve," I responded, not at all offended by what she was saying.

"You're a bitch," Lindsey blurted out. She was now standing up. The shock of what she had just said, apparent on her face. "I'm sorry," she squeaked, her hands coming to her mouth.

I laughed, "I know that, Lindsey. I was hoping that you would be a little more creative."

"You have no idea how long I have wanted to say that," she said laughing. I joined in. It was nice to laugh, even if it was at my own expense. "Ok, I'm sorry. Really. I shouldn't have said that. Okay. Back to Luke, you are lucky. He could have done what he did in front of everyone. Now *that* would have been embarrassing," Lindsey said, helping herself to the candy dish sitting on the counter.

"You speak as if from experience," I said, eyeing her curiously. *Surely Lindsey wasn't an executive assistant by day, and a biker chick by night.*

"No, it has never happened to me, but I have seen it. My ex-fiancé is in a bike club. I was there with him through the whole prospect period; a hundred and seventy-six days to be exact," she said. *I could tell she was trying come across indifferent, but I saw the pain behind her smile.*

"What happened between y'all?" I asked.

"He got patched in. Women were throwing themselves at him, just for a chance to ride with the club. He loved that life much more than he loved me. I was tired of the late night phone calls saying he wasn't going to make it home. Then, he got to where he wouldn't even call. I had enough and ended it. He was relieved. I knew it was what he wanted. He had been trying to push me away for months. That was before I moved here," she responded, busying herself in the kitchen, so that she wouldn't have to face me.

"What did you mean earlier when you said it could have been worse?" I asked, feeling a change of subject was in order.

"Well, in that world, it isn't about you. Luke is the president, right?" she asked, looking at me for an answer.

"I think so," I responded unsure.

"You think so, great. Well if he is, then he sets an example for everyone else. Now, how do you think it made him look to have the woman he brought with him, chatting up another man?" I looked at her with an impassive face. *I tried to think about what I had done, but I saw no wrong in it.*

"It wasn't as bad as what he was doing," I responded. "Bikers hug and kiss their family. By family, I mean the people who ride with them, fellow club members, other club members. It's a way of communication for them."

I just stared at her, not sure what she wanted me to say. "Ok, think of it like this, in the real estate world, you are the queen, the Alpha and Omega, top of the line. Nobody does real estate as well as you. In the bike world, that's Luke. You know how you tend to take three hour lunch breaks? Sometimes it's because you have business to attend to, sometimes you just want to go to 306 Front Street and eat, knowing good and damn well it will take an extra thirty minutes just to get through traffic. My point is that you can do that because *you* are the boss. But, what if I did that? What if your clients had to wait because your employee wanted to take a three hour lunch break? How would that make you look?"

She had me. I got it. I would have fired her on the spot if she had pulled some of the stunts that I pulled on a regular basis. I could do it because I was the boss. She did as I told her, that's how the business worked. Apparently, that was how Luke worked, too. Except, I was the one being told what to do.

"Hey, you still with me?" Lindsey asked, waving her hand in front of my face.

"I get it. But, I don't like it. Not that it would matter even if I did," I said, closing the subject. My phone began ringing in my pocket, and my heart fluttered at the sound. I knew who it was without looking. I glanced at the screen and saw Luke's name flashing. Without thinking twice, I hit the ignore button and sat the phone on the counter.

"What the hell are you doing?" Lindsey asked, looking at me like I had lost my mind.

"I'm not interested in anything that he has to say," I responded.

"Dallas, I thought we talked about this," Lindsey whined.

"No, we did not talk about this. And, we are not going to," I said stubbornly. I knew I was being irrational and that I would most likely regret it later, but right now, I didn't care. I had done nothing wrong and if Luke had expected me to act a certain way he should have told me.

"Fine. I'm hungry. Want a pizza?" Lindsey asked. I was glad that she was willing to let the topic die. My phone rang once again, and without looking to see who it was, I cut the phone off.

"I don't really have much of an appetite. But, I am in the mood for a good chick flick," I said smiling at her.

"Don't worry," Lindsey said flashing me a smile. "I have just the one."

I liked Lindsey's idea of a chick flick. I was full of M&M's and popcorn, completely mortified, and aware of the least little sound after watching The Texas Chainsaw Massacre and the Exorcist. I lay sprawled on the couch, my yawning uncontrollable.

"Would you like to spend the night?" Lindsey asked, mirroring my yawning. "If you promise not to question your sexual orientation, you can sleep with me." I laughed at her attempt to do a sexy pose while batting her long eyelashes at me.

"Sure," I replied sleepily. We made our way into the bedroom, Lindsey cutting off light switches as she went.

"Here ya go," she said, tossing me an oversized MSU t-shirt. I walked toward the bathroom to scrub my face and prepare for bed. Lindsey, who obviously had no shame, was already half naked before I had even left the room. Pulling my hair back, I washed my face carefully removing all traces of makeup. I stared at my shiny, clean face in the mirror. My big hazel eyes looked sad and the feeling was reflected in my heart. It had been a long day and although the movie was enough to deter me, I knew the night was coming and the memories of the day were flashing back, and becoming clear in my mind once again.

I missed Luke. I wanted to talk to him, but my pride would not allow it. Was it possible to miss someone so much? I had just met this man, yet I felt like I had known him all of my life.

"Ohhhh Dallllaaasss...," I heard a sing-song voice call from the bedroom. A slow smile formed on my lips as I left the bathroom to join my new found friend in her bed. I couldn't help but laugh at Lindsey's splayed body over the bed, rubbing my pillow and eyeing me seductively.

"Move it, bitch." Lindsey laughed, rolling back onto her side of the bed.

"It's good to see you smile," she said, without any trace of humor. "Wanna see something really cool?" I nodded my head, unable to contain my smile. Lindsey patted the bed and I climbed in under the covers. The bed dipped in the middle causing us to nearly be on top of one another, but it was extremely comfortable. The closeness didn't bother me at all. It actually reminded me of a sleepover. Lindsey grabbed a remote next to the bed and hit a button. Sounds of water falling on a tin roof filled my ears. I could also hear lightning and thunder. "I have to have this to sleep or else I will hear the house creaking and shit my pants, thinking someone is coming to get me," she said laughing, but I could tell she was serious. She hit another button and the lights went out, but when I looked up I found the ceiling above us was glowing with stars. "Pretty awesome, huh?" she asked without looking at me. *Wow.*

"Definitely awesome, I love it."

"Goodnight, boss."

"Goodnight, Lindsey and thank you, for everything."

"Mm hmm," was the only response that I received. I grabbed my phone, switching it on to set my alarm. I would have to get up early, so that I would have time to go home before work. My notification window lit up letting me know I had messages. *Answer the fucking phone* *Where are you* *I swear to God Dallas if you don't answer me...* *Wow...* several messages, all from Luke. My heart lurched as I read them. Even though they were rude and not exactly what I was hoping to hear, I couldn't help but feel excited that he tried to contact me numerous times. My phone pinged again with a new message. My breath quickened when I saw that it was from him. *I'm sorry about today. The world I live in is very different from yours. Please forgive me. I have returned your car to your home (personally) so no strange man has access to your private information. I hope to see you again someday. Keep my number and don't hesitate if you ever need anything.*

What the hell? He hoped to see me again someday? My heart fell, as the unfamiliar feeling of rejection took over. *He didn't want me. If he did, he would have asked to see me again.* The realization of it all consumed me and I had to fight hard to stifle a sob. I set my alarm and laid my phone beside the bed, then turned to stare at the stars above me. I closed my eyes and let the sound of the rain and the memories of Luke lull me to sleep.

Chapter 8

The following week passed by in a blur. Lindsey was off on Monday, courtesy of Luke, and Tuesday, courtesy of me. Back in the office on Wednesday, there was plenty for her to catch up on and an abundance of deals for me to close. Things around the office were much more relaxed, now that she and I had bonded. It seemed that more work was getting done and my appreciation for her had become more and more evident, considering I did both our jobs for the first part of the week.

Friday finally rolled around and she sank into the plush leather chair in my office with an exaggerated sigh. "Thank God, this week is over. I believe that we deserve a drink."

"I have to agree. How about you make us a reservation at Mahogany and we will let the company treat us," I said, smirking at her.

"Done," she said standing and making her way out of the office. I walked to the window, looking out at the busy streets of downtown Hattiesburg. The sleek, modern interior of my office was much different from the outside historical area. Bricks lined the one way street and made a rumbling sound when the cars passed over them. The rumbling seemed to get louder with the passing seconds. I soon realized that the sound I was hearing was not the bricks at all, but a motorcycle coming from a distance.

My heart leaped into my throat and the aching I had in my chest resurfaced as my thoughts turned to Luke. *It was him. He was coming to see me*. I had not talked to him in a week, but he was not far from my memory. *I could still feel his arms around me, his intoxicating smell, and his lips on mine*. My lips turned up in smile, but quickly fell when the bike passed right by my office, never taking a second glance, or slowing in the slightest. It was not Luke. I was suddenly aware of someone standing beside me. I turned to see a sad expression on Lindsey's face. Her apologies were apparent ,even without words.

"Let's go get that drink," she said with a reassuring smile. I nodded. Grabbing my purse, I walked out of the office with the loud pipes of a motorcycle ringing in my ears.

The restaurant was packed and loud. The atmosphere immediately lifted my spirits. The elderly couple in front of us at the reservation podium was turning to leave, disappointed because of the wait. "Sir, you are more than welcome to have my reservation," I announced to the elderly man who was assisting his wife. "We can sit at the bar."

The old man smiled kindly at me. "Thank you, young lady. It's our anniversary," he said smiling fondly at his wife. The feeling of gratification spread through me like warm honey as I watched the couple shuffle off to what would have been my table.

I noticed Lindsey giving me an odd look out of the corner of my eye and I shot her a *don't-start-with-me* look as we made our way to the bar. We sat at the bar and ordered a round of cosmos. The T.V. was tuned to a baseball game and the men around us were in joyful conversation over who would win. It was hard not to get sucked into the topic, considering we were the only two females in talking distance. My thoughts and worries about Luke were fading with each passing minute as the guys schooled us on baseball stats and kept the drinks coming. Laughter filled the room when we all took turns demonstrating the perfect batting stance. When my turn came, I was giggling uncontrollably, trying to look serious when I heard a whistle from behind me. I turned and saw the boyish face of Regg grinning at me.

"Regg!" I screamed, throwing my arms around his neck.

"Hey, beautiful!" he said, returning my hug. I stepped back, holding him at arm's length and my face fell. If he was here, chances were Luke was nearby.

"He's here. I know what you are thinking," Regg said, winking at me. As if he heard his name, Luke appeared, looking just as hot as I remembered. His ripped jeans gave me a view of his toned, tanned legs and the sleeveless t-shirt that he wore under his vest made his full sleeved tattooed arms available for my eyes. My breath caught in my throat when my eyes landed on his mouth. His lips were turned up into a smile, clearly enjoying my reaction. The stubble around his mouth reminded me of the pleasure it gave me when it was on my most sensitive area.

He stepped closer to me, returning the favor of undressing me with his eyes. I was still dressed for work in a cream colored silk blouse and black slacks. He started with my face, pausing momentarily at my cleavage that was barely visible through the opened buttons on my shirt. Then his eyes skimmed down my legs, all the way to my black Yves Saint Laurent pumps and back up to my eyes. I quickly regained my composure, and regarded him impassively.

"Luke, what a pleasant surprise."

"Dallas," he said stepping towards me and closing the distance. "You look absolutely beautiful, as always." He leaned in, causing my breath to hitch in my throat and planted a soft, chaste kiss on my cheek.

"You must be Lindsey," he said, turning from me and holding his hand out for Lindsey to shake. She stood staring at him wide eyed as he took her hand in his giving it a light shake. She finally managed to mumble something that resembled a hello. I rolled my eyes at her and turned to Luke again.

"We were just leaving," I said, managing to keep my voice calm and even.

"Really?" he asked, not hiding his surprise.

"No hell, y'all weren't. Y'all were over here flirting with these men," Regg chimed in, grinning from ear to ear. *He really had no filter.* Before I could respond, Luke smiled warmly at me.

"Well, who am I to interfere. I hope you ladies enjoy yourself. Ms. Lindsey, it was a pleasure to meet you." And with that, he turned and walked away. My eyes followed him all the way to the door. "Oh, and by the way, Dallas," he said, turning to walk backwards so he was facing me, "Stay away from them cowboys." He shot me a wink and a boyish smile that left me reeling.

"So, that's Luke?" Lindsey asked me, pulling me from my dreamy haze.

"In the flesh," I responded, holding up my empty glass to the bartender. "Let's get shitty, Lindsey."

"Yes!"

It was midnight when we finally made our way to the parking lot. I held my keys up, pushing the alarm button to remind my cloudy mind of where we were parked. We were drunk and giddy as we followed the sound of the horn blaring. Not sure of where it was coming from, we were singing loudly tunes from the musical "The Sound of Music," and filling in words we didn't know with "la- la- la- la." Our laughter ceased when our eyes fell on the two motorcycles sitting next to my car. Regg and a man that I didn't recognize were laughing and shaking their heads at us.

"Did y'all have a good time?" Regg asked, through his laughter.

"Yesssirr," I slurred, with a salute.

"Damn. How about we give y'all a ride home now." Regg said. It was a demand, not a question. *Shit. Are all bikers like this?*

"Nah, we're good," I responded, swaying slightly.

"Here," Regg handed me a helmet and took my purse and keys from me before I could respond. The other guy followed suit, taking Lindsey's purse and handing her a helmet. I started to protest, when Lindsey planted a finger on my lips and shook her head. "He's cute," she said, giggling and nodding her head toward the guy, who had 'PROSPECT' stitched on his vest. I decided not to argue. I owed it to Lindsey; although I was a little displeased that it was Regg that I would be riding with and not Luke.

I thought of Red, but quickly pushed the thought away. Maybe she wouldn't find out. Maybe, she already knows? Oh well, who gives a shit. I clambered onto the motorcycle, with the assistance of Regg. He grabbed my leg and pulled my foot onto his lap. With a disapproving look, he removed first one and then the other heel and handed them to PROSPECT. He dutifully took them and repeated the same process with Lindsey who was smiling ear to ear, and put them in his saddle bag.

I winked at Lindsey and held tight to Regg as he fired up the motorcycle and sped out of the parking lot. I couldn't help the feel of exhilaration I got. I should have been drunk when I rode with Luke. I laughed in Regg's ear and he shook his head in response. We headed east on Hardy Street and I wondered where he was taking us. But I didn't ask, I just enjoyed the ride. A small part of me was hoping that wherever we went, Luke would be there. The wind in my hair felt amazing. My arms were wrapped tightly around Regg. A twinge of nervousness surfaced when we took a sharp turn to the right, but I closed my eyes and quickly put it at the back of my mind. He pulled up into the parking lot of a hotel. One of the nicest hotels in Hattiesburg, I noted, and parked at the front entrance. Helping me off, he handed me my things and placed his hand on my back, leading me into the hotel. I looked back to see Lindsey wrapping her arm around PROSPECT, but he seemed oblivious to her.

"Reservation for Reggie Jones," Regg announced to the attendant.

"ID, Mr. Jones?" Regg presented his ID and we were soon being escorted to the elevator. My feet hurt, my head hurt, and I was on the verge of passing out. Lindsey didn't seem to be in any better shape. We walked down the hall of the hotel and Regg opened the door to a suite. He ushered us in and handed me the key.

"Do not leave. Someone will be here in the morning to take you to your car. Understand?" Fun Regg was gone and in his place was stern, demanding, no-nonsense- biker, Regg. I nodded my head in agreement, not wanting to argue- only sleep. "You have Luke's number. Call if you need anything." With that, Regg and the PROSPECT turned and left. I collapsed onto the bed and was asleep before my head hit the pillow.

I awoke the next morning with a start. As I sat straight up in the bed, I took note that I was fully dressed and smelled of booze. My hair was a tangled mess and it took me a moment to remember the previous night. As I looked around the large spacious room, I saw the balcony doors were open and a cool breeze was blowing in despite the hot weather we usually had for September. I heard the shower running, and not seeing Lindsey, assumed it was her. A light rap sounded at the door and I scrambled out of bed to see who it was. I opened the door to find an older gentleman delivering room service.

"Miss Knox?" he asks kindly.

"Yes, I am Miss Knox."

"Mr. Jones had this sent up for you." I opened the door wider to allow the man to come inside. With him was a cart covered in silver platters along with pitchers of orange juice, water, and coffee.

"Thank you so much," I said graciously, fishing a twenty out of my purse. He nodded in response and left, closing the door behind him. I uncovered the platters and found a little of everything- sausage, bacon, eggs, grits, pancakes, fresh fruit, bagels... *Regg had gone all out*. Lindsey emerged from the bathroom dressed in a robe with her wet hair piled high on her head.

"Mmmm, something smells delicious. Did you order this?" she asked, grabbing a piece of sausage and greedily taking a bite.

"No, apparently Mr. Jones had this sent up to us," I said mockingly.

"Well, thank God, I am starving." I shook my head at her and made my way to the bathroom. My appearance reflected the way I felt this morning. *Shitty.* I decided on a hot shower to help clear my head. As the hot water cascaded over my body, I let the memories of last night come back to haunt me. Luke had sent Regg and PROSPECT to check on me. *I knew it. Why could he not have come himself? Why did he even care? I was pissed that he sent Regg. I was pissed that he felt the need to control me. I was pissed that I was in this hotel. But, I was mostly pissed at myself.* My body and heart were betraying me. My nerves sung out with the hopeful promise to feel his touch again and my treacherous heart fluttered at just the thought of talking to him today. Even his voice possessed me. Without him even being here I felt his presence, because I knew deep down that he was responsible for me being here.

My strong will and never bending pride took over as a sense of pure rage engulfed me. Who in the hell did he think he was? I pushed aside the feeling of elation I got when my mind was made up that I would call him. Negative attention was just as good as anything. Maybe if I made him mad enough, he would show up just to reprimand me. The thought of him doing something crude to me as punishment sent chills down my body, causing me to shudder.

Ugh. Snap out of it Dallas. I quickly shut the water off and stepped out of the shower, adamant not to let my carnal instincts take over and determined to stick to my guns. Luke was wrong for what he did. In no way do I belong to him nor does he have any right to treat me as though I do. Determined to end this debacle once and for all, I towel dried my hair, put on a robe, and headed out of the bathroom to grab my phone. Of course, my plan fell through when my eyes met those ocean blue ones across the room.

Luke was here. Relief flooded through me as an overwhelming urge to jump into his arms took over. Somehow or another, I managed to keep my composure, and straightening my shoulders, I glared at him with my mastered impassive face. He was no fool, he could see right through me and I knew it. An arrogant smile spread across his face as he lifted his hands in the air in a surrendering gesture.

"I just brought your car back babe. That's all." His grin was that of a Cheshire cat and I wanted nothing more than to slap the look off of his face. His smugness was just what I needed to keep my feelings for him at bay.

"Oh no, that most definitely is not all," I said smoothly. Grabbing myself a cup of coffee, I took my time enjoying the look of shock that passed over his face. "I need to make a few things clear to you. I am not your fucking pet. I don't belong to you, nor do I need you looking out for me. I have been told by more than one person that there are plenty of women just lining up to be dominated by you. I am clearly not one of those women, so do yourself a favor and leave me the hell alone." There. That told him.

My cold hard stare bore deep into his eyes and his reflecting look was just the same. My eyes faltered momentarily, grazing over his body. He was so fucking beautiful. He stood staring at me with his arms crossed, giving me the full view of his taunt, hard muscles. I wanted those arms around me. His legs were slightly apart from one another giving his stance that of power. The look he bore into me was filled with such malice that I wanted to look away, avert my eyes to anything but him. I stood my ground, but the one second that I lost my composure did not go unnoticed. He knew I was bluffing. I could tell by the way his face softened and went from that of stone to skepticism. He sauntered toward me, removing the coffee from my hand and placing it on the dresser. Somewhere in my brain I registered the sound of the door closing and knew that Lindsey had stepped out leaving me alone with him. My breath quickened. My heart nearly beat out of my chest and I felt dizzy from his intoxicating smell. He leaned in, planting a soft kiss on my neck.

"Do you really want me to go, Dallas?" he asked in his dark, raspy bedroom voice. *I couldn't answer. I was trying to concentrate on not convulsing into an orgasm from his closeness.* "You don't like me taking care of you?" He kissed me further down my neck, pausing when he got to the base of my throat and then continuing back up. "I could take real good care of you. You need someone to look after you, Dallas-someone to hold you when you cry, someone to satisfy your needs, someone who isn't scared of a little intimidation. Have any of your other boyfriends made you feel this way?"

He continued the torturous onslaught with his mouth by moving my robe off of my shoulder, loosening the belt that held it closed. My panting grew louder and a soft moan escaped my lips when he nipped my shoulder with his teeth.

"Look at me," he demanded, pulling my chin up so my eyes met his. I could see that he was looking for an answer. I knew deep in my heart what that answer was, but I couldn't let him have complete control over me, especially after what he had done. I was still wounded from the way he talked to me at the bar. My heart still hurt from him sending someone to watch after me, when I knew that deep down if he was really worried about my safety then he would have come himself. Digging deep inside me, I found the courage to end this conversation before it took a turn for the worst.

"You need to leave, now." My voice came out much harsher than what I intended. A look of rejection and hurt passed over his face before he quickly hid it with his signature smirk.

"Okay babe, I'll leave. But, just so you know, I sure do miss that girl I met last week." He kissed me tenderly, almost reverently on the lips and walked out. I stood in shock, staring at the now closed door.

Why did I keep doing this to myself? If I wanted him, why did I put myself through such misery? There was nothing wrong with me falling for him. Why couldn't I put my stubbornness aside and actually enjoy something in life for once?

By the time Lindsey walked back into the room I was dressed and ready to leave. She took the silent hint and dressed quickly, grabbing a bagel before heading out the door. I sped from the parking lot, hoping to get away from his lingering smell and presence, but not before seeing him watching and waiting for me from the side of the building. Without a second thought, I pushed my rearview mirror up effectively blocking him from my sight. *If only it were that easy with my heart.*

Chapter 9

I pulled up next to Lindsey's car at the office. We had not spoken since we left the hotel, and the awkward silence between us was becoming more and more uncomfortable. She gave me a weak smile and got out. I stayed to make sure she was securely in her car, and then pulled into traffic to head home. I couldn't wait to crawl into my bed, in my dark bedroom and shut the whole world out for the next forty-eight hours.

A week ago, I knew exactly who I was. Life had given me just what I expected it to. Then, like a whirlwind, Luke had appeared and turned everything upside down. Now, I didn't recognize the girl that I saw in the mirror every morning. Every second of every day, I thought of him. I was happy and smiling, for no reason. He had changed me. In the small amount of time that I knew him, he had reminded me what life felt like. How it felt to love and appreciate things that money could not buy. He had given me Lindsey. My friendship with her was one I knew would last forever. He taught me humility. I found myself doing things for people that normally I never would have done. He had impacted my life, yet I pushed him away. And for what? Because he didn't want me driving home drunk? Because he made sure that I was taken care of? Didn't he warn me not to flirt with other men? I blew it. The only man who could ever potentially love me and capture my heart was now out of the picture.

Maybe I did need someone who wasn't scared of my intimidating ways and who could take care of me. I decided right then that if God was gracious enough to give me another chance with him, I would not push him away. Well, not for the things he had done in the past anyway. We would definitely discuss it, but I would not run from him. Hattiesburg was a small town. Surely I would bump into him. But, what if he no longer wanted me? What if I had ruined my last chance?

My phone rang out over the loudspeaker, and without even seeing who it was; I hit the call button on my steering wheel.

"Dallas Knox," I answered in my Monday thru Friday monotonous tone.

"Do you always answer your phone like that?" Lindsey asked disapprovingly.

"No, it normally rings only on work days. What is it?"

"Well, I wanted to remind you of the Mayor's daughter's engagement party tonight. We sent an RSVP. Do you want me to cancel?" Lindsey asked, regret filling her voice.

Who was I to ruin her weekend? "No, don't cancel. I'll be there. Arrange for us to have a limo. Y'all can pick me up at six."

"A limo?" Lindsey asked shocked, as if it were the first time that I had asked her to get one. "Don't you think that is a little over the top for an engagement party?"

"It's black tie isn't it?" I snapped.

"Yes, it is. I apologize. I don't know where my head is. I'll arrange for it to be here at five-thirty and we'll be at your place by six."

I hung up the phone without a goodbye. Lindsey was my friend, but business was still business and I didn't like to be questioned. Hell would freeze over before I showed up driving my own car while some of my most prestigious clients and competitors looked on. I agreed to this dinner for one reason only. Mayor Kirkley owned some properties that I was interested in purchasing. I already had an investor looking for something in that area and if I could land it, it would mean a huge profit for the company. Not to mention, that would mean that I owned over sixty percent of the commercial property in Hattiesburg. Tonight I would put Luke out of my mind and focus on business. If I was lucky, maybe some bachelor would come along and relieve some pent up stress. No, nothing to remind me of Luke. Tonight, I would be the Dallas Knox that I know. Tomorrow, I could go back to being the sap I had become.

After a nap, a bubble bath, and a quick masturbation session, I was completely relaxed and ready to begin dressing. The limo would be here in an hour, which means we would arrive at approximately six-thirty. Perfect. The party started at six, so that would give the other guests plenty of time to arrive before my grand entrance. I applied light make-up consisting of a little mascara, blush and a clear lip gloss and swept my hair into a knot just above my neck. A few tendrils fell, framing my face, but still they left my diamond teardrop earrings visible. I chose a floor length, pale yellow, satin gown that had a small train. The back was cut out and dipped low, starting right at the top of my perfectly toned ass. It was borderline inappropriate, but still looked classy. One row of rhinestones went across the back, right below my shoulders, keeping the dress held together. The front was cut low, covering both my breasts, but leaving the space in between open. I slipped on a pair of matching heels that were custom made for the dress, grabbed the matching clutch and turned to look at the vixen in the mirror. I would, without a doubt, be the talk of the town. My tanned skin contrasted perfectly with the pale colored dress, and although I was covered, the outline of the dress left little to the imagination. I sprayed on my most alluring perfume and headed out to make every man in Hattiesburg envious of the husband I didn't have.

The limo arrived at exactly 6:00 p.m. Henderson, the driver, quickly opened the door for me and assisted me by holding my hand while I sat.

"You look lovely tonight, Miss Knox," he spoke in his deep, yet warm tone.

"Thank you, Henderson. You look well yourself." He smiled warmly, and then closed the door. I looked beside me to see Lindsey gaping with her mouth open. "You okay?" I asked.

"Uh, you look hot, Dallas. Like, really hot," she said with real appreciation in her tone.

"Thank you. You look beautiful as well." And she did. Her hair was swept up on top of her head and her black, strapless gown was stunning. She smiled and leaned up, grabbing a couple glasses and a chilled bottle of champagne. We toasted to the night, the business and friendship- then to Henderson, leather seats and the rapper 50 Cent. Before we pulled into the Convention center, the bottle was empty and we were both light headed and tipsy.

This was no Hollywood movie premier, but for Hattiesburg, it was the main event. The time people went all out to make an impression on the ever important, Mayor Paul Kirkley. Mayor Kirkley had been in office several years now and had drastically improved the city. Some considered him a celebrity. He even had an article written about him that was published in *Time* magazine. His one and only child, Nathalie, was marrying her high school sweetheart, Mason, the son of State Representative John Blunt. Everyone who was anyone would be present tonight and I could not help but enjoy the attention that I drew once I walked through the door. Grabbing a glass of champagne from a passing waiter, I made my way around the room, smiling and making small talk with those I encountered. Seated at my table for dinner, were two very important potential clients and their wives.

By the time dinner was over, I had successfully landed three new properties, gained two new clients, and made a generous donation to a charity in which both clients' wives sat on the board. It felt good to be in control again. It was amazing what you could accomplish with a smile, a low cut dress, and a check book. Mayor Kirkley had been busy all night, but once his eyes landed on my dress, I saw my opportunity and took full advantage of it.

"Mayor Kirkley, what a magnificent party." I said cheerfully, kissing him on both cheeks.

"Miss Knox, I'm so glad you could make it. Are you enjoying yourself?" he asked, not able to keep his eyes from my cleavage.

"Oh, yes. Dinner was delightful and very rewarding. Thank you for arranging the seating for me," I said with a wink.

"My pleasure. Will you save a dance for me later?" he asked, eyeing me seductively.

"I'm looking forward to it." I turned and walked away, giving him a clear view of the back of my dress, then joined Lindsey for a drink, something a little stronger than champagne.

I gladly danced with anyone who asked. You never knew when that person could be of assistance to you. I danced with aldermen, firemen, county workers, and young bachelors; not once did I think of Luke. I had locked him in a box in the back of my sub- conscious and I was determined to keep him there until the night was over.

Mayor Kirkley had finally made his way around to me and I was anxious to get it over with, so that I could leave. *I had approximately three minutes to convince him to sell his land to me, and Mayor Kirkley was known for being a shrewd negotiator.* "Ahh, finally I get to dance with the most beautiful woman in the room," he said to me, sweeping me into his arms. He was a very good looking man. His tall strong body was flawless. He was once a bodybuilder, and when I placed my hand on his shoulder, I could feel his taunt muscles through his tuxedo.

"Well, I have to disagree with you Mayor. It seems that Nathalie is by far the most beautiful woman in the room."

"She is nothing more than a child, but you are *all* woman. Do tell me Miss Knox, why did you really come here tonight? To try and acquire some land I have, I presume," he said arrogantly.

"Why, Mayor Kirkley. I am shocked that you would think such a thing." I responded, appearing wounded.

"Oh cut the shit, Dallas. What do you want with that land anyway?" he asked using a tone that was all business.

"I'm thinking of combining all of my offices into one building," I lied smoothly.

"Some of that land, I could sell by the square inch. It is in high demand right now."

"And I plan to pay you top dollar. It will be at least five years before the property has enough commercial business surrounding it to even be worth anything. That is why I want to put my office out there. It will be the only real estate company on Ninety-Eight. Everyone else is downtown." I could tell that he was intrigued by my proposal. He was going to have to sell the property soon anyway and everyone knew that if anyone could afford it, Dallas Knox could.

"So there's no hot shot investor waiting to jump at the first opportunity to put a strip mall or other large business there?" he asked curiously.

"Not that I am aware of," I lied again.

"Okay, I'll tell you what. I'll send some figures over to your office first thing Monday morning. If you like 'em we'll make a deal," he said, not looking me in the eye.

"Do I look like an idiot to you, Paul? I know as well as you do, exactly what top dollar is for that property. Send me the paperwork. I'll take it to my lawyer and I'll have you a certified check by Tuesday morning." I was giddy, but managed to conceal it, feigning disinterest.

"Okay, but promise me that you will use Carmical Construction to clear the timber. I kinda owe the owner a favor," he replied defeated.

"Done." I gave him a quick nod and exited the dance floor, just as the song finished.

I joined Lindsey at our table and making a silent toast, drained another glass of champagne. Lindsey smiled knowingly. "So, what are the stipulations? I know he had some."

"Only one, Carmical Constr-." I froze mid-sentence. *Carmical Construction?* Surely it was not the same Carmical? My question was answered as a tuxedo dressed Luke entered the room and shook hands with Mayor Kirkley. *He was stunning.* Dressed in a black tux with a champagne colored vest and tie, he looked nothing like the biker-Luke that I knew. No, this Luke was all business and the power and attention he demanded when walking into a room did not go unnoticed by anyone, including myself. He drew the eyes of every woman in the room, and I was immediately jealous. This was my Luke. Well, maybe not this one, but the Luke under those clothes belonged to me and no one else. He seemed oblivious to the women who were gathered in small crowds around him, whispering and smiling. It seemed that he had eyes for only one woman, and I knew exactly who that was as soon as he turned and looked at me. I could feel the pull that was between us. The chemistry was there, even amongst all of the people, and I felt as though we were the only two in the room. In what seemed like only a second he was there, standing in front of me.

"Dance with me?" he asked, holding out his hand. His voice stood out over everyone in the room. I thought the chatter quieted down somewhat when I took his hand and allowed him to lead me onto the dance floor. My body tingled from his touch. I noticed that the band was leaving the stage, but a man sat on a chair with a single guitar and began playing one of the sweetest melodies that I had ever heard.

"I requested this song just for you," he said, looking deep into my eyes.

He pulled me close, placing his hand on the small of my back, just above my dress. I rested my head on his chest, closing my eyes and inhaling his scent. *Oh how I had missed these arms, that smell; this man.* I let the lyrics of Joshua Radin's *You Got What I Need* take me away.

I reveled in the feel of his arm's holding me close. The world had disappeared and it was just us. I sent up a silent prayer, thanking God for the second chance that he had given me. I finally had Luke in my arms and I wasn't going to let him go this time. The song finished and I looked up into his clear, blue eyes.

"Come home with me," he whispered. It was not a question but a demanding plea. Not being able to find my voice, I nodded in agreement and was rewarded with his breathtaking smile. Placing both hands on either side of my face, he kissed me. I opened my mouth allowing his tongue to slowly caress mine. I had never felt so cherished. This man, who was still a stranger to me, was showing a public display of affection in front of hundreds of people and in that moment, I was happier than I had ever been. He pulled his lips from mine and grabbed both of my hands, kissing them, and then led me from the dance floor.

Every eye in the room was on the two of us. I felt a little guilty for stealing the show, but the feeling faded when I noticed Nathalie wiping tears from her eyes and smiling fondly at us. Luke's truck was parked at the entrance of the building. He opened the door, and assisted me in then walked around to jump into the driver's side, pausing to receive my things from Lindsey, who was wearing a face-splitting grin. Luke pulled me across the seat, placing his arm around me and kissing the top of my head.

"Shall we, Miss Knox?" he asked, melting my heart with his smile.

"We shall."

Chapter 10

We rode to Luke's house in almost complete silence. The only sound being the classic country music filling our ears. We were constantly touching one another; me rubbing his knee or playing with the hand he had around me, him kissing my hair, my temple, caressing my shoulder and arm with feather like touches. I would occasionally glance up to admire his beautiful face and each time that he caught me he would give me his signature smirk. I couldn't believe how fond I was of him. My body was teeming with excitement. Every time he touched me, my body shuddered. I knew tonight would hold something special, and the days to come would be even greater. However, in the very back of my mind, where I hid things that I never wanted to think about, there was a hint of nervousness or uncertainty.

Pulling up to Luke's house, he got out first and then I slid across the seat to his open arms. He helped me from the truck, grabbing my hand and leading me inside. "Would you like something to drink? Eat?" he asked, opening the fridge and getting a soda.

"No, thank you," I replied nervously. The anticipation for what was to come had me hungry alright, but not for food.

"You look so beautiful tonight," he said, letting his eyes roam over my body. He made me feel shy and embarrassed for some reason. I smiled and looked at the floor, my cheeks scarlet; definitely not me. He walked over to me and lifted my chin up with his finger and then trailed it down my throat to my neck, then between my breasts.

"I want to kiss you all over. I have never craved the taste of someone like I crave you." A shudder ran through me causing my body to literally shake.

"Cold?" he asked, his voice low and husky.

"No," I replied weakly. Not being able to control myself any longer, I launched myself at him. My hands wrapped around his neck as my mouth claimed his. His answering kiss was just as passionate as mine and before long he had my hair undone and wrapped around his hand, pulling my head back to deepen the kiss. I moaned into his mouth, just enjoying the taste of him. He didn't even have to fuck me, just kiss me and I would be satisfied.

He pulled away from me suddenly. We were both breathless, staring at one another in the kitchen. I thought he was going to tell me no, that he wasn't ready or that I wasn't ready or that this is wrong, but Luke had a way of surprising me often, and this time, like all the others, he didn't disappoint.

"I want to make love to you, Dallas. I want to show you how a real man cares for a woman. I would never hurt you. I only want to protect you. Please, come to bed with me."

What the hell was I supposed to say to that? A simple "let's fuck" would have been good enough for me. I wondered why he felt like he needed to go into such detail about it. I wondered if maybe it was his way of apologizing for what had happened. Deciding that was a good enough excuse for me, I agreed to go to bed with this man. I wanted the same things that he wanted. *I needed those things.* My head had just started nodding when he scooped me into his arms and carried me to his bedroom.

Luke sat me down on the bed and went around the room lighting several candles that I had not noticed before. How romantic. He turned the lights off and I lost my breath at the sight of him in the glow of the candle light. He was perfect. Dangerous, sexy, sweet, handsome, and tonight he was all mine. I smiled at the thought.

"Something funny?" he asked amused.

"I am just happy to be here, with you," I said sincerely. A looked claimed his face, as if he were thinking very hard about something. He pulled his jacket off and laid it over the dresser, then his shoes and socks. I was getting my very own Luke strip tease. He walked up to me, loosening his tie, taking his vest off, and laying it with his jacket. I struggled to swallow at the sight of him. I stood up, unbuttoning his shirt as fast as I could. His body was like air to me and at that moment I couldn't breathe without it. He sensed my need and grabbed both of my hands in one of his, while he deftly undid the buttons with the other. He let go of my hands to undo his cufflinks, never letting his eyes leave mine. Once his shirt was off, I stepped back to admire his chest and arms. His abs rippled down his stomach and the muscles in his arms were so well defined, that it was like looking at a painted picture. My finger traced one of the tattoos on his arm, a tribal one that ran from his shoulder to his wrist. I grabbed his belt and very slowly slid it off and let it fall to the floor. He swallowed noisily and I was pleased with the effect that I had on him. It seemed to fuel my desire, because in record time, I had his pants down and was staring at the large bulge in his boxer briefs.

"My turn," he said, causing me to glance up to his face. His smirk was there and the arrogance was evident. I didn't care. He had every right to be conceited. He trailed his fingers up my arms and back down again. Grabbing my shoulders, he slowly turned me so that my back was to him and pushed my hair to the front of my shoulder. With one hand, his skilled fingers, unsnapped the string of rhinestones. He slid his hands from my neck down to my waist, taking my dress with him. It soundlessly fell to the floor and pooled at my feet. "You are so beautiful."

I could feel his breath on my neck as he kissed his way from my ear to my shoulder, then down my arm. He planted a soft kiss on the palm of my hand, and then twirled me around to face him. In that moment, in the candlelight and completely naked in front of him, I was more appreciative of hot wax and spa treatments than I had ever been. His eyes roamed my body, taking everything in from my hard nipples to my yellow stilettos.

"So beautiful," he murmured, claiming my mouth with his. I melted into his arms. Even though there was no physical way that I could get any closer, I continued to push my body against his. He gently pushed me onto the bed. He grabbed my shoes and slid them off, then pushed my legs apart, exposing my most intimate parts.

"Tonight, you are all mine. I am gonna savor every part of your body that my mouth touches." His blues eyes were blazing with heat and his face was full of hunger. His voice was low and deep each time he spoke. He kissed my feet, sucking each toe as if it were a delicious treat. His mouth made its way up my leg, kissing and nipping my skin as he went. When he got to my inner thigh, he kissed the tender tissue in the crease of my leg causing me to moan out loud. Just when I thought that he would hit it home, he skipped over my throbbing center and began the same torture on the other leg.

"Please," I moaned. My back was arched off the bed and my eyes were screwed shut. The pleasure was almost too much to bear.

"Shh, baby. I'm going to take care of you. That's what I'm here for. I promise you, it will be well worth the wait. Are you on birth control, Dallas?"

"Yes," I managed to say. I was unable to focus. His words, along with his torturous tongue, drove me mad. Finally, his tongue made contact with my sensitive, wet flesh. The first flick of his tongue almost sent me over the edge. His tongue circled my clit over and over. My moans and cries, I was sure, could be heard for miles. I moved my hands to grab the back of his head, but his were faster and restrained me.

"Calm down, baby," he whispered. When his breath blew over me, I couldn't hold back any longer. My orgasm racked through my body as his mouth took over, licking, sucking and kissing me from my entrance to my clit. The orgasm rocked on for what seemed like forever, and when I finally came down from it, he was climbing over the top of me licking and kissing his way up my stomach to my firm breasts. He sucked softly on my nipples, each flick of his tongue causing me to jerk. "Look at me, baby." I slowly opened my eyes to see his beautiful face staring down at me. Seeing that my juices were visible on his perfect lips instantly made me hotter. His look was serious when he spoke. "I need you to tell me if it's too much, ok?" I nodded my head in agreement, remembering how big he was. I took a deep breath and tried to prepare myself for what was to come. "We are going to take this real slow." With gentleness that I didn't think possible, he slid partially into me. I felt myself expand under him. "Breathe, baby. I won't hurt you." I let out a big breath, and when it regulated, he inched in further. He felt so good inside of me. *This wasn't so bad.*

"More, please," I begged. *I wanted to feel him deep inside me. I wanted every bit of him.* He kissed me passionately, keeping my mind off of his large cock that was now buried inside of me.

"You feel so good. So wet, and hot just for me."

"Yes," I breathed. *I wanted him to know that no other man could ever make me feel like he did.*

"You okay?" he asked, searching my face for clues.

"Yes, please Luke, fuck me. Please." *I wanted to feel him move inside of me. I needed to feel him.*

"No, baby. No fucking this time. Just slow love making." He said, kissing my neck, my face, my lips. *I loved hearing him talk to me.* The more he said, the wetter I got. Every little endearment was like a breath of air. My heart fluttered each time his lips touched me. I had never felt like this before. Slowly, Luke began to move. It wasn't painful but a little uncomfortable. I lifted my legs to wrap around him and winced as he thrust deeper. "Be still." His tone had a bite to it, but he kissed me and I immediately forgave him.

He picked up rhythm and the feeling intensified. It was no longer uncomfortable. His mouth never left my body, constantly kissing my lips and neck and breasts. I lifted my pelvis and matched him thrust for thrust. *I could feel myself building.* I wrapped my arms around his neck and kissed him deeply. I moaned in his mouth and his growl from deep in his chest was enough to push me over the edge.

"Come for me, baby. Let me feel you while I'm inside you." My screams were of pure pleasure, this orgasm even more intense than the other. As I came apart beneath him, he drove into me- taking full advantage of my relaxed muscles. I was on the verge of passing out from ecstasy, when he rammed into me, filling me completely.

When I came to, he was still inside me, kissing my neck and face. Ever so slowly, he eased out of me and instantly I missed him. *The feeling of him inside of me, the way he constantly kissed me, the sweet things he said to me, it made me feel like a woman.* He worshiped my body. There was not a place on me that he had touched that didn't feel as if it were on fire. He laid beside me and tucked me into him. My head rested on one arm and with the other one he had a firm hold on my waist, rubbing tiny feather like circles on my stomach. His soft voice broke the silence.

"You okay, babe?"

"Yes," I managed to say, although it came out as a whisper. A soft chuckle came from behind me. I wanted to turn and look at his face, but my body was so relaxed, I didn't think that I had the strength.

"Why did you run from me?" My body tensed. I knew we would eventually discuss this, but I was hoping it would not be in my post-coital state.

"You know why," I responded, my voice somewhat stronger.

"No, I don't. I asked you not to do something and you disobeyed me. You deserved what you got." He said, never raising his voice.

"Disobeyed you?" I struggled to turn over so I could see his face. *How dare he use the word disobey with me? I was a grown woman for crying out loud.*

"Yes, disobeyed me. I told you not to be associating with other men and you did it anyway." His facial expression was completely impassive and his voice was still soft. *God, he was gorgeous.*

"First of all, I am not in the fifth grade. I am a grown woman who does not live by a set of rules. You can't just tell me to do something and expect me to do it when you were over there hugging and kissing on every woman in the bar." I was now fuming. Sweet, sexy Luke was gone and in his place was this guy that I had yet to meet.

"Ah, now we are getting somewhere. You were jealous." He gave me his signature smirk and it was like throwing gasoline on a fire.

"I most certainly was not jealous. I don't give a shit what you do. If you want to hang on every piece of trash you encounter, that's fine with me, but don't expect me to sit there and watch it," I seethed. I stood up and headed to the bathroom. *That son of a bitch, how dare he try to blame this on me. Damn right, I left; why the fuck should I stay?*

"You are a feisty bitch, aren't you?" I turned to see Luke standing in the bathroom doorway. He had pulled on some basketball shorts. For the first time, I notice his calves. Damn. How did he do that? They were muscular and tan and just the right size. *Wait, did he just call me a bitch?*

"Did you just call me a bitch?" I asked him, completely taken aback by what I thought my ears had heard.

"A feisty bitch, to be exact," he responded, still smirking. I could see the challenge in his face. Well if he wanted a fight I was going to give him one. Before I could lash out at him, he spoke again. "Why don't you tell me why you really left? Tell me the truth. How will I ever know if you don't talk to me? Is that your answer for everything? To run?" He looked so confident standing there, talking to me. His words were hypnotizing. He was so calm and collected when he talked and I was a stick of dynamite, whose fuse had already been lit.

"Do you want to know why I left?" My voice had risen and my body was shuddering with rage. "I'll tell you why, because you drag me to this fucking bar in the middle of no fucking where, then leave me at the mercy of some fucking body else why you hug and kiss every bitch that walks through the door. Then," I said quickly as if he might interrupt, even though he was propped against the door looking slightly amused and not giving a single impression that he was about to cut me off, "You made me feel like shit, because you wouldn't even introduce me to your friends or co-workers or whatever the fuck they are and I talk to one guy, one fucking guy, whom I haven't seen in years and you drag me out of the building like I am a fucking rag doll, push me up against the wall, close me in and cuss at me, not even giving me the chance to speak. What the fuck was I supposed to do, huh? Walk back inside so I could look like a complete fool in front of everyone? No fucking thank you. If you think for one minute that I am gonna let you tell me what to do then you are fucked up in the head, you egotistical, self- centered son of a bitch." I sucked a big breath in and stood there panting, staring at him. He stared back at me with a small smile on his face and his eyebrows lifted as if he was impressed.

"You finished?" he asked. He would have been better off spitting in my face. *I hated fighting with someone who refused to fight back. What was the point of an argument if he was just going to stand there and stare at me?*

"You damn right I'm finished." I pushed passed him and made my way back into his room, scooping my clothes up off the floor.

"Dallas, just calm down," he said exasperated.

"Calm down?" I was in his face now and his look had suddenly changed from that of amusement to a clear warning for me to shut up. Finally, I was getting a reaction. "Don't you fucking tell me to calm down! You started this shit!" I said, putting my finger in his chest. His breathing had become heavier and he was losing his composure. *Well, bring it on, LLC.*

"Hush, Dallas. That's enough," he said, struggling to stay calm. I knew that I shouldn't push him too far but of course, I let my mouth overload my ass.

"Fuck you!" I screamed. *That was the wrong thing to say.* He grabbed my hands and roughly pushed me onto the bed.

"Fuck you? I don't mind if I do. Let's see how smart your mouth is when I'm finished with you." Without another word of warning, his shorts were off and he was coming towards me. I was filled with excitement and nervousness all in one. He was mad, but I had seen him madder and he didn't hurt me then. But my instincts kicked in and I scrambled to try and crawl off the opposite side of the bed, but he grabbed my ankles and pulled me back to him. I was on all fours and frantically trying to escape his tight grasp. He wasn't holding me hard enough to hurt me, but firm enough so that I couldn't get away. The cat and mouse game had me soaking wet. *I was so horny, but if he wanted it, he was going to have to work for it*. A harsh slap landed across my ass and was immediately followed by another one that hurt equally as bad. I cried out from the pain, but was so turned on by it that the feeling quickly faded to a delicious sting.

"Stop it!" Luke yelled at me. He now had a firm hand on my waist and had managed to wrap his other hand in my hair, holding my head back and making me stay in place. My breasts rose and fell with the harshness of my breathing. I felt Luke lean across my back and he put his mouth close to my ear. "I am going to fuck you until you beg me to stop, and even then, I'm going to keep driving into you until I think you have learned your lesson." My response was a strangled moan, full of passion and wanting. "I know you want this, so I'm not going to give you an option of saying no." His voice was low and deep. The coldness in it sent a shiver down my spine. "If it becomes too much, just lift your arm and I'll stop. Do you understand?" I tried to nod my head, but I couldn't move it. "When I ask you something you will answer me with words. Do you understand?"

"Yes," I managed to choke out.

"What are you going to do if you can't handle it, Dallas?" He asked, blowing his breath on my ear.

"Lift my arm," I said nervously. *Fuck, this was exciting and intense and nerve racking.* He leaned up, letting go of my hair and slowly eased into me. *It felt so fucking good.* I was so wet from my arousal that I welcomed him in, my pussy stretching to accommodate him. When he pulled out, I was expecting him to fuck me slowly until he knew that I was ready, but *I was wrong*. He rammed into me over and over again. My cries were a mix of pain and pleasure. He was so deep inside me, filling me and fucking me mercilessly. *I knew this was a punishment fuck, but I loved every minute of it.*

"You learned your lesson yet, Dallas?" He asked through gritted teeth. *Hell, no.* This was too wonderful for him to stop now.

"Fuck. You," I responded with as much malice in my voice as possible.

"Wrong answer, baby." He rotated my hips, putting me at a different angle and slammed into me deeper. I blacked out momentarily. It was too much, but it still felt so good. It felt better than an orgasm. I was afraid to come, not being sure if my body would hold up afterward. He drove into me harder and faster, and I couldn't hold back anymore. My body exploded into an orgasm and somehow, Luke found a way to drive deeper.

"Stop," I tried to tell him, but it came out as a whisper. I tried to lift my arm, but my limbs were like wet spaghetti noodles. He wasn't hurting me, but my body couldn't take anymore. I collapsed on my face and immediately passed out.

When my eyes fluttered open, I was under the covers and in Luke's arms. I turned my face slightly and saw those blue eyes watching me intently. I gave him a shy smile, slightly embarrassed by my actions.

"Feel better?" he asked me, kissing my forehead.

"Much," I answered. *It was amazing how much better I felt. I was completely relaxed and felt... perfect.*

"Would you like a hot bath?" His voice was low and soft, just as it had been when he made love to me.

"With you?" I asked, hopeful.

"Of course." His smile was so infectious that I couldn't help smiling myself. "I'll go run some water, why don't you help yourself to the kitchen. I have some wine in the fridge." I nodded in agreement as he rose from the bed, walking to the bathroom. My eyes followed his perfectly sculpted back, marked with my claws of passion. I smiled to myself, remembering what had just happened. He was like night and day and I was falling in love with both sides of him. I made my way to the kitchen, taking him up on his offer of wine. I drained one glass then filled another. Back in the bathroom, Luke was standing naked in front of the mirror, shaving.

"Going somewhere?" I asked him. He looked at me in the mirror and smirked saying, "No, I just thought that your smooth skin might appreciate it."

I looked down and noticed the chaffed marks between my legs. "You don't have to do that," I muttered, embarrassed. I looked like I had some kind of rash.

"Really, babe. It's my pleasure. I plan to spend a lot of time pleasing you. I don't want you giving me any reason why I can't." He smiled sweetly at me and I couldn't help but smile back. How thoughtful of him. Thirty minutes ago, he was fucking me unconscious; now he wanted to shave to keep from chaffing me. *Oh the irony.* He rinsed his face, and then gestured for me to get in the tub. The water was hot and very inviting. I sat down feeling slightly uncomfortable. The soreness between my legs was becoming more and more intense the more I moved. "You sore?" Luke asked, eyeing me warily.

"I'm fine," I answered quickly. I didn't want him to take it easy on me just because of a little pain.

"You are a terrible liar," he said with that familiar smirk. He climbed in behind me and pulled me back against his chest.

"Mmm. This feels nice," I said, running my hands up and down his legs.

"Yes, it does. Do you want to wash your hair?" he asked, twirling a length of my hair around his finger.

"I need to," I responded sleepily. "But it can wait." The hot water along with all the sex had my body so relaxed, all I wanted was sleep. Luke took a sponge and filled it with body wash and began massaging my shoulders and arms with it. I leaned up so he could wash my back. It felt so good to be pampered and I was going to take full advantage of it. *Luke seemed to enjoy catering to me, so who was I to impose on his happiness?*

"Let's take a shower," Luke said standing and bringing me with him. He stepped out of the tub and held my hand to help me out, then pulled me into the shower. He angled us both so that the first jets of cool water were not hitting us. When the water warmed, we moved, standing under it. Luke washed my hair, massaging his strong hands into my scalp. I leaned back against him, letting him support all of my weight. "Stay awake for me, baby. Just a little longer, I promise," Luke said to me. *I couldn't believe that I was letting him bathe me. Who was I and where in the hell was Dallas Knox?* I noticed Luke's hands were no longer on my body and I turned to see him bathing himself.

"Want me to wash your back?" I asked surprised by the fact that I really wanted to. He gave me a smirk then handed me the sponge and turned around, placing his hands on the shower wall. I took my time, washing him slowly. Enjoying the way the water and soap trickled down his back, over his toned muscular ass, and onto the shower floor. I must have lost track of the time, caught up in the pleasure of bathing him, because he broke through my thoughts saying "Hey babe, I think I'm clean."

"I'm sorry," I said quickly stepping back with the sponge. I was so scared I would do something wrong to disappoint him. Not because I was afraid of a punishment fuck. Lord knows I would be instigating fights in the future to get that again, but I wanted to please him and make him happy. *It made me happy.*

"Stop apologizing for everything darlin'. It's not a big deal." He was smiling down at me. The water dripping off his face was so sexy, I was afraid that I would need another shower-*a cold one.* Luke shut off the water and we stepped out of the shower. Grabbing a towel, I dried my hair and body, then wrapped myself up and followed him into the bedroom. He handed me a black t-shirt and I slipped it on and climbed into bed. I watched him as he slid on his tight, gray boxer briefs and climbed in beside me.

"How are you feeling, and don't lie to me," He asked me firmly. I loved all of his personalities, but this one was my favorite; in charge, no-nonsense, bad ass, biker boy Luke.

"I'm sore, more than I thought I would be, but it is a delicious feeling," I answered truthfully. The aching between my legs was intense, but the reward of having him at my side was worth it. Luke surprised me when he leaned down and kissed me. His mouth was so velvety soft on mine that I wasn't sure if I was imagining it or not. His warm tongue slid over my lips and I opened my mouth, inviting him in. He held onto the side of my neck, tilting my mouth up to his and rubbed his thumb softly across my jaw. It gave me chills, the way he kissed me. It was almost as good as his love making-*almost*.

"Good night, baby," he said, kissing my head and pulling me into his arms. I was asleep as soon as I closed my eyes.

Chapter 11

I opened my eyes and Luke's chest was staring back at me. I was still folded into his arms. His slow, deep breathing let me know that he was fast asleep. It was still dark outside and I wondered just how long I had been out. I remembered what woke me when the cramp in my stomach started again. I slid out of the bed and made my way to the bathroom. *Oh God, please no, Lord please, no.* I chanted silently on my way to the bathroom. The nausea was setting in and I knew that I was going to vomit. *Probably that nasty ass lamb from the party, or all the liquor that I consumed while I was there.* The mayor probably poisoned me. I made it to the bathroom and managed to close the door before my body jerked into the first dry heave. *I hated to throw up.* I would rather have my leg amputated with a spoon. I wasn't very graceful with it either and I knew it. Chances were, this bathroom was gonna look like it belonged to a middle school on chili day by the time that I was through. I dry heaved again, trying to keep the noise to a minimum and trying to hold down the food that was forcing its way up my throat. I knew it was coming. It was inevitable. I managed to pull my hair behind my neck as my retching began.

"Dallas!" I heard Luke call from the bedroom. *Oh shit, just what I didn't need.* Forget what I said about wanting Luke to take care of me. Right now, I just wanted him to leave me the hell alone. I tried to tell him to stay away, but I couldn't even catch my breath. I flushed the toilet, hoping the swirling water would distract me from the nausea. *No such luck.* It just kept coming. After my stomach was empty, I sat dry heaving, my whole body convulsing with each horrible gag. Hands were in my hair and a cold rag was on my neck. He was here. Rubbing my back and keeping my hair out of my face. My body finally calmed and my stomach settled. I laid my head on the toilet, trying to catch my breath. Luke handed me the towel from around my neck and I wiped my face, blowing my nose in a not so discreet way.

"I'm okay. Just go back to bed," I said, trying to push him away with my weak arms and failing.

"Fat chance, babe," he replied. I knew without looking at him that he had that damn smirk on his face. I leaned up, wiping the residue of my vomit from the toilet. "I'll get that, babe, come on," Luke said, placing his hands on my shoulders, waiting for me to stand.

"I got it. Just go away. Please." I was mortified and the last thing I wanted was for Mr.

Perfect to see me like this. I struggled to stand and he helped me, holding onto me while I went to the sink to wash my mouth. *Fuck it.* He could stay. I didn't have the strength to argue with him anymore. My face was pale and my still damp hair was a mess.

I washed my face, rinsed my mouth and brushed my teeth with the new tooth brush Luke handed me. Noticing my shirt was no longer clean; I took it off and carelessly dropped it to the floor. Luke never spoke, just stood there beside me. I never looked at him. *How could I?* I made my way back to the bedroom and crawled in the bed, turning my back to him. If I had my car, I would have left right then.

Luke laid down beside me, pulling the covers up with him. He rubbed my back, my ass, and my shoulders. He was so attentive. *How in the hell was he single?*

"Why are you single?" I blurted out.

"I have been waiting for you," he responded, kissing my head. *Good one, Luke.* I smiled to myself, wondering how many times he had used that line. I lay awake for a long time after that. When I finally did dose off, Luke's tireless arms were still caressing me.

Mornings in Luke's arms are indescribable. I have never felt so safe and secure and loved as I do when I am in his arms. I knew there was no way he could love me this soon, but it was nice to think about. We were still in the same position as when I went to sleep, so I couldn't see his face. I wanted to turn over so I could admire him, but I didn't want to wake him, and I wasn't sure that I was ready to wake up completely myself.

His arm moved from my waist and I quickly closed my eyes. For some reason I didn't want him to know that I was awake. I was sure it had something to do with attention, but I didn't want to admit that. I felt him lean up, like he was looking over at me. He brushed the hair out of my face and planted a kiss on my temple, then got out of bed.

I could hear some noises that sounded like they were coming from the kitchen.

Deciding not to spend all day in bed, I got up and rummaged through his drawers, finding a pair of basketball shorts and one of his many black t-shirts. In the bathroom, I noticed that the color had returned to my face. I looked well rested and was only slightly sore. I piled my hair on my head and brushed my teeth, then struck out to find Luke. He was in the kitchen, wearing nothing but pajama pants that hung low on his waist. He looked scrumptious. He spotted me and his face lit up into a smile.

"Good morning, beautiful," he said cheerfully. I smiled shyly, crossing my arms and looking at the floor. He always knew just what to say to make me blush. "I'm making us some breakfast. It's quite a delicacy, too. You may have heard of it before." He held up a packet of instant oatmeal and I laughed.

"Sounds great," I said, taking a seat at the bar.

"Orange juice or coffee?" he asked setting both on the bar in front of me.

"Juice, please." He poured me a big glass and I greedily drank it all. He smirked at me, refilling my glass.

"I was thirsty. You know dry mouth from the... well from last night." I looked down at my knotted fingers, not meeting his gaze.

"Well, I have plenty," he said turning and taking the steaming kettle from the stove. Thank God, he wasn't going to elaborate on what happened last night. He fixed us both a bowl of oatmeal and sat down beside me. The oatmeal smelled fabulous and I was starving. It tasted just as good as it smelled and I couldn't remember ever being able to make it taste this good.

"Dallas, I want to make us official," Luke suddenly said. I looked up to see him watching me. *Wow. I couldn't believe this was actually happening. Did people even do that anymore?*

"Are you asking me to be your girlfriend, Mr. Carmical?" I asked dramatically. He laughed and dropped his stare to his hands. *Was he embarrassed?*

"I'm serious, babe. I want you in my life." *He was serious. This un-believably hot guy wanted me in his life.*

"Luke, I...," I couldn't find the words. *How was I going to tell him that I wasn't the girl he thought I was?* I pushed myself away from people. I had lived in a bubble for years for a reason. "Luke, you don't want to be with me," I said defeated.

"Oh, I don't?" He seemed surprised, but I could tell he was just being facetious.

"Look, I'm fucked up. I have issues. I'm not like most girls," I said, staring at my hands in my lap.

"Baby, I can do fucked up, and I have issues myself, everyone does." He turned in his seat so that he was facing me. "I know you are not like most girls. That is why I'm so attracted to you. Do you have any idea how many women throw themselves at me just because I am the President of an MC? But you, you like me, for me. For the man I am without the vest. I want you in every aspect of my life. The club, the job, my family... I want you to be a part of it."

I felt like the breath had been knocked out of me. He was laying his feelings out on the table and I had nothing to offer in return. I had no group of friends to introduce him to, my job consumed my entire life and my family was pretty much non-existent.

"Luke, I don't have anything to offer you in return. I mean- I am self-centered and often ruthless, I have absolutely no empathy, I'm jealous and controlling and everyone thinks I'm a bitch. The only reason people even tolerate me is because of my name." I was on the verge of tears. I had always known all of those things, but it cut deeper when I said them out loud.

"Hey," Luke said taking my face into his hands and making me look at him. "You are also kind, and beautiful and thoughtful. And, who cares what everyone thinks. They don't know the Dallas that I know. You are an amazing woman." His voice was so sincere and his face so thoughtful, that I almost believed him. "If it makes you feel better, we won't make any promises. Let's just try this and see where it leads." Luke was amazing. He knew more about me than I knew about myself. It was clear to him that I had commitment issues and he was willing to revise the invisible "normal" contract between two people, just to make me comfortable. I would be a fool not to keep this man. I nodded my head in agreement. "So, that's a yes? You will be my girlfriend?" he asked, sheepishly. The comment immediately relieved the tension in the room and set my mind at ease.

"Yes, Luke. I will be your girlfriend," I said, smiling back at him. A broad smile broke out across his face and he leaned forward, kissing me deeply. When he pulled away, I was breathless.

Luke didn't waste any time. The first thing he did, after we finished breakfast was take me to his "Harley Room." I remembered the room from the last time that I was in here, and just like before; the beautiful motorcycle was parked in the middle of the room. "I was three years old when I rode my first Harley. My grandfather, Pops, took me around the yard. I still remember it. Most kids were scared of the loud pipes and the big burly men that drove them, but not me. I have loved them since that first ride," Luke said passionately. "When I was sixteen, my father bought me a truck. He wanted me to have things that he never did. He was so proud when he handed me the keys. I had it for less than an hour before I traded it for an old Harley my Pops had at his shop," he paused, laughing to himself. "My dad was so pissed. He didn't speak to me for over a week. It took him years before he accepted my lifestyle. Now, even though he doesn't agree, he is one of my biggest supporters."

"Why didn't your father ride?" I asked, intrigued with his story.

"My Pops wasn't much of a father to my dad. He was constantly in and out of jail. When he did get out, he couldn't get a respectable job because of his record. The bike world welcomed him with open arms. Once he knew all the connections, he and another guy started their own club."

"Connections?" I asked. I knew what that meant, but I wanted him to tell me.

"Another time, babe. I want to show you something," he said, effectively changing the subject.

He took my hand and led me outside to his shop. The inside looked like a honky-tonk. There were pool tables and a juke box, a bar that ran the length of the building and pictures of motorcycles were hung everywhere. Behind the bar, I could see bottles of whiskey and tap beer available. I half expected someone to show up and take our order. In the back of the shop, there were two large double doors that were locked with a padlock. Luke presented a key, unlocked the doors and pushed them open. A huge table was centered in the room. Around the table were large brown leather chairs that looked like something an executive would sit in. What was most amazing to me though, were the large, framed shadow boxes that covered the walls housing leather vests with different patches on them. I felt like I had stepped into a museum.

"The boxes are fire and bullet proof, so even in the worst circumstances, they are protected. These two here belong to the founders of the club. My Grandfather, Pops, and his lifelong friend, Gill." Luke said, leading me to the head of the table and pointing to the two boxes on the wall behind it. "They did time together in Parchman, a five year stretch in the seventies. When they got out, they went their separate ways. My grandfather joined in with an MC out of Louisiana and Gill moved to Texas. After about two years, they reunited and decided to start their own club. That's how the Devil's Renegades MC began."

I was amazed at the history in the room. Founders and members were listed on the wall and a shrine made for each and every one of them. Each box held their vest and a personal keepsake. I noticed that Pop's keepsake was a coloring page that had been scribbled on and the name James was printed on the bottom in a child's handwriting.

"My father drew that for him when he was very young. Pops kept it with him for years. He said it was the only memory that he had of my father ever loving him," Luke said, melancholy ringing loud in his voice.

Poor Luke, it must have been terrible growing up in the middle of a family feud. I couldn't imagine having to choose between my parents and grandparents. Even though I was lacking in the family department, at least when they were alive; they all got along. I smiled at him and grabbed his hand reassuringly. "It was a long time ago, babe-water under the bridge," he said, kissing my hand.

He showed me the other vests, housed in the shadow boxes around the room. I soon learned that they were called "cuts." They all belonged to former members, all of whom had passed on. "We have meetings here weekly, and hold a formal church once a month. All members are expected to be present at church. It's the time that we discuss business, upcoming events, and any problems that may affect the club."

"Where do you sit?" I asked.

"At the head of the table," he said to me as if that was something that I should have known. I laughed. *Of course he did.*

"So, where do I fit in with all of this?"

"You don't." He said matter-of-fact. *Oh.* "You are with me. If things work out, I would love for you to become my ol' lady." Luke was back in biker mode.

"Ol' lady? What the hell is that?" I asked. *It sounded horrible.*

"It's not disrespectful, babe. It's actually the complete opposite. Being an ol' lady has its perks, especially if you're the president's ol' lady," he said smirking at me.

"I don't like the term "ol' lady." It sounds silly," I said, frowning. *I liked babe, a lot better*.

"Ol' lady is used as an endearment. It might sound silly to you in the outside world, but in my world, it's the most respectful position a woman can have."

"Well, what will I have to do?" I asked.

He laughed, "Let's get you through one day at a time. If you see this is something that you want and can handle; then I'll tell you more and we can take the next step. The girls can really help with these things. I know you don't like them that much, but at one time they were right where you are. Red knows a lot about this lifestyle. She is kinda the go-to girl in the club, and can help you with any questions you have. Tomorrow night we go out for steak night at a local bar and grill. I would really like you to come. You will get a chance to meet everyone and see if this is something you really want."

This was a lot to take in. I wanted to find out what this life was really about. I had become so attached to Luke. I knew I couldn't be happy without him in my life, so I was willing to take a chance. Plus, my curiosity had gotten the better of me.

"I would love to go," I said, walking up to him, putting my arms around his waist and burying my face in his chest. He kissed the top of my head and engulfed me in his arms. I could stay here all day, but I knew that if I wanted to be off in time to go out tomorrow night, I would have to work today. "I have enjoyed this weekend so much. And thank-you for sharing all of this with me," I said, squeezing him a little harder.

"My pleasure, babe. I really want us to work. Just promise me that you will keep an open mind."

"I promise." I meant it, too. I would not let my jealousy come between us again.

"I have some things to do this evening. Would you like to stay and have dinner with me later tonight? You can do anything you want. I won't be gone too long," he asked, looking down at me. As I looked up at his handsome face, I tried to find a flaw about his appearance but everything was perfect. *Lucky bastard.*

"Do you have a computer?" I asked. I could work from here. *That would give me another night with Mr. Wonderful, and perhaps I could do something to piss him off and earn myself a delightful, punishment session.* The thought excited me.

"I do. Come on. I'll show you where it is." He took my hand and led me out, locking the doors behind us.

Back inside, Luke presented me with his laptop and headed off to get ready. I opened my email, finding over fifty messages that I needed to respond to. My company was huge. I had offices all over Mississippi, and even though each office had its own management team, all major decisions had to come through me. My employees often emailed me personally; asking for favors, whether it was advances on their paychecks or a discount on a property. I usually had Lindsey sort through them and give them a generic response, but last week I had to answer them myself and I found that some conditions were serious. Since then, I have decided to respond to each one of them, personally. Perhaps I needed to hold church with my employees. The thought reminded me of Luke, and even though he was in the next room, I missed him. *Well, he was my boyfriend.*

I walked into his room and found that he was not in there. I could hear him in the bathroom, so I decided to stay until he came out. When the bathroom door opened, I was glad I did. Sprawled out on the bed, I had the best view in the house of Luke's incredible body. He didn't notice me at first. I heard him humming a song to himself and wondered what it was. He had his back to me and I watched while he shimmied into some underwear. I couldn't help it. I walked up behind him and put my arms around his waist. I registered his surprise, but he immediately relaxed when he glanced over his shoulder and saw that it was me.

"You snuck up on me, babe."

"Sneaky, sneaky," I giggled, quoting one of my favorite movies. He turned around and picked me up. I put my legs around his waist and my arms around his neck, giggling once again.

"What's so funny, gorgeous?" he asked, mirroring my smile.

"Nothing, I just get excited when I watch my boyfriend dress."

"Well, if it will make you smile like that, then I'll let you watch more often." He kissed me sweetly and butterflies fluttered in my stomach. "I love seeing my girl happy. Would you like to sit and watch the rest of the show?" *His girl.* I loved how he said that. I nodded enthusiastically and he sat me on the bed. *What in the hell was wrong with me?* I was giddy and felt like a love-struck teenager.

Luke glanced at the clock on the wall, and to my disappointment, dressed a little too fast for my liking. He looked hot in a pair of khaki pants and a white button down dress shirt. He slipped his belt on, grabbed his wallet and keys and leaned down giving me a kiss. He smelled so delicious that I wanted to lick him all over. I wondered where he was going, but I figured if he wanted to tell me then he would. He had not asked me to go and I couldn't help my disappointment. Not that I would have went anyway, but it still would have been nice to be invited. I pouted like a petulant child, and when he saw my frown, he knelt down in front of me and stuck his lip out.

"Why so blue, panda bear?" he asked, mocking the catch phrase for an old commercial and making me laugh.

"Do you have to leave?" I asked, still frowning.

"Unfortunately, baby, I do. Riding a Harley and making love to you don't pay the bills, although I wish it did." I smiled in relief. He was going to work. I admired his dedication, which was much like my own.

"Well, hurry back or I may be forced to do something that will result in you reprimanding me," I said grinning.

"Oh, baby. How I wish you would." He kissed me hard, leaving me breathless and stood to leave. "Call me if you need anything. I'll be back as soon as I can." And with that, he was gone.

Chapter 12

The next few hours flew by as I busied myself with work. I responded to every email in my inbox and went back to review some previous ones that I had over looked. My office in Tupelo contacted me about some rental properties that they were having some issues with. Apparently, the tenants had been somewhat destructive and had not held up to their end of the deal. They had received a notice of eviction, and were now making threatening calls to the office manager.

I didn't have many homestead rental properties; I usually just dealt with commercial properties unless I purchased a company that already had them. This was one of those cases. And it was not the first time that we have had issues with these properties. When people moved out, I did not rent the houses to anyone else. I fixed them up and sold them.

I only had two tenants left. One was an elderly lady whose children wanted her in a rental house, because of some issues with her life insurance. They claimed she couldn't have any property in her name and it was easier for her just to rent. It sounded shady to me, but they always paid on time and the woman was very kind.

The other property, housed a median income family. I had attempted to contact them on several occasions to see if they would be interested in a rent to own deal, but I never received a response. My branch manager was at his wits end, so I emailed him; letting him know that I would be there Tuesday to handle the matter myself. I would go talk to the family and see if there was a way that we could work something out that wouldn't include them trashing the place, or me throwing them out on their asses.

My phone rang and I scrambled to the other room to find it. It was Luke, and my pulse immediately quickened when I saw his name. "Hey, baby!" I answered.

"Baby? And what 'fraid tell have I done to receive that endearment?" Luke asked laughing. I never used pet names, so I was just as shocked to hear me say it as he was.

"Do you prefer Luke?"

"You can call me whatever you want, as long as you don't call me late for supper, and speaking of which, what would you like?" After last night, I really didn't want anything heavy.

"How about something light?" I asked, hoping he didn't have a big rib eye steak in mind.

"Something light, hmm. How about a grilled chicken salad?"

"Sounds delicious." Just saying it made me realize how hungry I was. It was already two o'clock. *Where had the time gone?* "Okay, I'm gonna swing by the store. I'll be there in about an hour. Anything else you want me to pick up?" he asked and I could tell he was in a really good mood.

"No, just hurry. I miss you." It was out of my mouth before I could stop it.

"I miss you, too, babe. I promise to hurry," he said, sounding very pleased with my confession.

"Okay, bye."

"Bye, babe." I hung up the phone and fell back onto the bed. I felt as if I were living in a dream. *How did I get so lucky?*

I decided to make use of my time and hopefully make time pass faster. I cleaned up the bedroom, making the bed and picking up our clothes off of the floor. In the bathroom, I wiped the counters down and rinsed out the tub, taking note that Luke's house was very clean. The floors were spotless and everything was dusted and in its place-other than the few items that we had strewn around last night.

Luke must have a maid. The thought agitated me, but I tried not to dwell on it. Having nothing else to do, I sat down on the leather sectional in the living room and switched on the T.V. Luke had all of the channels that satellite offered, including the movie and porn channels. I flipped through until I found a sitcom re-run, and then settled into the side of the couch.

Not long after I settled in I heard Luke call from the kitchen, "Honey! I'm home!" I took my time, turning the T.V. off and pulling myself from the couch. I leisurely made my way into the kitchen. *I didn't want to appear overly anxious to see him, even though I was*. Luke was digging something out of the fridge when I walked in.

"Hey, baby," he said smiling at me when he looked up. I didn't realize how much that I had missed him until that moment.

"Hey, yourself," I said sauntering towards him and taking him by surprise when I pulled him to me in an embrace.

"Did you miss me, babe?" he asked, gathering me into his arms. I nodded into his chest, and breathed in the scent of him.

"Well, that makes two of us." He kissed the top of my head, then lifted my face to his and kissed my lips. I would never tire of his kisses. "Let's eat." He grabbed two boxes from the bag on the counter and sat them on the bar. "I didn't want to waste what time we have cooking, so I just picked us something up from a restaurant."

That satisfied me, because I knew that I would have to go home all too soon. I climbed onto the bar stool and sat down. The salad was delicious and I was eager to finish so that I could be back in his arms. We talked a little about the club and he informed me of the officer ranks. Tiny was the Sergeant at Arms, meaning he was the club's security. It relieved me to know that Luke had such a tough guy looking after him. The club's vice president, Worm, was someone I had yet to meet, but Luke assured me that he would be there tomorrow night. I wasn't surprised at all to find out that Regg was the Enforcer for the club. He was pretty much Luke's right hand man and answered only to him.

I asked him why he sent Regg to watch me that night and his answer surprised me. He wanted to come himself, but was afraid that I wouldn't listen to him, so he sent Regg. He knew I was comfortable with him and that if he asked him to do something, he knew without a doubt that it would be handled. He had a sense of pride when he spoke about his officers and it was very admirable. He also mentioned that War was the Secretary and Coon, who I had not met either, was the Treasurer. I was excited about meeting them all tomorrow night; it was the ladies that I had the biggest problem with.

By the time we finished eating, my head was hurting from all the new information that was packed in it. Luke came with a lot of baggage. When he took his shirt off in the kitchen and I got a sneak peek at his abs before his under shirt slid back down; I was reminded of why his baggage didn't bother me at all. The t-shirt he was wearing underneath his polo was tight fitting on his arms. It looked shockingly white against his tanned skin and I was anxious to see him with it off. Luke seemed oblivious to my staring as he gracefully made his way around the kitchen.

"Did you get dessert?" I managed to ask, my voice low and full of hunger. Luke turned to stare at me and he smirked when he noticed my eyes looking over him hungrily.

"Well, I thought about it," he said walking towards me. "I must have looked at that menu a thousand times, but nothing seemed as tasty as Dallas."

I swallowed audibly, my breathing becoming shallow and my body heating. He was standing in front of me and I could feel the heat from his skin.

"Ever since I woke up this morning, there has only been one thing on my mind. Do you have any idea how hard it has been keeping my hands off of you?" He ran his finger down my cheek, then lifted my chin and put his lips to mine. The kiss started out slow and tender, then quickly morphed into a kiss of passion and need.

Fueled by my need for him and my desire to please him, I started undoing his pants. All I wanted at that moment was to have him in my mouth. I wanted to look up and see him coming apart. I broke the kiss off and looked into his eyes. Desire and need for me was just as evident on his face as it was on mine. His lips were slightly parted and his breath had quickened. He looked so fucking sexy, his blue eyes staring into mine. I sank to my knees on the kitchen floor in front of him and freed him from his boxer briefs.

Before he could harden completely, I took all of him into my mouth. He threw his head back and let out the sexiest moan that I had ever heard. Placing my hand at the base of him, I slid it back and forth, while I licked and sucked the head of his enormous cock. Once he hardened completely, he was so big that my mouth could not accommodate all of him. My hands grabbed his thighs, while he placed his on the back of my head, holding me still. He thrusts his hips slowly, giving me as much as I could take.

"Relax, baby, I want you to take more." The sound of his voice willed me to comply. I opened my mouth wider and relaxed my throat. He slid into me deeper, still moving slow but keeping a steady rhythm. I didn't have much of a gag reflex, but that didn't apply to him. He was huge. There was no way that I could take all of it. He pushed deeper, causing my eyes to water. "That feels so good, baby. I love looking at you on your knees." His voice was deep and throaty.

Seeing the effect that I had on him and hearing his voice, made me forget my discomfort. If it pleased him, I would do it. He pulled out of my mouth and slid his pants down, taking his underwear with them, then peeled off his t-shirt. I was still on my knees, looking up at a completely naked Luke, stroking himself in the kitchen. *It was so fucking hot.*

I loved being told what to do. *Who would have thought?* I wanted to be submissive to him. My body was craving his command and he must have sensed it. "Stay on your knees, but I want you naked. I want to see all of you." His voice had taken on a dark tone and the pleasure it gave me was shown by the increased wetness between my legs. I slid my shirt off, then never getting up, managed to slide my shorts down my legs. I was now kneeling before him, completely naked. "Do you want some more of this cock, Dallas?" He asked, still stroking himself. I nodded my head and he glared at me.

I wasn't sure what was wrong, and then remembering his command from last night, I answered him. "Yes, please."

"Good girl." *Good girl*? *Fuck, that was hot.* I felt like a dirty little slut and loved every minute of it. He grabbed my head with one hand, while his other one grasped his hardness, guiding it into my mouth. He pushed so deep, I had to control the gagging, but as soon as he reached the point where I couldn't take anymore, he pulled back and began again.

"Look up at me, baby. I want you to see how good this makes me feel. I want you to see how much you please me." A moan came from deep in my chest, and even though it couldn't escape my mouth, he heard it and I could tell it pleased him more. My eyes burned and watered, my jaw was sore from my mouth being open so wide, but the feeling of pleasure was more intense than either of those. He let go of my head and pulled out of my mouth. I immediately leaned forward and grabbed him, putting the head of his cock back into my mouth. I ran my tongue from the base to the head, greedily taking him.

"Stop, baby. If you don't, I'm going to come in your mouth." I sucked harder, taking him deeper than I ever thought I could. *I wanted to feel him come apart. I wanted to taste him.* The look on his face told me that he wouldn't take long. He looked so good standing above me. The groans that escaped his mouth, his harsh breathing, the twitching in his legs, it was all signs that I was pleasuring him.

"If you want it, baby, you got it." He gripped the back of my head with both hands and fucked my mouth. He never pushed too far, but he gave me as much as I could handle. A strangled, guttural sound escaped his mouth as his hot burst of cum slid down my throat. *He tasted absolutely delicious*. I swallowed every bit of his release, being sure not to waste a drop.

Assuming Luke was a one nut wonder; I stood up on my shaky legs and chastely kissed him, gathering my clothes from the floor.

"What are you doing, Dallas?" he asked his voice still in command. I just stood there staring at him. What did he mean? I knew how the game was played. Never suck a man's dick until he comes. If you do, be sure to have what you wanted first. If not, you would be left high and dry. I was fine with that from Luke; giving him pleasure was like pleasuring me.

He grabbed the clothes from my hands, tossing them back to the floor, and then had me in his arms, kissing me so hard it almost hurt. He picked me up, wrapping my legs around his waist and carried me into his bedroom, never breaking the kiss. Gently, he laid me down on the bed, and covered his body with mine.

"No good deed ever goes unpunished, babe," he said, sliding two fingers inside me. My moan was so loud it surprised me. I was still slightly sore from yesterday but his fingers were just the right size to not cause me any discomfort. He worked his fingers in and out of me. His mouth found my hard nipples and sucked with just the right amount of pressure. He knew exactly what to do to me and the feeling was mind blowing. He slid down my body, his fingers still inside me. His mouth found my clit and when I began to come, he finger-fucked me harder. I moaned loudly, my fingers clawing at the covers beneath me.

Before my mind could register what was happening, he was inside me-moving in and out of me with ease. He didn't bury himself completely in me and I was thankful for that. I didn't know if I could take it.

He sat up, pushing my legs far apart and grabbing my thighs, lifting my ass off the bed. The feeling was so intense that within moments, I was coming again. As soon as my body started to shudder, he drove deeper filling me completely. When my breathing slowed, so did he. He placed his thumb on my clit, rubbing small circles around it. "I want you to come for me again, baby."

"I can't," I moaned breathlessly. *It was already too much.*

"Yes, you can," he breathed in my ear.

"Please, I can't handle any more." I couldn't. My body was not strong enough.

With one arm he lifted me again and he hit the spot. I shattered beneath him and he slammed into me, flooding me with his release. After a moment, Luke pulled out of me then pulling the covers back, placed me underneath and showered my face with kisses.

"Sleep, baby."

I woke after an indeterminate amount of time. I lay there gathering my thoughts. Over the past two days, I had done nothing but sleep, eat and make love to the most amazing guy that I had ever met. *I could get use to a life like this.* I looked over at the clock and jumped out of bed. *Shit.* It was Monday morning and I was late.

"Luke!" I yelled, while jumping in the shower. I screamed as the cold water blasted me. "Luke!" I yelled again. I was hoping that he would call Lindsey for me and have her bring me some clothes to the office. If he could get me there in an hour, I would only have to reschedule my first meeting.

"Dallas!" Luke sounded frantic.

"I'm in here." I was rinsing the shampoo from my hair when he jerked the shower door open.

"What's wrong?" he asked breathless.

"Will you call Lindsey for me?" I asked, hurriedly washing my body.

"Are you fucking kidding me?" he asked, furiously. "I thought something was wrong. I was under the carport when I heard you yell, and then you screamed. You scared the shit out of me, Dallas."

"I'm sorry, but can you yell at me later? I'm going to be late. Will you please call Lindsey for me and ask her to bring me something to wear to the office and move my nine o'clock appointment? If we hurry, I can be there by ten." *I didn't have time for this right now. I had a lot of shit to do today.*

"Dallas, its eight thirty in the evening." *What?* Luke opened the cabinet under the sink and threw me a towel. "Don't you ever do that shit to me again," he said, pointing his finger at me. "Get dressed." He stormed out of the bathroom and I was left standing there feeling like a complete idiot. I dried off then rummaged through his dresser to find a t-shirt. Luke walked into the bedroom, on the phone carrying a duffel bag.

"We are leaving now just get somebody out here," he growled into the phone. "No, the prick was on foot. He was wearing yellow and blue colors. Yes, I'm sure; do I look like a fucking idiot to you?" His eyes found mine, and then scanned me from head to toe. "You ready?" he snapped.

"I just need some pants," I mumbled. *What was wrong?* I had never seen Luke so furious.

"Come here," he said to me, still holding the phone to his ear. I slowly approached him. He was kneeling down, digging something out from under the bed. When I was close enough to touch him, he turned and grabbed a pair of sweats out of the dresser. "Look, I don't have time for this shit. I am taking Dallas home. I'll call you on my way back through." He hollered into the phone, and then ended the call, sliding his phone into his pocket.

Still on one knee, Luke held out the pants for me to step into. He looked tired, angry, and somewhat worried. I started to ask him what was wrong, but he cursed under his breath and grabbed his phone from his pocket. "What?" he snapped again, but this time he sounded a little exasperated. I held onto his shoulders while he dressed me.

When my pants were on, he stood, grabbed my hand and the duffel bag and led me out to the carport. "I'm pulling out now," he said to the person on the other end of the phone. Luke opened the driver's side door of the truck and ushered me in. I moved across the seat and he climbed in behind me. I noticed when we pulled out that the shop doors were open.

"The shop door is open," I said softly.

"It's called a clubhouse and I know," he said seething. *Geez. What was up his ass?*

"What's wrong?" I asked cautiously. He was still on the phone, but he must have been put on hold.

"Nothing. I'll drop you off then I have some stuff to handle. I'll pick you up from work tomorrow."

"Luke, have I done something wrong?" I asked. I wanted him to talk to me. I thought if I played my innocent card that he would open up. Someone came back on the line and my question went unanswered. I only caught tiny bits of his conversation after that and none of it made sense to me. He was being very evasive and it bothered me.

Something had gone wrong and either he was hiding it from me or someone had pissed him off and he was taking it out on me. Either way, I wanted some answers. When he hung up the phone, he immediately turned the volume on the radio up and I knew that I wouldn't get anything from him.

We soon pulled into my driveway and he opened the gate without a problem. Pulling under my carport, he answered his phone, once again, ignoring me completely. Before I could even open my door, he had his truck in reverse; ready to leave. I had never felt so alone or hurt. I found my hidden key and unlocked the door. I replaced the key in its hiding spot, and then entered the house leaving Luke and all his problems in my driveway.

Chapter 13

At that moment all I wanted was to crawl under the covers of my bed and cry myself to sleep. So many questions were on my mind. *Why was he being so ugly to me? Was he mad because I got my hours mixed up? Was he mad because I asked him to call Lindsey?* He could have taken two minutes to talk to me. Even if he didn't want me to know, he could have had the courtesy of telling me that it was none of my business. If it was about me, then I deserved to know. Instead of talking to me, he had hollered or just not said anything at all.

Neo greeted me in the living room and even he could tell that something was wrong. I patted his head and he dutifully followed me into the bedroom. I crawled under the covers, Neo in tow, and was crying before my head hit the pillow. *How could a man make me so happy one minute, then have me in tears the next*? Ever since I met him, my life had been turned upside down. I cried more in the last two weeks than I had in my entire life. I was so sick of this. One minute he was mad, then he was happy, then he was a sex God, then he was bossing me around. He was giving me whiplash with his mood swings, and I was starting to regret ever meeting him. I wanted to be myself again, someone who didn't have time for a man or a relationship.

"Dallas," I heard Luke call from the kitchen. I was hoping that if I didn't answer he would just go away, even though deep down I knew I didn't want him to. I could sense Luke's presence. I didn't even have to turn over to know that he was behind me. I tried to keep my breathing level, but my snotty nose betrayed me and I sniffed.

"Dallas, baby, I'm sorry," Luke said, crawling under the covers with me and wrapping me in his arms. The sweet sound of his voice and the touch of his strong hands made me cry harder.

"Why are you so fucking mean sometimes? I didn't even d-do anything," I stammered. "And if I d-did why don't you just tell me."

"Shh, baby. You didn't do anything. I just didn't want to worry you. Protecting you and taking care of you is what I want to do more than anything, and earlier I couldn't do that," he said, rocking me in his arms. "While you were sleeping, I was in the Harley Room, tinkering on my bike, when I heard the kitchen door close. I assumed it was you so I didn't pay any attention to it. A few minutes later, I sensed something was wrong and went to find you. You were still in the bed sleeping, but the door was open. I heard a glass break and ran outside to find someone had broken into the club house. The guy took off through the woods and I was beginning to chase him when I heard you holler my name. Then I heard you scream and I panicked. I called the club and they told me to get out; that they would handle it. I wanted to handle it myself. I wanted to track him down and hurt him, but I knew that I couldn't leave you. I'm not use to feeling like that Dallas. It's very new to me."

Oh wow. I had no idea. My tears had stopped, but my body tensed with worry. *What if something would have happened to him?* Luke was busy looking after me, but who was looking after him? I remembered the sickening feeling that I had at the bar when he went outside to fight those guys. I didn't even know him then, and now that I did; that feeling had only intensified.

"I'm so sorry," I whispered, turning to bury my face in his chest.

"You did nothing wrong," Luke said, looking me in the eyes. He looked like he had aged a few years in just the past several hours.

"Please, don't leave me," I begged. *I was not worried about my own safety*. No one could get to him out here, but if he went back to his house then he was fair game. He had said many times that he wanted to protect me. I knew that if I asked him to stay, that he would. Especially if he thought that I feared for my safety. He looked torn and I felt like shit. I knew he wanted to be there with his brothers. He didn't like sitting on the sidelines, but his safety was not only important to me but to everyone else, too. If someone was after Luke, then this was the safest place for him to be.

I heard a phone ring and realized it was mine. Who would be calling me?

"I got it," Luke said, leaning over and grabbing my phone from my clutch on the end table. "What you want, Red?" Luke asked, answering my phone. "Really?" *What was she saying?* "Okay, hang on." He handed me the phone and rolled his eyes.

"Hello?"

"Dallas, do you have a blue pair of heels?" Red asked, surprising me completely.

"Um. Yeah, I think so."

"Can you please go look and maybe tell me what other colors you have?"

Well, this was weird. "Yeah sure, hang on," I said, getting out of bed and heading into my closet. Luke was concentrating hard on his phone and paying no attention to me. "Okay, I have several different blues I ha-."

"Dallas," Red said, cutting me off. "Listen very carefully to me. I don't care what you do or how you have to do it, but I need you to keep Luke there tonight. I can't go into detail, but please.

Consider it a favor for the club." I knew whatever was going on was not good, and the urgency in Red's voice was enough for me to do anything she asked.

"Okay, I can do that," I answered her. "Is everything okay?"

"I'll talk to you tomorrow, and Dallas… Thank you." She hung up and I walked back into the bedroom to find Luke still lying in my bed.

"What did she want?" Luke asked, never looking up.

"To borrow my Jimmy Choo's, but they're the wrong size." I said, quite convincingly.

"Babe, I have to go," he said standing. *Shit.* I had to think fast. I thought I had convinced him to stay, but apparently not.

"Luke, please don't leave me," I whined.

"You will be fine, darlin'. I promise, no one is going to mess with you out here. Come, lock the door behind me."

"Luke, wait!" I said a little too anxiously.

"Baby, nothing is going to hurt you. They were after me," he said soothingly. I ran into his arms and without even trying, I was sobbing into his neck.

"Whoa, babe. Are you that upset?" He asked, smoothing my hair and kissing my cheek.

"Yes. Please, don't leave me." I begged, exaggerating my sobs.

"Baby, I won't let anything happen to you, but I have to go. I'll send a prospect or I'll take you to Lindsey's."

"I s-saw him, Luke," I announced, surprising myself when I said it.

"What?" Luke asked, pulling me from his chest so he could look at my face.

"I saw him. He was standing beside me and he touched my face." There was a special place in hell for liars as good as myself, but this was my last resort and I prayed it would work.

"He touched you?" Luke asked, completely shocked by my admission. I nodded my head, and with an enormous amount of effort, I forced my body into sobs and shudders. I felt him dig something out of his pocket. Without letting go of me, he grabbed his phone and dialed a number.

"Tiny, I'm staying at Dallas's. Call me in the morning and let me know what you find. Be careful, brother." I didn't hear Tiny's response, but I knew he was glad that Luke was not coming.

"Come on, baby, let's go to bed." Luke pulled the covers back and after undressing, joined me in the bed and wrapped me in his arms. "Baby, I am so sorry. No one will ever get that close to you again. I promise." I felt guilty for lying to him, but I was asked to keep him safe and that's *exactly* what I planned to do.

Luke and I didn't get much sleep that night. It seemed his phone rang every hour-waking me and him. He would get up and go into the next room to talk, but I stayed awake until he came back each time. When my alarm went off at seven o'clock, I felt like I had just gone to sleep. I drug myself into the shower, hoping the hot water would wake me. I wondered what had become of the man that broke into the clubhouse and why did he do it? Tonight, I would see Red and squeeze as much information from her as possible.

When I came out of the shower, Luke was still asleep in bed. Not wanting to wake him, I slid into my closet and closed the door behind me. I dried my long hair as quickly as possible, curled the ends, and applied my makeup using only some light blush, mascara and coral colored lip gloss. I chose a sleeveless, white crepe dress that came to just above my knees and accessorized it with a thin orange belt around the waist. I grabbed a pair of bright orange pumps to match the belt, some diamond studs for my ears, and my usual watch and bracelet. Satisfied with my appearance, I packed a quick bag for tonight; consisting of some jeans, a white fitted t-shirt and my black ankle boots with a low heel. I walked out of the closet to find Luke no longer in bed.

"Luke?" I called. Wondering where he had wandered off to.

"I'm in the kitchen, babe," he answered. Luke was sitting at the bar with two steaming cups of coffee in front of him. As I approached, he turned to stare at me and his eyebrows shot up in surprise, but he quickly recovered, giving me his signature smirk. "You look good, babe. Real good. The color orange suits you."

I walked into his arms, planting a kiss on his lips with a loud smack and sat down to join him. "Well, what's the news?" I asked, picking up my coffee and taking a big sip. *Damn, Luke could make some good coffee, just how I liked it; strong and dark.*

"Nothing, yet. The guy took off. We don't even know who it was." He looked like he was thinking hard, and I didn't want our morning to be anything like last night so I quickly changed the subject.

"Where are we going tonight?" I asked, flashing my best smile. His eyes softened and he smiled back.

"Shenanigans. Ever been there?"

"Once, a band I like played there. The Glitter Boys."

"Ah. Gotta love The Glitter Boys," he said playfully. Luke seemed to be in a good mood, but I could tell he had a lot on his mind. I was hoping that having a break from me would give him plenty of time to handle it. I still felt like a jerk for lying to him, but I kept reminding myself that it was the right thing to do. I knew in my heart that he would have done the same for me.

"I have to go. Make yourself at home. I'll see you around five." I leaned over, giving him a quick kiss and left.

Chapter 14

At nine o'clock, just as I was about to start my first meeting of the day, a large bouquet of flowers were delivered to me. The card read, "missing you already." My heart fluttered at such a sweet gesture. Luke knew how to brighten my day. At ten o'clock, another delivery was made. This time it was a dozen white roses, a balloon that had a picture of a black lab on it, and a card that read, "Neo misses you, too. He also watered the roses." I giggled like a schoolgirl and inhaled the sweet scented roses.

The situation at Luke's was bad, but still he managed to let me know that he was thinking of me. I decided to send him a message. Picking up my phone, I texted him- *you are amazing-thank you.* He never responded, but at noon another bouquet was delivered and it took my breath away. It was so big, two men carried it in. The arrangement was full of bright, colorful flowers and roses. It smelled wonderful. This time the card read, "These flowers hold no comparison to your beauty. The smell of them, even as intoxicating as it is, smells nothing of the sweetness that is of you. The soft, velvety petals are not as pleasing to touch as the satin of your skin. You have captured my heart and it now beats only for you. I hope your day is as wonderful as you are- Luke Shakespeare." I laughed out loud at his signature.

Tears fell down my face as I grabbed my phone once again. Who was I kidding? *I was in love.* I was head over heels in love with a man that I hardly knew. I didn't care that it sounded preposterous or that things were moving faster than I ever could have imagined. I didn't care what people thought or what they had to say.

Lucas Carmical had captured my heart, too, and I wanted him to know it. I wanted everyone to know it. *I love the flowers. I love the poetry. I love that you are thinking of me. I love your motorcycle. I love your club. I love the fact that you want me to be a part of your life. But more than flowers and motorcycles and clubs and friends and poetry- I love you.*

I quickly sent the message before I chickened out and laid my phone on my desk. Less than a minute later, it vibrated notifying me of a message. I fumbled with it, dropping it twice on the floor before my shaky hands could grasp it tightly and read the message waiting for me. *I can't wait to hear you say those words to me.* *That's it? He wasn't going to say it back?* Sure, he had said that I captured his heart, but I thought he would tell me he loved me. Lindsey walked in, saw my face, and immediately asked what was wrong. I quickly told her the whole story.

"Maybe he wants to tell you in person," she said smiling.

"You think?" I asked hopeful. She shrugged.

"Maybe. Your one o'clock is here a little early. You want me to send them in?"

I needed the distraction. "Yes. That would be great," I said, busying myself with the paperwork on my desk. Lindsey retreated and I put Luke out of my mind to mentally prepare myself for my next meeting. I couldn't dwell on him. I had business to attend to and the last thing I needed was a distraction. When the door opened, I stood to shake hands with Mrs. Griffith but instead found myself staring at Luke. I was like a deer caught in headlights. No wonder I loved him. *Who wouldn't?* He was everything that I could have ever imagined.

He stood in the doorway looking tall, breathtakingly gorgeous and all man. His jeans were faded and worn. His solid white t-shirt was loose in the waist but tight around his arms and chest. His leather vest was unbuttoned and the gray and orange patches that he wore stood out against the blackness behind them. That damn smirk was on his face and his eyes were sparkling. Today was the first time that I had ever seen him in a hat. It was black and turned backwards with the letters 'DFFD' monogrammed in orange on it. This was my Luke; my boyfriend, my lover, my everything. He stepped in and closed the door behind him. I could see Lindsey and Terri, my part time file clerk, staring open mouthed into the room.

"Tell me," he said, staring at me with a darkened stare. I felt my temperature rising and the hair on the back of my neck standing up. How did he have this effect on me?

"Tell you, what?" I asked, more breathy than I had intended. His eyebrows shot up and a surprised look crossed his face.

"Forgotten already? Or did the flowers just inspire you to say something that you didn't really mean?" *So, this was the game that he wanted to play.* He wanted me to tell him. Well, he was going to get his wish. I was going to tell him the truth. I did love him and if he refused to say it in return, well, that was a risk I was willing to take.

Shit. What was happening to me? Before I could even open my mouth, he was standing right in front of me. His hands found my face and he tilted my head back to trail kisses down my neck. "I want to hear you say it, baby." I was breathing heavy. My body was on fire, and so was my heart. I had never wanted to give a confession as much as I wanted to give this one.

"I love you, Luke. I think I loved you from the first time that I laid eyes on you. No one has ever made me feel the way that you do." His continuous kisses across my neck and throat were pure torture. *God, I loved this man*. When I was in his arms, whether it was in a bar, or a bed, or my office; I felt like it was the safest place in the world. He was my universe. His eyes met mine and I knew in that moment that whether he said it or not, he loved me. Love for me consumed him. His eyes told the story. They were filled with love and passion and need, just for me. *I was cherished by this man*. He kissed me hard. The need to touch me evident in the way he held me tight and the movement of his tongue. Every nerve in my body tingled and my stomach was full of butterflies. *Would it always be like this?* Yes, it would. There was no way that I could ever tire of this man or his touch.

"You. Complete. Me," he murmured between kisses. I laughed in his mouth.

"That's. Not. Very. Original." I responded between kisses. He pulled back from my face and I opened my eyes to see him smiling.

"Well, you stole my lines. What you said to me was exactly what I had planned to say to you." He kissed me again, both of us making it hard to keep a smile from our lips. A light tap on the door interrupted us as Lindsey peaked her head inside.

"Your *real* one o'clock is here."

"Okay. Give me just a minute," I replied regretfully. I wish I could just leave and spend the day with Luke.

"It's cool, babe. I have to go, too," Luke said pulling me into his arms and tucking my head under his chin. I inhaled the scent of him and squeezed him harder. *My Luke.* I would never tire of knowing that.

"I love you, Dallas. I know it's crazy to fall for someone so fast, but you are the first thing that I think of when I wake up and the last before I go to sleep. I think you are amazing and sexy and smart and I have thanked God every day for putting me in that bar that night." He pulled back and lifted my chin so that my gaze met his. "You once told me, love like what your mother and father had doesn't exist anymore. Well, I am here to tell you that you are wrong. No one could ever love anyone the way that I love you." Tears filled my eyes and he quickly kissed them away. The intimacy he showed me and the words he said to me were everything I had ever dreamed of. Some people live their whole lives not finding their true love, but in just twenty-six years, I had found mine. "I'll see you at five. I love you," he said, looking at me with those ocean blue eyes that were filled with love and adoration.

"I love you too, Luke." He closed his eyes and swallowed at my words. He kissed me once more, then taking my hands into his, kissed my fingers before backing out of the office and leaving.

The rest of my day was a blur. I found myself smiling for no reason at all. *Well, I knew the reason.* When I was happy, it seemed everyone in the office was happy, too. I called Scott to let him know that I would be in the Tupelo office around ten tomorrow morning and the relief in his voice was so apparent and my mood was so good that I promised him a three day weekend the following week. I contacted Tammy, an old colleague of mine, and she agreed to have dinner with me Tuesday night. Hopefully, she could give me the scoop on the family that occupied my property. I owned a small bed and breakfast in Tupelo and was pleased to find that it was available for my travel dates. Looking at the clock, I realized that it was time to get ready for my night out with Luke.

My mood slightly faltered when I remembered that I would be surrounded with women who absolutely hated me, but I wouldn't let that or anything else ruin my day. Luke loved me and that was enough motivation for me to endure whatever the night offered.

I changed clothes and re-applied my makeup, noticing that I needed no additional blush. My cheeks were red enough. Pleased with my appearance, I practically skipped into the front of the building to wait for Luke.

Before I could make it there, I heard the rumbling of motorcycles in the distance. I opened the front door and stepped onto the sidewalk, letting the warm September breeze pass over me. About fifteen motorcycles approached and I realized that they did not belong to Luke's club. They all wore colors of red and gray and every one of them seemed to be staring holes through me.

Figuring they were some of Luke's friends and fueled by my good mood, I waved and smiled at them. None of them attempted to wave back, but continued to stare. When they reached the end of the street, they turned left heading downtown and disappeared from view.

Moments later, Luke arrived with the PROSPECT from the night at Mahogany and another man that I didn't know. When he motioned for me to jump on, all my thoughts of the red and gray bikers were quickly forgotten.

Riding with Luke this time was much different than the last time. I was relaxed and comfortable, and much happier than I ever remembered being. I wrapped my arms around him, holding him tight and delighting in the feel of him in my arms and the smell of him in the air.

Chapter 15

We pulled up to Shenanigans, which was a local bar and grill that made every day feel like St. Patrick's Day, and had drinks so stiff that you felt the luck of the Irish was within you. Luke gracefully slid from the bike and held his hand out to me while I gracelessly climbed off. He introduced me to his V.P., Worm, and his wife, Luci B. Worm was a tall slender guy with a deep voice and his height was magnified standing next to his petite wife, who smiled kindly at me. They both hugged me as if I were a part of their family. *Maybe this night wasn't going to be so bad after all.* Luke grabbed my hand and we walked in to find the whole left side of the bar filled with bikers. Each one stood up as Luke walked in and he took turns hugging each one and introducing me as "Dallas," but never giving me a title. *I didn't complain. Hell, at least he was actually acknowledging my presence.*

Regg and Red were there, along with Tiny and War, who I had remembered meeting a few weeks ago. I was slightly embarrassed remembering what had happened the last time that I was with them all, but if they knew anything of it; I couldn't tell. There were also a lot of people there that I had not met. All were patch members and their women, who I assumed were their ol' ladies. There was Coon and Carla, Octane and Juggs, Buck and Baby, Kev and Gypsy, Boss Hogg and Texas, Scratch, Bear, Crash and three PROSPECTS. Everyone greeted me warmly and each person hugged me. I could feel the love in the room that I was in. Atleast until Maddie sashayed her way from the back and into Luke's arms. He never let go of my hand, but returned her hug and asked, "Maddie, you remember Dallas?"

I could see in her eyes that she would rather eat shit than acknowledge my presence, but she surprised me by saying, "Yes, I do. It's good to see you again, Dallas. How is your head?" The bitterness in her voice and her ending comment made me want to slap that sour look off her face, but instead I just answered her in the most polite voice that I could manage.

"Eat me, Maddie." I had not realized that all eyes were on me when I said it. Everyone in the club seemed to be waiting for my response from the moment that she had walked in. Luke shot me a disapproving look, but everyone else seemed to find it humorous because the whole bar erupted in laughter. Maddie rolled her eyes and stormed off. I heard several comments like, "I told you" and "You owe me a beer" and I knew that my reaction toward Maddie had been wagered. I silently wondered who bet against me. That kind of information might be valuable in the future.

Everyone was chatting away-laughing, talking, and flirting. I saw why Luke loved his club so much. Everyone seemed to be family here and other than Maddie, they all seemed to accept me as part of it, too.

I sat at the head of the table next to Luke, and from my seat, I had a clear view of everyone around us. Worm and Luke seemed to be in deep conversation about something and Luci B, who sat next to Worm, was laughing and chatting with Red. Coon and Carla were in their own world. They seemed so in love with one another. I felt like I was intruding just by watching them, so I allowed my eyes to leave them and fall on Juggs, who was adjusting her breasts in her shirt, which seemed pointless considering Octane was constantly playing with them. Buck and KD, along with Scratch, Bear and Crash were listening intently to Kev, who must have been telling a joke, because they all erupted with laughter. Gypsy rolled her eyes and shook her head at Kev, obviously disgusted at what he said. The PROSPECTS were nowhere to be found and neither was Maddie.

Tiny came up behind us and tapped Luke on the shoulder, motioning for him to come outside.

With a nod of his head, every man at the table stood and followed Tiny out.

"Good luck, babe," Luke whispered in my ear.

"Thanks, a lot," I responded laughing. He laughed with me and leaned down, kissing the top of my head, and then walked out. My eyes followed him and I had a big goofy smile on my face when my eyes fell on all the women at the table. They were all staring at me open mouthed, as if I were an alien.

"What?" I asked.

Red was the first one to recover. "Nothing, it's just good to see Luke happy," she said smiling. The other women nodded in agreement and choruses of "yeah" and "that's right" rang out from all of them while they busied themselves with their phones and drinks and averted their eyes to anything but me.

"So, Dallas, you are in real estate?" Jenn asked from the end of the table.

"I am. I own Knox Companies." Jenn almost choked on her drink. I wanted to kick myself for opening my mouth.

"*You* are Dallas Knox? Oh, my God! I had no idea."

"That's me." I responded a little embarrassed. For some reason, I didn't want these women to know who I was. The public already had stereotyped me into what they wanted me to be and I wanted these women to not know the real me, but the "me" that Luke knew.

"Wow. That's impressive. You know, I used to work for a real estate company. That was a long time ago though. KD is actually fixin' to take the exam to get her real estate license," Jenn said recovering from her shock.

"Really? Well KD, I hope you will consider my company. I could probably pull a few strings to get you an interview," I said winking at her. They all laughed.

"Oh, my God! That would be so great!" she said, her face lighting up. KD would be good for business. She definitely fits the part. She was attractive and outgoing and seemed like she could be very persuasive. Red had made her way down the table to me and reached out to take my hand in hers.

"So, I hear y'all are official?"

I looked down at my lap smiling. "Yes, we are. He really is amazing, Red."

"Yes, he is. But don't underestimate yourself, Dallas. You must be pretty great, too, to land a catch like him." Her smile was genuine, as were her words. These women were not much different than me. I had expected them all to act like Maddie and treat me like an outsider, but since I had arrived, none of them had made me feel the least bit uncomfortable or out of place. I felt like I had known them all for forever.

Red leaned in close to me, her face taking on a serious expression, "Okay, I am going to lay a few ground rules out for you. This is your family. There is nothing these ladies would not do for you. They don't trust you right now, but that comes with time. If you are with Luke, then you are with them. Don't do anything to draw too much attention to yourself. Be friendly, but don't suck ass. They can see straight through the bullshit. Be genuine, respectful and above all, loyal. If you see your sister in trouble, it is your place to help her. If a man wants to join in with this club, he has to prospect. It's the same for the women. Until you prove your loyalty, you will never be accepted. Don't let their charm and looks fool you, these women can be very ruthless, and that includes me." She sat back and seemed satisfied with what she had just told me. I felt like it was a speech she had given many times. I appreciated the knowledge and her honesty, but it worked both ways. These women would have to earn my trust too. I knew better than to judge a book by its cover. I was a threat to all of them, especially Red. If I stepped in, her position would belong to me and I wasn't sure how much she would like that. She was good at what she did, but if I was going to be with Luke, then I would have to learn her role and to prove I could do it; I was going to have to be better than her.

"Who is Maddie with?" I asked. She was my biggest problem and I had to cross that bridge before I could build another one.

"Maddie is a long story, but in a nutshell, she is a part of this club. She isn't with anyone, but her history with the club is a long one. I'll leave the rest of that story up to Luke to tell."

Well, I had already violated one rule. I had not shown any respect to Maddie, nor had she shown any to me. I guessed that was why nobody seemed to care what I said to her earlier. Right then, a commotion at the pool tables across the room drew our attention.

"Here we go," Red said rising and heading across the bar. The other women stood and followed suit. I sat still, not sure what to do. *Should I follow? Should I stay? Was this really my business?* KD turned to look at me and discreetly motioned with her hand that I should join them. I could tell that she didn't want any of the others to see what she was doing. She was helping me out. I was sure it was because of the job that I mentioned earlier, but it was still a nice gesture.

I joined the others and saw that Maddie was nose to nose with another woman, who I noted was wearing red and gray colors. I remembered the bikers that I had seen earlier and silently wondered if she was with them. I had not seen them when we pulled up, but there was no mistaking the man propped on the pool table behind them. He was one of the bikes from the pack that passed my office, and although there was a feud going on before him, it was me he was watching. I walked closer, trying to get a better look and saw one of our guys, wearing a PROSPECT patch, pick up his phone and call someone. He was standing right next to Maddie, in between the guy on the pool table and her. A cold chill went down my spine as I made eye contact with the man staring holes through me. It was as if he knew me, and it was hard for me to pull my eyes from the large scar on his face. I remembered him leading the pack I'd seen earlier.

Escalating voices caused me to turn my attention to Maddie, who had her finger in the face of another girl. "You know better than to have your trashy ass in here," she yelled. That was the last thing said before the fight erupted. Several other women in red and gray were there too, standing behind the woman and cheering her on. My instincts kicked in and I ran closer. Someone grabbed my arm and I whirled around to see the cold eyes of the man from the pool table staring into mine. He had greasy black hair, small beady eyes, and looked like he was drunk or strung out on drugs.

"Well hello, sleeping beauty," he said to me. I jerked my arm from him and surprisingly, he let me go. I turned around and found myself in the middle of the fight. I looked over to see that all of the ladies from the club were involved in some way. Some were separating women who were fighting and some were fighting themselves. I had never seen anything like it. These grown women were literally fist fighting like teenagers. I looked down to see that two women had jumped on Maddie and she was doing her best to fight them off. I was sure that she deserved it in some way, but a fair fight was a fair fight. Besides, Red said she was a part of the club and my job was to help if any of my family was in need.

Putting my hatred for Maddie in the back of my mind, I allowed my fighting skills from my high school and college days to resurface, and leaned down to pull one of the girls off of her. She swung her arm around, with absolutely no aim and I dodged it with ease and planted a blow to her face with my right hand and quickly followed with one from the left. By the time she retaliated, I was in full fight mode and she didn't stand a chance. I had always been told that I was a good fighter. My record was 13-2, not that I was keeping count. I hit the girl, who was about my size, on the tip of her nose, and I knew she was down for the count. Blood gushed from her nostrils and she was too busy holding her face to see the punch coming that put her on her ass. I looked down and saw Maddie getting pummeled by a girl with a roll of quarters balled up in her fist.

These bitches fight dirty. Well, two could play at that game. I gave the girl a swift kick to the ribs, allowing Maddie enough time to recover from her fetal position to rein blows on top of the girl's head. I was grabbed and lifted into the air as the guys came in from outside and broke up the fight. Within seconds of Luke barking orders, the fighting ceased and everyone was standing around looking at one another. The bar was silent as he walked over to the woman lying on the floor and pulled her to her feet.

"What the fuck are you doing here, wearing this shit?" Luke asked her and pulled on her vest.

"Frankie sent me. He has a message for you," she responded trying to sound tough, but I could tell that she was intimidated by Luke. *Hell, who wouldn't be?*

"Oh yeah? Well, you tell Frankie that if he has something to say to me then he knows where I am, and not to send bitches to do his dirty work. Now, you get the fuck out of my town and it would be in your best interest to burn this shit. If you ever flash those colors in my presence again, I'll cut them off of you myself." The coldness in Luke's tone had me shivering. He was a force to be reckoned with and everyone in this bar knew it. He looked down at the girl like she was nothing. Like a scolded child, she hung her head, and along with the four other women, she left the bar.

"Everybody whole?" Luke asked the room, his eyes finding mine, giving me a once over, then walking up to Maddie. Luke put his hands on either side of her face, moving her head as if to look her over. "You good?" he asked her.

"Yeah. I'm good." Luke let her go and she glared at me, spitting blood onto the floor. *Why was she so pissed at me?* I just saved her ass.

"We're out, bill me," Luke announced to the bartender, but made it loud enough for everyone to hear. No one dared to utter a word until we were outside.

All of the women seemed to know their place and what not to say. Apparently when Luke was in a pissy mood, everyone knew to stay out of his path. Red shot me a wink and a smirk, and although the other women tried to hide it from the men, I could see satisfaction and approval on their faces.

Luke had hardly looked at me since the scene unfolded, but when I went to put on my helmet, he grabbed it from my hands and stared at me. I could see the concern behind the fury in his eyes.

216

"You okay, babe?" he whispered. Scared that I would say the wrong thing, I just nodded my head. He shot me a look of warning and I quickly remembered his rule.

"Yes, I am okay." My lips parted and my breath quickened at the thought of a lovely punishment fuck. *How did he do this to me?* He was obviously on to what I was thinking about because that damn smirk was on his face, again. It relaxed me a little. At least he wasn't mad. He put my helmet on then kissed my swollen, bruised knuckles and I climbed on the bike behind him. I noted that everyone else was seated on their bikes and ready to go, but no one cranked their motorcycle until Luke did. We pulled out onto the highway and I wrapped my arms around Luke. We were going fast, like really fast, and the motorcycles behind and beside us were only inches away. I looked to my right and Luci B was watching me intently. She gave me a reassuring smile and I waved at her; only realizing how stupid it looked *after* I did it. Riding so close to everyone made me nervous. I looked in Luke's rearview mirror and could see the pack behind us. The synchronization was amazing. When one moved, they all moved.

By the time we got to Luke's, I needed a stiff drink. I followed Luke and the others into the clubhouse. The window that had been broken was now repaired. Luke led me to the bar and swiftly kissed my cheek before going behind it and pouring us a drink. It was a shot of some kind of liquor, but my nerves were strung so tight that I didn't question it as I through it back and let the burn soothe me. Luke gave me a wink, walked around the bar, and then unlocked the door to the room with the large table. The guys, without having to be told, walked in behind him; the last one closing the door. I noticed one of the PROSPECTS stood guard outside of it and the others fell in behind the bar, making drinks and busying themselves. "Why are they not in there?" I asked Red, who had taken a seat next to me.

"Only patch members sit at the table and they have not reached that phase yet. They have to prospect for a minimum of one year before they are even considered for a cut." *Wow.* A whole year and even then, they may not make it.

"Why do they do that?" I asked, turning in my chair to look at her.

She laughed lightly. "Ask them." I had a sense that this was some sort of test or challenge.

"Can I do that?"

"What? Ask them a question?" There was a mischievous glint in her eyes and I knew that unless I found out myself, I would never know.

"Excuse me," I said to the PROSPECT standing behind the bar. He looked to be in his mid-twenties and had an attractive face with big green eyes that were framed with dark eye lashes.

"Yes, ma'am?"

"Why would you want to prospect for a year for a club, when you're not even sure you will get in?"

His answer came almost immediately, as if it was as natural as breathing. "For the brotherhood, ma'am."

I looked at him expectantly, hoping he would elaborate. When he didn't, I decided to push further. "What does that mean exactly?" He had my full attention. I was expecting him to say something about getting women or how bad-ass his cut would look, if and when he got it, but he surprised me.

"Ma'am, in the real world there is no such thing as loyalty. I have been betrayed by my friends and even my own family, but with this club, I never have to second guess my potential brothers. I'm willing to take a year of my life to work hard and prove my loyalty to the club, so that one day, hopefully, I will have the honor of wearing a Devil's Renegades patch and ensuring a lifelong brotherhood with some of the most honest, honorable and respectable people that I have ever met. Don't you think that's worth it, ma'am?"

I was shocked. His last statement hit home with me. I knew he was not trying to be a smart-ass, even though it kind of sounded that way. Did I think it was worth it? I *knew* it was worth it. I had seen the way these guys were with each other and it amazed me. This life was not for everyone, but for PROSPECT MARTY, it most definitely was. I could relate, because it was worth it for me, too. "Yes, Marty, I do." I smiled at him and he smiled back, passing me another shot.

"Excuse me, ma'am." He turned and headed to the other end of the bar, checking on the ladies and making sure there was nothing that they needed.

"Such manners he has," I said to Red, who was eyeing me. "Rule number one, be respectful. When the guys are prospecting, they are walking on thin ice. Some of the things they do may seem a little overboard but the meaning for it is there. There is not a man in that room who did not go through the same thing."

"What's the meaning?" I asked.

"The greatest thing a man possesses is his pride. That is not something that is easily given up. If a man is willing to swallow his pride for the club, that is a true sign of loyalty. Women will come and go. Material items can be replaced, but pride is something in your soul, something a real man cannot live without. So, when these guys have to lower themselves to waiting on grown men hand and foot and doing things that belittle them; their pride is taken. But, respect is earned in its place." Red seemed to be in deep thought over what she just said. I could tell she was struggling with something. I decided to drop the subject and move to another more important one.

"Why did you need Luke to stay with me last night?"

"It was not safe here," Red said to me as if the answer was obvious.

"Well, I know that, but Luke is a big boy."

"Well that 'big boy's' safety is the most important thing right now. He was safer with you than he was on his bike alone and vulnerable trying to come back here."

Alone and vulnerable? Was someone after Luke? "I don't understand. Why would anyone want to hurt Luke?"

Red laughed, "You'd be surprised." That was her only answer. She took a draw from her beer and turned to me, curiosity consumed her expression.

"What did you say to him to make him stay?" That awful feeling I had in my gut resurfaced. I didn't want to relive what I did last night. Lying to Luke was one of the hardest things that I had ever done. I felt like shit for making him choose between me and the club, and I was ashamed at the feeling of satisfaction I got when he chose me.

"It was bad. Let's just leave it at that." I couldn't look at her. She nudged my shoulder and placed her hand over mine.

"Hey, look at me." I turned to meet her serious gaze. "You did the right thing, Dallas. Thank you. And speaking of doing the right thing...," Red said raising her voice. The chatter died down and Red walked behind the bar, grabbing a bottle of tequila and lining up a row of shot glasses. She filled them and everyone grabbed one and turned to me.

"To Dallas, for standing up and taking care of business when business needed taking care of. I am proud to call you my sister."

"To Dallas!" The ladies all said in unison and through back the shot in my honor. Red was already refilling glasses. Luke was going to have to carry me inside at this rate. I forced the drink down my throat and looked up into the eyes of the ladies standing before me. I wasn't sure if they wanted a speech or a thank-you or what, but I was glad I had already had several shots of liquid encouragement and my voice came out smooth and strong.

"It is an honor to be a part of this family. Thank you for welcoming me with open arms; to love, loyalty and respect." I raised my now full shot glass to the women and once again, as if they had rehearsed this a million times, they chanted in unison. "Love, loyalty and respect."

I took the drink easily this time and looked over my shoulder to see Luke and all the guys standing behind us. Luke had a very pleased smirk on his face and it seemed the others were pretty happy, too. I figured a happy Luke meant a happy club. He sauntered over to me and once again, we were the only two in the room. I wanted him to kiss me. I could feel his mouth on me everywhere and my breath was ragged and shallow.

"You seem to have made some friends," Luke said smiling down at me, but not touching me. *I almost whined as I shifted, trying to draw his attention to my body.* He leaned down and whispered in my ear, never letting his body touch mine. "You will have to wait, baby. We have a house full of company." A groan escaped my lips before I could catch it and his amused expression didn't sway me in the least.

"Fuck the company."

He through his head back and laughed, "Not much longer, baby, I promise."

I suddenly remembered my trip tomorrow and the realization must have been all over my face because his expression turned to one of concern.

"What's wrong?"

"Nothing, I am just wishing that I didn't have to work tomorrow." *I wasn't sure why I hadn't come out and told him about my trip, but it made me feel somewhat rebellious and I liked that.* He smiled at me, the worry gone from his eyes.

"Well, we still have the night. Stay with me?" *Like he had to ask.*

Chapter 16

It was after midnight before everyone left. I was exhausted and knew I had a long drive ahead of me, but when Luke pulled me into his arms; sleep became the last thing on my mind.

"Take off tomorrow. I'll take you to the beach." I pulled back to look at him. He was smiling so big that his cheeks must have been hurting. I was tempted to say yes. The beach with Luke would be incredible, a whole day of seeing him completely shirtless.

"I have to go to Tupelo tomorrow," I said pouting.

"Tupelo? For how long?" he asked incredulously. My eyes looked everywhere but at him. *Why did I suddenly feel like I had done something wrong?* "When were you going to tell me, Dallas?" He asked in a stern voice.

"I didn't know until Sunday and with everything going on, I didn't want to bother you." He dropped his arms from around me and stalked into the bedroom. *Did he seriously want a fight?* "Luke!" I called, stalking after him. "What the hell is wrong?"

"Nothing," he stated, not looking at me.

"Something is wrong." He was undressing to get in the shower and the fight went out of me as I stood there watching. He had his back to me and I watched as his muscles flexed when he took his shirt off. He was completely naked when he turned around and finally spoke.

"Get undressed." I was slightly taken aback by what he said. I stood there in shock, not sure what to do. Luke walked slowly towards me. The darkness in his stare was so intense that I had to look away. When he was only inches from my face, he stopped. I could tell that he was mad, but was trying to control it. "You belong to me. When you decide to just up and leave the city, I need to know about it." I wanted to slap him and tell him that I belonged to no one, but when I opened my mouth, he silenced me with just a look. "Raise your arms up, Dallas." He spoke with authority in his voice, but so softly that I had almost asked him to repeat it. I raised my arms and he pulled my shirt over my head and then unclasped my bra. He grabbed my belt loops on the front of my jeans and pulled me up against him. Luke was pissed. I remembered seeing him this way only twice before. Once at my house and the last was when I left him at the bar. This could go either way and I knew it. I was scared to death even as a thrill of excitement coursed through my veins.

"A man broke into my house yesterday. He came into my bedroom and touched the face of the girl that I love. Yesterday, she was so beside herself that she could not be alone. Today, it's as if nothing happened. Then, this incredibly frustrating woman plans a trip, out of town, and somehow forgets to tell me about it. Now, I am not sure what the fuck is in her head, but I can assure you that within a matter of minutes she will think twice before she ever does that bullshit again."

His voice was full of malice, his eyes like stone and I had never wanted him more. I raised my arms around his neck to bring his face down to mine. I kissed him hard, pulling the back of his head down to me and letting my tongue invade his mouth. I could tell that he was torn, but when he groaned into my mouth, I knew I had him. He pulled back from me and viciously ripped my pants off. He was like a predator and I, the prey. I didn't care that he had just ripped the buttons from a pair of my favorite jeans, or that I was probably not going to be able to walk tomorrow. At that moment, all I wanted was him. He grabbed me around my waist and lifted me onto the counter.

"I love you so much. I don't know what I would do if anything happened to you." His confession came out like a strangled groan. I could tell that he was in pain and worried-about me. It seemed that sex was his release and I wanted him to know that we were okay. I wanted him to know that I was okay and that I was sorry. We couldn't get enough of each other. Our kisses were not enough and even though our hands wandered freely over each other's bodies, I knew we wouldn't be satisfied until he was inside me. He wrapped my legs around his waist and in one swift movement was inside me. I cried out from the harshness of it as he covered my mouth with his. Luke's arms were resilient and he lifted me with ease, pushing in and out of me.

"Stop. It's too much," I moaned between kisses, but it was not too much. *It was just enough*. He slammed into me harder and a whimper escaped my lips.

"You can take it, baby. This is what you want, what you need and most definitely, what you deserve." His voice was softer this time, hypnotizing. Luke knew my body better than I did and just as he promised; the feeling was phenomenal. I could feel myself building and I threw my head back, allowing Luke to take full advantage of my throat. "Tell me whose pussy this is, Dallas," he growled into my ear.

Fuck me. "It's yours, Luke, I'm yours."

"Come for me, baby," he whispered into my ear. His strong arms lifted me high, and then pushed me back onto him, so that he was buried deep inside me. I came apart on top of him, crying out his name. He came with me, as his mouth found mine. When he broke the kiss, I was breathless and could do nothing more than lie my head on his shoulder. I silently hoped that he wouldn't put me down. I feared that if he forced me to stand, my legs would buckle. He must have known that, because when he slid out of me, he boosted me up higher, tightening my legs around him and carried me into the shower. "You okay, babe?"

"No," I pouted. He chuckled into my ear and I was happy to know that the tension was gone. We were back to normal.

"Someone is grumpy. Usually you're in a good mood after we make love," he said to me. I could feel his smile even though I couldn't see it.

"That wasn't even close to love making. You fucked me, hard, and now I won't be able to walk tomorrow."

He laughed at my reply and kissed me on my head. "Well, I'll just have to make it better." I wasn't sure what all that would entail; but the promise gave me a delicious chill. He pulled my legs from around him and stood me under the water. "Let's get you clean. Someone has a big day tomorrow." I could see the disappointed look in his eyes, but he kissed my head and gave me a tight smile, and I knew he was trying to be reassuring. We bathed quickly and Luke found me a t-shirt to sleep in before crawling into bed behind me.

I was expecting him to wrap me in his arms, but instead, he crawled between my legs and without any warning, placed his mouth on my sensitive flesh. My back came off the bed at the feel of his tongue, so soft and velvety smooth. He moved his mouth over me slowly, devouring and worshiping my most intimate parts. It was only a matter of minutes before I was moaning his name and coming once again. He kissed up my stomach, stopping to suck my nipples softly before kissing me tenderly, and then slid in beside me. I was so exhausted that I couldn't even respond when he whispered in my ear, "Good night, my love."

The ride to Tupelo, so far, was long and uneventful. I smiled at myself remembering how wonderful my morning had been. Luke had surprised me with breakfast in bed, consisting of instant oatmeal and orange juice. He was in a much better mood this morning and I wondered if he was happy to be rid of me for a few days.

We still had not had a chance to talk about what had happened the other night. Every time that I tried to bring it up, he changed the subject or distracted me with his mouth or hands. I figured whatever was going on, was either not that important or so important that he didn't want to tell me.

I remembered that Red owed me a favor and since she made been sure to put her number in my phone, I figured that it wouldn't hurt to call her. Using my car's hands free device, I dialed Red's number in hopes of getting some answers about just what in the hell was going on.

"Dallas?" Red answered, sounding worried.

"Hey, Red, do you have a minute?"

"Of course, what's up?" It sounded like she stopped whatever she was doing and walked to another room. I thought I was prepared to talk to her, but I wasn't sure this was the right time. I started to chicken out and make up some phony excuse as to why I called, but she interjected before I could. "Dallas, you can talk to me about anything. That's what I'm here for." Her voice had lowered and I could tell that she was being sincere. I needed her. I needed a friend and although I had Lindsey, I needed someone on the inside to talk to.

"He won't tell me anything," I blurted out. "I have tried talking to him, but he keeps distracting me. I haven't pushed him. I have only asked him a couple of times, but he doesn't want to tell me anything. I understand that this may be none of my business, but I can't help but feel like it is." I sucked in a deep breath and waited for her response. I hadn't realized it, but my eyes burned and I knew that I was going to cry. *Damn. Why did I have to be such an emotional wreck?*

"Yes, it is your business. You deserve to know the truth about what is going on. I was hoping Luke would tell you this himself, but since he wants to be an overprotective asshole, I'll tell you." I wiped the tears from my face and sat straight up in the vehicle. Red had my full attention. "As you know, Sunday night a man broke into Luke's house. We figured that he was hoping to catch him alone, but when he saw you; he freaked out." A chill ran through me as I thought of how panicked Luke had become when he thought that I had been hurt. I swallowed nervously, willing Red to continue. "We are not sure if the broken window on the club house was intentional or not. It may have been a ploy to get Luke's attention or to see if you would come outside."

Oh shit. Good thing I wasn't a light sleeper, because just like in all of the scary movies, I would have gotten up to investigate.

"At the bar the other night, the woman that Maddie was fighting with is an ol' lady to a rival club. They are not allowed in Hattiesburg, but for some reason they have been showing up lately. We're not sure, but we think it has something to do with Luke." My mind started to spin as I remembered the red and gray colors that the lady at the bar had been wearing. They matched the ones on the motorcycles that had passed my office just yesterday. *Was that something that I needed to share?*

"Where were their men?" I asked, silently praying she would say that they knew where they were.

"Who knows? They are not allowed to be around these parts. The only way that the girls pulled it off was by bringing their cuts inside hidden in their purses. After the guys walked out, they went to the bathroom to put them on. That's when Maddie confronted them."

"Red, I saw those guys," I said softly. *I didn't want to start a war, but this seemed pretty important.*

"What guys?" Red asked confused.

"The guys that wear red and gray cuts. They passed by my office yesterday just before Luke got there."

"Did you tell Luke?" Red practically shouted at me.

"No, I didn't think about it. I had no idea who they were."

"Dammit, Dallas!" Red yelled. I could hear someone, who I thought was Regg, in the background asking what was wrong.

"I'll call you back." She hung up and I was left wondering what crime I had committed this time. I was getting tired of them expecting me to act like I knew what the hell I was doing. I was new to all of this. How in the hell was I supposed to know who was allowed and who wasn't? My phone rang, distracting me from my thoughts and I glanced down to see that it was Luke calling. I cringed at the thought of him chewing my ass.

"Hello?" I tried to sound cheery, but my voice betrayed me. I sounded like my underwear was stuck in my ass.

"Hey, baby." Luke's smooth silky voice took me by surprise. I was expecting his wrath, but instead he sounded like he missed me and was excited just to hear my voice. "Dallas? You there?"

"Uhh... Yeah, baby. I'm here," I stuttered. *I was such a loser.*

"I just got a call from Red. She was freaking out on me. Is there something you want to talk about?" *Why was he being so calm?*

"You're not mad at me?" I asked cautiously. *Maybe this was the calm before the storm.*

"No, babe. Why would I be mad at you?" he asked shocked. *Wow. This was a turn of events.*

"I just thought since I didn't tell you about those guys that you might be mad."

"Babe, you had no way of knowing who those men were or what they wanted. I'm sorry that I have been so evasive the past few days, I just didn't want to worry you." *Damn, he was so sweet.*

"I love you," I said breathlessly. He had a way of removing the air from my lungs, even over the phone. Luke laughed softly.

"I will never tire of hearing you say those words to me. I love you too, baby, now talk to me. What's on your mind?" Knowing he was not mad at me and that I could speak freely, I spilled my guts.

"Yesterday, I was standing outside my office when I heard all of these motorcycles. I thought it was your guys, but they were wearing red and gray. I thought they might be friends of yours, so I waved, but none of them waved back. There was a guy in the pack. He had a large scar on his face. When we got to Shenanigans, he was there, too." Luke was eerily quiet on the other end and fearing the silence was a bad sign, I quickly continued. "He was sitting on the pool table when the fight broke out and he grabbed my arm and said something to me."

Luke spoke before I could continue and I knew that he was trying to control his anger. "What did he say to you, Dallas?'

I swallowed hard and spoke so softly that he asked me to repeat it. "He said, 'Hey there, sleeping beauty'."

"That mother fucker! Where are you staying?" Luke screamed.

"The Abbey." *Why was he asking? Was he coming to stay with me?* I was suddenly excited. *Why had I not asked him to come in the first place?* "I am sending someone up there." My heart fell. Once again, he would send someone instead of coming himself.

"Don't worry about it. I'll be fine. Stacy will be there. I will be sure to let him know what's going on." I said defeated.

"Who in the hell is Stacy?" Luke asked confused.

"He is a friend of the family. He has a black belt in karate and is trained in martial arts. I promise that I will be fine." I knew Stacy would be more than a little excited at the thought of hurting someone.

"Dallas, I can send someone. It's not a problem," Luke stated. *No shit, it wasn't a problem. There were people lined up to be at his beck and call. Too bad it wasn't him who wanted to be here for my safety.*

"No, I will be fine, really." *Why did I let this bother me so much? He had enough shit to deal with. He couldn't drop everything just to drive two hundred and fifty miles to be with me.* I got it, but it still hurt. "I better go. I'll call you tonight," I said and abruptly ended the call. I didn't want any more apologies, excuses or possible solutions. I only wanted to get through the next few days and then back home. Maybe then, Luke would take me to the beach and fuck me senseless. That would surely fix this melancholy mood that I had slipped into.

Chapter 17

I pulled up to The Abbey and it was even more beautiful than I remembered. The large, three story Victorian house had served as a bed and breakfast for over one hundred years and was located just off of the Natchez Trace. The home was sentimental to me. It was the first property that I purchased when I decided to expand my business north. The old cobblestone driveway was worn and the familiar rumble of the stones beneath my tires made me feel like I had stepped into another century. The large white porch wrapped all the way around the house and opened into a garden at the back. White wicker rockers littered the front porch. Ferns and flower baskets hung from the ceiling along with a large wooden swing that could seat at least five people. I climbed out of my car and was met by Stacy, at the end of the stairs.

"My favorite girl!" he exclaimed, smiling at me. I walked into his arms and allowed him to engulf me in a hug. "You look more and more like your mama every day," he said, holding me at arm's length and looking me over.

It had been a long time since I had a conversation with someone that knew my parents. My dad had taken Stacy under his wing when he was younger and he had been like an uncle to me for years. Stacy moved to Mississippi shortly after I did and he had been the only one to attend my college graduation and my Masters Award ceremony. I had not seen him in over a year, but he still looked exactly the same. His salt and pepper hair was unruly on his head and his age was apparent around his eyes and mouth, but he was still very attractive. He was only a few inches taller than me and his lean muscular figure could still be recognized under his jeans and t-shirt. At forty-two years old, Stacy was still smoking hot.

He was the reason that I came to Tupelo. When I found this place, it was him that I hired to do the renovations. He now lived here and kept the maintenance up to date on the house. "Well, let's get you settled and then we can catch up." I nodded in agreement, knowing that Stacy was going to be mighty surprised with everything that I had to tell him.

When I walked into the house, I couldn't help the smile that stretched across my face. This place was amazing. The large wooden door opened into a sitting room that was full of antiques. The aged furniture, along with the huge staircase, made you feel like you had just stepped into a plantation home from the eighteen hundreds. To the left, a swinging door led into a massive kitchen and on the other side of that was a dining room that had enough private tables to accommodate everyone in the house. To the right of the sitting room, there was a smoking parlor and a library. I was hoping to spend a little time in there before I left.

I climbed the long staircase to the second floor, and then a narrower one to the third floor and walked into what would be my home for the next few days. I sat my things down on the settee, exhausted and very glad that I had an elevator installed after I purchased this place. I knew that if I had a tough time climbing all those stairs, it would be impossible for someone in their sixties or seventies to do it, and considering they were my best customers, it was the best money spent on this house.

I was glad only a few people were staying here this week. It wasn't often that this room was available and it was, by far, the best in the house. The room was large and spacious with twelve foot ceilings, plush burgundy carpet and a king sized canopy bed that was raised off the floor and had steps surrounding it. An old vanity table, complete with a wash bowl and water pitcher, sat on one side of the double doors that led to the bathroom, and a dark wooden chifferobe sat on the other. The bathroom housed an oversized claw foot tub and a double sink with lights that looked like old lanterns. But, the best part of the room was the balcony that overlooked the garden below. I could spend hours out there and do nothing more than look out over the garden and day dream.

I grabbed my cell and called Scott to let him know that I made it here and would come by the office sometime around four and to not leave until I got there. I also sent a quick text to Luke letting him know that I made it and was sorry for being a bitch and hanging up, then unpacked my clothes before heading downstairs to the kitchen to meet up with Stacy.

In the kitchen, I could smell corn and crab bisque simmering on the stove. The smell made my mouth water and I wandered over to get a bowl. Unlike other bed and breakfasts, this one was full service. We had a cook on call twenty-four, seven who would cook anything that your heart desired, within reason. Mrs. Pearl, Mrs. Jackie and Mrs. Gladene had been cooking here since long before I was born. They were sweet and wonderful and full of life, but they would snap on your ass if you so much as breathed wrong in their kitchen.

"Jackie told me to make sure you got a big bowl of that," Stacy said, entering the kitchen. "She always said you were too skinny."

It surprised me that Jackie would even consider cooking something for me. Last time we spoke, she called me a spoiled bitch and I was quick to tell her that she could find another job. She just laughed, which made me angrier. She knew that she was irreplaceable and so did I. If I fired Jackie, I might as well say goodbye to Pearl and Gladene too, and if I did that, I would lose all of my business. People drove from miles around just to eat Mrs. Pearl's cornbread dressing.

"The old bitch probably poisoned it," I muttered.

"So, what brings you up here?" Stacy asked jumping right to the point.

"Well, I am having some problems with some renters and I came to straighten a few things out," I answered while fixing myself a large bowl of bisque and joining him at a table.

"Sounds fun, but enough about work. How has life been treating you?"

I smiled up at him. "Good. Really good. I met someone," I confessed trying to gauge his reaction.

"Dallas, that's great! I am so happy for you. Tell me about him." This was going to be the hard part. I was hoping that Stacy would keep an open mind and not be too judgmental, but I was afraid he would jump the gun on this one.

"Well, his name is Lucas Carmical. He is from Hattiesburg and we met a few weeks ago." I knew I was being short with him, but I didn't want to confess all of his secrets. Hell, I didn't even know all there was to know about him.

"What does he do? How did you meet him?" Leave it to Stacy to cut straight through the bullshit. I didn't want the remainder of my time spent with answering questions, so I figured that I might as well go ahead and get it all out there.

"I met him at a bar. He actually saved me from being molested by this guy and we have been seeing one another ever since. He is in the timber business, is extremely good looking, and takes care of me. Oh, and he is the President of a motorcycle club." I said the last part rather fast, hoping he didn't hear me, but of course I didn't get that lucky.

"A motorcycle club, huh? Which one?"

"The Devil's Renegades," I said not making eye contact.

"Hmm. That's cool." *Was that all he was going to say?* "I am glad you met someone. I am even gladder that this someone is down to Earth and not some spoiled rich kid like you usually go for. I would really like to meet him."

I was shocked at what he said, but I tried to conceal it. "Of course. I was hoping that he could come with me, but he had some prior obligations."

"I see. Well, I look forward to meeting him one day." Stacy patted my hand then got up to help himself to some bisque. I started to tell him about the other group of bikers, but no need to go stirring up anything right now. If they came, and I highly doubted that they would, we would deal with it then.

Chapter 18

My Tupelo office was located downtown in a shopping center. It was small, but with the amount of business that I had up here, it worked. Scott greeted me as I walked in the door.

"Hey, Dallas!" he said, a little too cheerfully. I noted that the office was clean and everyone was superbly dressed. There was no doubt in my mind that this was a result of me coming.

"Give me the files on both of those properties," I said. I was back to being a shrewd bitch and I could tell the effect it had on everyone. Scott scrambled to his desk to grab the files and I felt a pang of guilt when I noticed how he acted around me. His brow had beads of sweat on it and he appeared to be a nervous wreck.

Had I always been this intimidating? I wondered what made me realize this now, even though I knew in the back of my mind what had caused this. *Luke. He was making me weak.* I didn't like it, but I had to admit that the high I got from being nice to people was much different than the one I got when I was a being a complete bitch.

"Oh Scott, calm down," I said exasperated. I don't know who I was more aggravated with, me for trying to change who I was, or him for being such a pussy. "I'm not gonna bite you, relax." I took a seat at the chair in front of his desk. He paused, looking at me curiously.

"Yes, ma'am," he said with one quick nod of his head. I could tell my words had done absolutely nothing to relax him. Hopefully, he would lighten up by the end of the week.

"Have you heard from them today?" I asked looking over the file in front of me.

"No. I 've tried to call them every day, but I haven't received an answer."

"Okay, well, I'm having dinner with Tammy tonight. Maybe she can give me some insight. I'll call you in the morning." I left the office in no better mood than I had arrived in. Maybe a few drinks with Tammy would loosen me up and help me keep my mind off of Luke. He had not responded to my message and I hated it when we didn't communicate. It seemed like every time we took one step forward, we took two back.

I confirmed my dinner with Tammy, and then tried Luke once more. I called and after the phone rang for what seemed like forever, I got his voicemail. I slung the phone onto the passenger seat hoping to break something in the process. I hated being ignored. I bet if sweet Maddie would have called, he would have picked up. *Ugh!* I had to stop doing this to myself. Luke was probably just busy. I would try him again after dinner and if he didn't answer, only then I would worry.

Dinner with Tammy was a flop. I learned absolutely nothing about the tenants and after the first fifteen minutes, we moved on to another subject. She didn't seem to mind that our meeting was cut short. Two drinks and one appetizer later, I was out the door.

Stacy sat on the swing with a beer in hand and I gladly accepted when he pulled one from the ice chest between his feet and offered it to me.

"Long day?" he asked, giving me a crooked grin.

"Shitty day is more like it. How was yours?"

"The same." We sat there in the swing not talking. It was nice to just relax and enjoy the fall air. October had shown its face and I welcomed it with open arms.

"Luke's club is having issues with some people and I have gotten involved." I wasn't sure where that had come from. I wasn't even thinking of the club, yet here I was telling Stacy. It must have been the sense of danger that lurked in the back of my sub-conscious.

"Involved, how?" Stacy asked turning to look at me. I told him the story of the break-in and the fight at the bar and the red and gray vests that seemed to show up wherever I was. "That sounds pretty serious, Dallas," he said concerned. I gave him a tight smile and shrugged my shoulders. "Well, don't worry, honey. Nothing will bother you here. Not as long as I'm around."

I knew Stacy meant what he said. He would have no problem stopping anyone who tried to get through that door. I wasn't worried in the least, so I just patted him on the leg and walked inside. This day had been enough. I was ready to go to bed and hopefully figure some of this shit out.

I climbed the stairs figuring that I needed the exercise after the fried cheese and two mixed drinks that I consumed, and walked to my room totally exhausted. I was winded just from the two flights and that was highly unusual for someone as fit as myself. I passed it off as stress, then climbed into bed and prayed for a better tomorrow.

I could hear the motorcycles in the distance. I knew that he was coming for me. Luke would save me. I was hanging over a ledge with nothing to hold onto but a tree root. The raging water below me was littered with sharp rocks, and I knew that even if I managed to dodge the rocks, I would still drown in the swift current. The noise became louder, my heart sped up. He would be here soon. I wiped my forehead with my free hand and found it soaking wet. I wondered how the sea spray managed to reach me all the way up here. My hair was wet, too. I must have fallen in and then climbed out. I was confused and scared and panting. I had never been scared of anything. What had scared me?

The motorcycles pulled up to the edge of the cliff and I tried to scream for Luke, but no matter how loud I screamed, he couldn't hear me. He walked to the edge of the cliff and looked down. He held his hand out to me. I reached for him, but he was too far away. Just a few more inches and I would be safe. I looked up into his eyes, but instead of seeing his blue ones, all I saw was black. This was not Luke. This guy had a large scar on his face and was laughing at me.

"Good-bye, sleeping beauty," he said to me in a sickening sweet voice. He produced a small hatchet from his back pocket. I thought he was going to kill me, but as he swung it, he connected with the tree root and then I was falling.

I sat straight up in the bed and breathed deep, trying to catch my breath. My chest hurt and I could feel the congestion building there. My whole body was soaking wet and I was burning up.

I decided on a hot shower to hopefully clear up some of the congestion in my chest. I climbed from the bed and made my way to the bathroom. It seemed like a lifetime passed before I made it, and my limbs felt as if they were made of lead.

After showering, I felt a fraction better. I decided that the soaked sheets on my bed would not be very comfortable, so I pulled the comforter from the bed and curled up on the settee to sleep.

A loud banging in my head woke me. The light pouring in from the doors leading outside hurt my head. The banging continued and I realized it was coming from the door.

"Come in," I said, but it came out as barely a whisper. I had not moved from the settee and once again, I was covered in sweat.

"Miss Dallas, you got a phone call and if you don't get outta that bed, you gonna be late for work." I recognized Jackie's voice. I didn't care if she hated me or that I despised her, right now, I needed some help. Something was wrong with me. I couldn't move, my breathing was shallow and I felt like someone was sitting on my chest.

"Jackie," I tried to say a little louder, but again, I heard nothing. I could hear people talking in the hallway and then I heard a key in the door unlocking it.

"Dallas!" I opened my eyes to see Stacy gaping at me. "Oh, my God! How long have you been like this?"

I must have looked pretty bad because everyone just stared at me with worried and shocked faces.

"Stacy, go downstairs and tell Gladene that I need her to come up here. Help Ms. Pearl with the breakfast, and Gladene and me will handle Miss Dallas." Stacy looked torn, but Jackie shooed him away with her hand. "Go on now."

Stacy left the room and I watched Jackie through my heavy lids. She looked worried and I didn't blame her. If I looked half as bad as I felt, I would probably die any minute. She was probably worried about losing her job and for some reason, I found that funny.

I tried to laugh, but I couldn't get my body to cooperate. Gladene came bursting through the door and stopped in her tracks when she saw me. *I mean, really*? I couldn't look that bad. I felt myself slipping from consciousness once again. If I could just sleep this off, I would feel better tomorrow.

"Oh no, Miss Dallas," I heard Jackie protest. "We need you to stay awake for us, until we can figure out what's wrong."

"She's got the damn flu, that's what's wrong," Gladene chimed in. There was no way to tell how old either of them was, but I guessed in their mid-fifties. Both had hair that was cut short, but stylish and their large robust bodies were equal in size. They could have been twins. Their skin was a dark caramel color and was wrinkle free and flawless. *I hated them.*

"Well, help me get her up and in the bathroom," Jackie demanded, pulling the covers off of me.

"She better be glad that I got my damn flu shot," Gladene mumbled. I tried to give her the finger, but I couldn't lift my arm. Jackie didn't much like me, but Gladene truly despised me. They lifted me with ease and carried me to the bathroom, sitting me on the toilet and holding me up, while arguing with each other over who got their flu shot first. I told them to shut up and just help me get a bath, but once again, nothing came out and this was not the time to be a smart ass. I was at the mercy of these two women, both of which didn't like me.

"Okay, Miss Dallas, we gonna help you get a cool bath and see if that brings your fever down a little. Then, if you want to, you can rest and we will see how you feel when you wake up." *I batted my eyelashes in agreement since that's the only part of my body that seemed to be working.* Soon, I was undressed and in the tub while Jackie and Gladene bathed me with a gentleness that I didn't think either of them capable of. *I would have to remember to give them a raise.* They hauled me out once I was clean, but before they could dry me off, I was sweating again.

"That's a good sign, Miss Dallas. You need to sweat that fever out," Gladene said.

"Thank you." It was the first words that I had managed to say, and even though it was just above a whisper, they heard me.

"Come on, let's get you some clothes on," Jackie ordered, but I could see the softness in her eyes.

Gladene changed the sheets while Jackie shoved medicine down my throat and forced me to drink some water. I only managed a few sips, but she seemed satisfied enough. I felt like I had run a marathon. The strength it took just to open my mouth was equivalent to climbing a mountain. They hoisted me into the bed and closed the blinds, darkening the room. I needed to tell Scott that I wouldn't make it today and check my cell phone to see if Luke had called. I wouldn't tell him I was sick because I didn't want him to feel obligated to come up here. Not that he would come anyway; he would probably just send someone to make sure that I didn't die. My anguish must have been written all over my face because Gladene was staring at me concerned.

"You gonna feel better real soon, Miss Dallas. Doctors don't make house calls anymore, but I'll call Dr. Pritchett to see what he thinks. He will be coming down this weekend, anyway. We will get Ms. Pearl to pay him in cobbler and don't you worry about Mr. Scott at the office. I called him first thing this morning and he said that he would handle everything. Oh, and a Mr. Luke called and I told him that you was busy, but I'll let him know what's going on when he calls back. Stacy told us you found you a man." I watched Jackie as she scurried around the room talking fast and jumping from one subject to another. *I rolled my eyes at her.* Gladene threw her hand on her hip and pointed at me.

"See, that's why you ain't ever had a man, cause..."

"Gladene, leave the girl alone or at least wait until she's better." If they left after that, I didn't know it. When I tried to blink my eyes, they wouldn't open and the darkness settled in.

Chapter 19

It was cold, *freezing cold.* My body convulsed with shudders. I felt like I couldn't breathe and the movements were making me even more winded. People were in the room with me, but I was not sure who they were. Stacy was the first person to realize that I was somewhat awake.

"Hey, honey," he said, his voice soothing me.

"D-doctor. I need to go to the h-hospital," I stammered. *Enough of this trying to be brave shit. I wanted a hospital room with IV's and medicine and white fluorescent lighting.*

"They're coming, honey. The ambulance is on its way," he said to me from a distance. *He should have gone with Gladene and Jackie to get that flu shot.*

"Who called the damn ambulance?" I could hear Jackie's voice hollering over everyone else's.

"I did, Jackie. Damn! Have you looked at her?" Stacy said running his hands through his hair.

"Of course, I have looked at her! That's why I called Dr. Pritchett and he's on his way over. There ain't no need in getting all worked up when we know what she has," Jackie said staring at him with her hands on her hips.

"How in the hell do you know what she has? This ain't the old days, Jackie. There are doctors, who work in actual hospitals, who can help her. She needs fluids. She hasn't eaten in over twenty-four hours and she's dehydrated."

I appreciated the fight that Stacy was putting up for me, but I wished that he would do it in the hallway. My head felt like it was going to explode. I heard the sound of sirens and everyone rushed from the room at the same time. *Did they really have to turn the damn sirens on?* I figured I could close my eyes and enjoy the silence until they got here.

It was the next day before I opened my eyes again. Sunlight poured in from the windows and judging by the brightness, I could tell that it was well into the afternoon. I looked around the room and sent a prayer up that Stacy had won and I was in the hospital. The room was large and spacious and covered in flowers. I wondered who they were from.

The bouquet next to my bed was a dozen white roses and I smiled at the thoughtfulness. I knew that Luke had sent them in leu of Neo. *Was Luke here?* My pulse quickened at the thought. *He was here. I knew that he would be.* The door opened and I glanced up to see a nurse entering the room.

"Well, hello there!" She said excitedly. "There are a lot of people waiting to see you. How are you feeling?" I felt like shit. My whole body ached and even my hair hurt. My mouth was dry and tasted like something had died in it.

"I feel great," I said forcing a smile. I didn't want her to refuse visitors just because I felt bad.

"Honey, you can lie to anyone you want, but I will not tolerate you lying to me. Now, let's try this again. How are you feeling?" I smirked at her persistence. She was young and feisty and reminded me a lot of myself.

"I feel like I was hit by a train, but I want to see my visitors," I said holding her gaze. She would not deny me that. I wanted my Luke. *I needed him.*

"Of course, you do. After I check your vitals, I will give you one hour and then it's back to resting up. We need to get you well and out of here." I didn't argue. An hour was better than nothing at all and although I would never admit it to her, our short conversation was wearing me out.

My vitals seemed to be fine. My pulse was a little fast and my blood pressure a little low but she told me that was normal. I was wearing a catheter, and the thought almost made me vomit, but she said it would be best if we left it in until the doctor said otherwise. I needed to remain immobile until he made his rounds again, which would be in about six hours. She helped me wash my mouth out, gave me some ice chips, and then sat me up in the bed. I was ready for my company and even though my eyes were getting heavy again, I fought through it with the thought of seeing Luke fueling my stamina.

"I'll send them in," she said turning to leave. She left the door open and soon the room was full of people. Stacy was first, coming over to kiss my head and tell me how good it was to see me awake and myself. Next were Jackie and Gladene, who both looked relieved that I didn't die, but not much more. Red and Gypsy were there with Regg and Kev, all four fussing over me as if I was a newborn baby. I was unable to register much of anything they said. I had only one question. *Where was Luke?* Red gave me a wink and a reassuring smile and I knew that she had some information to share with me, but didn't want to do it in front of everyone.

"Well ladies, now that we know she is gonna be alright, I reckon we better head back," Stacy said forcing me to look at him. His eyes were bloodshot and he looked like he had not slept in days. "We'll be back first thing in the morning." I gave him my best attempt at a smile. He squeezed my hand, and ushered Jackie and Gladene out of the room.

"So, how ya feeling?" Red asked pulling up a chair next to my bed. Regg and Kev had taken a seat on the couch on the other side of the room and Gypsy sat across from then in a reclining chair.

"Where is he, Red?" I asked not beating around the bush.

"He couldn't make it, Dallas. He sent us the minute that he found out you were sick. I have strict instructions to be at your every beck and call. I even brought my bag to stay with you until you are well enough to travel," she said as if that were better than him actually being here.

"What do you mean, he couldn't make it?" I tried to sound firm and demanding, but I had no fight left in me. I was hollow inside. Him not being here felt like someone had sucked the life out of me. He was all the medicine that I needed, yet once again, he put his club before me and sent someone else to do what he should be doing.

"There is a lot that you don't understand, Dallas," she said lowering her voice. "This is a tough time for the club and Luke has been trying to handle some things lately that he just can't walk away from. I told you before, this club is his life, but you need to know that he would rather be here with you than anywhere else in the world."

I didn't believe her. If he wanted to be here then he would. She was defending him like she always did, like she always would.

"I know you are upset, but one day you will understand and hopefully appreciate the sacrifices that he makes for this club."

"I don't give a shit about the club!" I yelled. "He is the one who wanted this. One minute, he tells me that he loves me and he would do anything for me and then when I really need him, he isn't here. I can't take this, Red. I have given up everything for him. I'm not even the same person anymore and what has he given to me? Huh? Tell me, Red! Tell me what sacrifices he has made for me and our relationship. I'm with him *not* the club." Tears streamed down my face as I fought to keep my shallow breathing under control.

"He is the club, Dallas. I know you don't understand this now, but I hope you will soon." I could see the pained look on Red's face. I knew that I shouldn't take it out on her, but I had to take it out on someone and since Luke wasn't here, she would have to suffice.

"Look darlin', we know you're upset, but believe me, he wanted to be here. There are some things that were planned a long time ago, shit that was set in stone and he had to be there to sign off on it. I promise you, as soon as he can get away, he will be here," Regg said from the foot of my bed.

I hadn't even realized that he had walked up. His words put me somewhat at ease, but still left me feeling empty.

Jenn came to sit next to Red and held my hand in hers. "I have known Luke for years and I have never seen him as smitten with someone as he is with you. Trust us, when we tell you that he wants to be here. I know this is a lot to take in and we have all been through it, but we are your family and we will help you get through this. By this, I don't just mean the sickness. I mean everything. We are here for you."

Jenn reminded me of a motherly figure, her soft voice and warm caresses on my hand had me feeling better about the whole ordeal. I needed to think this over and my eyelids were getting heavier with each passing second. I would sleep on it and maybe by tomorrow I would have some kind of conclusion to this fucked up life style that I had decided to live in. Unable to respond, I just nodded my head at them and closed my eyes. Sleep. I just needed a few hours of sleep and I would be fine.

I woke to someone shaking me and calling my name.

"Dallas, Dallas, come on, wake up." I opened my eyes and saw a girl that I didn't recognize standing next to my bed. She looked worried and very anxious.

"Who are you?" I asked, my voice thick with sleep.

"Listen to me. We don't have much time. You have to get out of this hospital. I don't care what you do or how you do it, but you must get out, now." *What the hell?*

"Why?" I asked trying to sit up in bed and get a better look at her. It was dark outside and the lights were off. I could only make out part of her face and nothing more.

"I, I have to go." She was out the door before I could ask her anymore questions. Maybe my meds were too strong, or not strong enough. *That was weird.* I needed to find out who she was, but my thoughts were interrupted when the nurse came in.

"Hey, girl! How about we get this catheter out and let you do a little moving around." I nodded my head in agreement. Hopefully, I could walk to the shower. I was starting to smell funny. The nurse removed the catheter and took my vitals, which were perfect. Maybe I would be out of here sooner than I had thought.

"Do you know who that girl was that just left?" I asked the nurse while she helped me into a sitting position on the side of the bed.

"What girl, honey? It's two o'clock in the morning. Ain't nobody here except you and me. We ran the other ones out of here because they had not had the flu vaccine. We still aren't real sure if that's what ya got. The blood work hasn't come back yet."

What? I was so confused. *Shit, maybe I had imagined it.* I shook my head to try and clear my thoughts, and then with a lot less energy than I thought I would need, I made it to the bathroom.

I owed Red. She had pulled through for me. I was able to shower with my own shampoo and body wash and she hadn't only bought me a brand new set of pajamas, she washed them, too. After I was clean and dressed, the nurse helped me to the recliner in the room and I sat feeling much more refreshed. I was still tired and my body achy, but it was tolerable.

"I am so fucking hungry," I announced, more to myself than the nurse. She looked at me with a raised eyebrow and I remembered that my language was probably not suitable for her ears. "Sorry," I muttered.

"The doctor is on the floor. I will see if you can have some jello or something light." *Fuck the jello. I wanted a hamburger. Maybe one of those Wards' big one with chili and cheese, or a chili cheese dog covered in onions and mustard.*

"You need anything before I go?" the nurse asked interrupting my imaginary buffet.

"Would you hand me my phone, please?" Someone, probably Red, had been kind enough to put it on the charger for me. She brought my phone to me and left the room. I must have pissed her off with my foul language. Oh well, I was the patient.

My phone had been turned on silent, so the notification tone that would have gone off twenty-three times went unheard. I had text messages from Lindsey letting me know that she had everything under control. I had one from Scott telling me that the tenants were moving out over the weekend. A few more were from various people from the office expressing their concerns, which surprised me. The greatest surprise was the eleven missed calls and the two text messages I had received from Luke.

I love you babe. Sorry I can't be there for you. Call me when you can. *I miss you so much it hurts. I love you.*

Luke was so frustrating. *What could be so important that he couldn't be here?* Well, there was only one way to find out. I didn't care that it was almost three in the morning. I dialed Luke's number and held my breath as it rang.

"Yeah," came a groggy voice from the other end of the line.

"Hey, stranger," I said. I was still upset with him, but just hearing his voice had me smiling.

"Dallas?" His voice was clearer and I could picture him sitting up in the bed.

"It's me," I replied still smiling.

"Hey, baby! How ya feeling?"

How did I feel? Lonely... Hurt... Betrayed...

"I'm feeling better. Sorry to call you so late, but I just woke up."

"Don't apologize, baby. I'm glad you called. What has the doctor said?" I could hear Luke up and moving around. What I would give to be there with him right now. I choked back my tears and forced my voice to remain steady.

"I haven't seen him yet. I think it's the flu, but it hasn't been confirmed. This is the first time that I have gotten out of bed since I have been sick. What are you doing?" I didn't want to talk about me. I wanted to talk about why he had not been here to see me.

"Baby, I know you are upset, but I promise when you get home, I am going to tell you everything. That may not sound like a lot to you, but it is the greatest thing that I have to offer. I have kept you in the dark because I don't want to lose you and I'm afraid you will run when I tell you what I have been avoiding since the first night I met you. You deserve to know, Dallas, and I have been selfish for keeping this from you. It kills me to know that when you need me, I can't be there."

"I understand, Luke," I said stopping him before he could tell me anymore. "I'm fine, really. I should be home in a few days."

I had made up my mind. Luke was everything that I had ever wanted in a man. His complicated world had turned me upside down, but I loved it. I loved his friends and the relationship that they had. I wanted that for myself, but most of all, I just wanted to be with him. Being without him these past few days was tough, but not as tough as it was before I knew he existed. I would take Luke anyway that I could get him, and if that meant I had to come in second then so be it, because only one day with Luke was better than a lifetime without him.

"I will make it up to you, baby. I know you are tired of hearing that, but it's the truth. I'm not perfect by any means, but I am a better man with you. Please don't leave me." His plea tugged at my heart. "Give me just a little time, baby. I promise it will not always be like this." I knew he wanted to tell me right then what was going on, but I trusted him. More than I had ever trusted anyone. "I'm not going anywhere. I promise. Go back to sleep. As soon as the doctor comes in, I'll text and let you know what he says."

"No, you call me. I always have my phone on me. If you need anything or you just want to talk, call me." I smiled at how fast he had gone from love struck Luke to biker bad boy, LLC.

"I will. I love you, Luke."

"I love you too, baby. I'll talk to you soon." I hung up the phone feeling a little better about my situation. My glory was short lived when the doctor walked into the room.

"Hello, Miss Knox. I know the hour is unusual, but since your schedule is messed up and I just so happened to be on the floor, I thought I would stop by."

The doctor was an older gentleman with hair as white as snow and kind brown eyes. He pulled a chair up next to me and took at seat.

"Miss Knox, I want you to know that no one other than myself and the lab techs know about the results of your blood work." I felt like I was missing a piece of the puzzle, but I just nodded so that he would continue. "Do you know anyone who would want to hurt you?" His question caught me completely off guard.

"Excuse me?"

"We found a small amount of arsenic in your system. Whoever poisoned you knew exactly the amount to give you to make you disoriented and sick, but not enough to kill you. The fluids that we gave you when you were admitted helped push it through your system. I'm hoping that was the case, and not the alternative-which is where they would have given you too much, causing your heart to stop immediately. The reason that I am leaning towards the first conclusion is because if the dosage would have been more, your heart would have stopped instantly, and arsenic would have without a doubt shown up in an autopsy report."

My head was spinning. This was too much. *Who could have poisoned me, and if they were brave enough to do so, why not just kill me?*

"The police have not been notified, but my suggestion for you is to make that your next step." *The police? I would not want all the publicity. I could see the tabloids now-"DALLAS KNOX MILLIONAIRE BACHORLETTE POSIONED BY IRATE CO-WORKERS."*

"No police. I don't want this all over the news and papers." He shook his head as if he understood and patted my knee.

"It was a close call, Miss Knox, but you will be just fine. I'm going to keep you today and you can go home tomorrow morning. The side effects will last a few more days but your strength will return soon enough. Just take it easy for about a week."

"Please don't tell anyone about this. I would like it to remain between you and me," I said pleadingly.

"As you wish, Miss Knox."

"Hey doc, I need one more favor. Is there any way I can get out of here in a few hours. My vitals were good and I really need to get home. I have a lot to figure out." He seemed doubtful. "I promise to rest as soon as I get home. I'll call daily and let you know how I am doing and I will follow up with my family doctor next week."

He smiled at me and shook his head, "You are not going to stop are you?"

"No, sir. I really just want to go home and be with my family."

"I can understand that," he cleared his throat and his expression turned serious. "Bed rest for at least the next three days. I mean it. You must call my office first thing Monday morning and let me know how you're feeling. If you have any problems, any at all, you go straight to the emergency room. Understood?"

I smiled in relief. "Yes, sir."

"Noon and only if your vitals remain good."

"Thank you, doctor." Before he even left the room my mind was swimming. I took a deep breath and gathered my thoughts. *I would not tell Luke about the poison*. He had enough on him and I still wasn't sure who could have done this. It very well could have been Jackie or Gladene. I knew they didn't like me, but I didn't think they hated me so much that they wanted to poison me.

The only other people that I had come into contact with were Scott and Tammy. There was no way that Scott could have done it. I was only around him for a few minutes. I had several drinks with Tammy, but I don't remember her acting suspicious in any way.

This was absolutely insane. I didn't want to think about it. It settled better with me if I just pretended that nothing was wrong. The only person in danger was me and I would be leaving here soon enough, and be back in the arms of Luke. Maybe I could even stay with him until I was better. No, I would need to go home. I didn't want to wear out my welcome, plus I had Neo to look after. *Shit!* I grabbed my phone and called Luke.

"Hey baby, something wrong?" Luke's worried voice was now wide awake. I imagined him showered and dressed and sitting at the bar drinking coffee. *I would give my left leg for a cup of that coffee right about now.*

"Dallas?" *Damn it. Focus Dallas.*

"Hey, uh, sorry. Look, I hate to ask you but I need a favor." I asked, still trying to erase the mental picture of his throat moving in that oh so sexy way that only Luke was capable of. *I had a conclusion to my problem...I was horny.*

"Sure, babe, anything." "If you go to town today, could you swing by and check on Neo for me? He is probably curled up somewhere pouting. He has plenty of food and water, but if I had known that I would be gone this long, I would have made other arrangements for him." *I was such a terrible dog mother.*

"Sorry babe, no can do." *Was he seriously telling me no? I mean, I know he had shit to do, but really?*

"I'm judging by your silence that you are calling me everything under the sun. It's good to see that you still have your spark, but before you bite my head off, I picked him up yesterday and he has been here at the house with me." My whole body warmed. Luke might not have been here in person, but his thoughts were with me.

"You really are amazing," I breathed.

"I know." I could tell he was kidding, but his cockiness was still there and it made me smile; my first real smile since Tuesday.

"I need another favor." I knew this one he would be glad to give.

"Anything." His voice was like caramel and it had me squirming in my seat. *Asshole.* He knew what he was doing.

"I'm getting released today at noon. You reckon Red would come pick me up? I can't drive for the next few days."

"You're getting out?" The excitement in Luke's voice was unmistakable. *My baby missed me.*

"I am. The doctor said it was the flu and that I could go home. I just needed to take it easy for the next week or so."

"I'll call them now. I gotta go, baby, but I'll see you when you get home. I love you."

"I love you too, Luke." I hung up the phone and sat there smiling to myself. *Everything was going to be okay.* My stomach growled at me, reminding me of how hungry I was, but the excitement of seeing Luke and the drowsiness that was setting in won over my hunger. I would get a little more rest, and hopefully by the time I woke it would be noon.

Something smelled fabulous, like body wash mixed with cologne and something else I couldn't quite wrap my brain around. *I had smelled this scent before. I had tasted it and craved it.* Only one thing could smell this good- Luke. My eyes fluttered open and when I saw him standing next to my bed looking down on me, nothing else mattered. *Luke was here.*

He had come to take me home, but something was wrong. Luke's face was full of worry. His eyebrows were creased and he looked like he was going to cry any minute. He wasn't looking at my face, almost as if he were ashamed to. He was in deep thought about something and I was sure that whatever it was had to do with me. I lifted my hand, finding his, and when his eyes met mine all of the worry drained from his face and was replaced with pure joy.

"There's my girl," he said bringing my hand to his lips.

"I'm hungry." *Really Dallas? You haven't seen the man in days and that's the first thing that you tell him?* He threw his head back and laughed my favorite laugh.

"Well, as soon as you are ready, I'll feed you," he said smiling his full megawatt smile.

"What time is it?" I asked sitting up. "What day is it?" Luke moved to assist me until me feet were hanging off the side of the bed and I was sitting straight up.

"Just after one and it's Saturday. The doctor came in around eleven-thirty and cleared you to leave. He said just to let you rest and when you woke I could take you home. I have strict instructions to make sure that you get plenty of rest and don't overdo it for the next week. He said you would be hungry and you are cleared to eat whatever you like, but you have to drink plenty of fluids. Here is the paperwork. You just need to sign and turn it in at the nurse's desk before you leave." *Damn. That was easy.* I felt rested and was ready to get the hell out of here. I wanted a hot shower with real water pressure and a hamburger and French fries and a coke and a hot fudge sundae. Just the thought of it had me up and moving to get ready.

"Hang on baby, damn. You're move faster now, than you ever have," Luke said. *I could tell he was trying to be stern, but it wasn't working.*

"I'm fine. I'm not gonna break, you know," I said sitting down to use the bathroom, not bothered at all by the fact that he was standing there watching me. I would never take for granted being able to pee on my own ever again. *Catheters sucked.*

Luke busied himself by packing my things in a duffle bag Red must have brought it all in. I stood up and looked in the mirror. *Holy hell.* My face was pale and slim. My eyes were hollow and lifeless. My tangled nappy hair looked like a rat's nest. Luke had definitely seen me at my worst. *Even I had never seen me this bad.*

I looked over at Luke and as always, he looked absolutely amazing. He wore jeans and a baby blue polo that complimented his eyes and hugged him in all the right places. His plain white ball cap was turned backwards on his head. He looked good enough to eat, and I was hungry.

I gazed down at my wrinkled pajamas and bare feet. Tears sprang to my eyes when I looked up into his. "Are you ashamed of me?"

He smiled and pushed a lock of hair behind my ear, "No, beautiful. Even at your worst, you still take my breath away." His sweet comment made me smile; my tears forgotten. He leaned down and ever so softly planted a kiss to my dry, chapped lips. When he pulled away, I quickly ran my tongue across them savoring the taste of him on my mouth.

He smiled down at me and shook his head. "I brought you another change of clothes. When I went to get Neo, I grabbed a few things for you." He walked back into the room and presented me with a bag containing the red strapless summer dress and gold sandals that I had attempted to wear the first time he was at my house. "I really like this dress, but if you want something more comfortable, I brought this, too." He said pulling out a neon pink Nike jump suit and some Nike Shox.

I laughed, "How about the sweats today and the dress after I've had a real shower and a chance to shave my legs?"

"I could shave you," he said wiggling his eyebrows. My stomach flipped. The thought of him shaving me did delicious things to my insides. "I know that look. Come on and get dressed, or we will never make it out of this hospital," Luke said laughing. I agreed.

After I was dressed, my teeth brushed and my hair piled on my head, my Greek god and I headed out. Luke held my hand in one of his and with the other carried both bags and led me to the nurse's desk.

"Miss Knox, we're glad you're feeling better," the lady at the nurse's station said while ogling my man. I decided to let her slide. *Hell, I couldn't blame her for looking.*

"Thank you," I said signing the papers and handing them back to her.

"Also, here is Dr. Yarborough's card. He asks that you call him on Monday." I took the card, nodded my head and headed toward the elevator.

"Is the doctor fond of you, Miss Knox?" Luke asked once we were inside.

"Not that I'm aware of, why?" I asked curiously. What was he playing at?

"It's not every day the good doctor gives his business card to the patient for them to follow up with personally." *Shit.* I just shrugged my shoulders in response as the elevator descended and we landed on the second floor parking garage.

Chapter 20

As soon as we stepped out of the elevator Luke had me in his arms. He hugged me tightly holding me close to his chest. I wrapped my arms around his waist and inhaled the scent of him. "God, I missed you." He whispered in my ear, showering me with kisses. "I'm so sorry that I couldn't be here." I silenced him by placing my finger over his lips.

"Don't. You're here now and that is all that matters." *And it was*.

He smiled and kissed my forehead then scooping the bags up off the ground, he led me to the truck. I expected him to open the passenger side door, but he didn't.

He stopped and said, "I feel like you have been gone for months instead of days. I want you next to me." I didn't argue. I liked being up under Luke. I was relieved when I was finally seated. Just the short walk had winded me. "You okay, babe?" Luke asked concerned.

"Yeah, just a little tired... and hungry."

"What do you want to eat?" he asked pulling the truck from the parking spot and driving one handed while the other arm was wrapped around me.

"Ward's. I want a Big One combo with fries and a coke and a hot fudge sundae," I said resting my head against his arm.

He smiled. "Anything for you, darlin'."

We pulled into the nearest Ward's, which was only about a block away. I managed to scramble from the truck with only a little assistance from Luke. "I can carry you, baby. Just wrap your arms around me." He said looking down at me while I was leaned up against the side of the truck. His offer sounded wonderful. Being completely immobile for three days was taking its toll on me.

"People will laugh and stare," I said pouting.

"Who gives a shit," he responded, not caring.

"No, I'm fine. Let's get in here before I eat you." I said forcing a smile and trying to make a joke. Luke was skeptical, but slowly walked me with his arm around my waist into the greatest fast food chain in the South. I didn't have to repeat what I wanted. Luke ordered my food and sat us at a table near the front. Probably so I wouldn't have to walk so far.

When our food arrived, I couldn't help the excited smile that broke out over my face. *This was going to be fabulous.* I never looked up as I shoveled half the burger in my mouth and dipped my French fries into my ice cream.

"Um, there is plenty more where that came from. You can slow down, ya know."

I took a break, long enough to look up at him and hold his gaze, while I took a large pull from my coke, keeping my face impassive. He was the first to look away, smirking. I continued eating and when I caught him looking once again, the amusement faded when I opened my mouth-full of food.

"Very classy, babe," he said laughing. I joined in with him and sat back full and satisfied. I had only eaten about half, but it had taken me less than five minutes and I had never felt more pleased with my decision to come here.

"You ready?" he asked willing to give up over half of his food to leave with me. I shook my head and waved a hand at him.

"Nah, go ahead. I need to sit a second." He shook his head laughing under his breath.

When I'm at home, alone and I finish eating a big meal, my favorite thing to do is to belch and relieve the pressure. I would never in a million years have done that in front of Luke, so I don't know if it was my body's way of thanking me, or God's way of punishing me for the sin of gluttony, but before I could stop it, the loudest most obnoxious belch came from my mouth, drawing the attention of everyone in the building. I quickly covered my mouth and was sure that I was seven shades of red when Luke's face slowly rose up to meet mine. "Oh, my gosh. I am so sorry. I don't know what happened," I said mortified. I was surprised to see Luke doubling over with laughter. I had never heard him laugh like that before. There were actual tears running from his eyes and down his face.

"You think that's funny?" I asked amused.

"I swear, I knew that was going to happen. Damn, baby. You deserve a medal for that one," he said still laughing.

"Well, I'm glad you find it so funny," I said straightening in my chair and trying to hold on to what dignity that I had left.

"Oh, come on, babe. Don't be mad. It was funny," he said trying to suppress his laughter.

"Whenever you're finished, I'm ready."

He stood up and disposed of our trash, then stood next to me and bowed, holding his hand out to me. "Who says chivalry is a lost cause?" he asked grinning like a fox eating yellow jackets. I couldn't help but grin with him as I took his hand. I glanced out at the people looking at us around the restaurant. Everyone seemed to be smiling and sighing as if they were looking at a couple in love.

I followed Luke out the door and once in the truck I laid my head on his shoulder once again. We *were* a couple in love. I loved this man and in my heart, I knew he loved me too.

"Will you come home with me, babe?" Luke asked while tilting my head up to look at him. "I want to take care of you. I need to." At that moment, he could have asked me to jump off a bridge and I would have. The yearning and need in his eyes had my heart feeling as if it would burst.

"I would love that," I said pulling his face to mine and kissing him. The kiss was soft, sensual and intimate, just what I needed. My whole body warmed and tingled with his touch. He wrapped his arm around my waist and I curled into his side. I didn't want to think about anything. I only wanted to live every moment as it was given to me. I knew first hand that life was short and I would not take it for granted. I closed my eyes in hopes that I could rest for a few minutes. I was full and tired and the past couple of hours had me weak and exhausted. Just fifteen minutes, and I would be fine.

I awakened with a jolt. Luke's grip tightened around me as the truck swerved off the road. "Fuck!" Luke yelled. I opened my eyes and we were on the side of the highway.

"What's wrong?" I asked sitting up. I looked at the clock and it was a little after three. I had only been asleep about twenty minutes.

"Blow out. I just put new tires on this truck," he said mostly to himself. "Stay in here." I watched him in the rearview mirror as he bent down and surveyed the damage. He returned to the truck to retrieve the tire tool and I noticed the look on his face was that of confusion and something else; worry?

"Everything okay?" I asked cautiously. He smiled, but it didn't touch his eyes.

"It's fine, babe. Just a flat."

I wondered what was on his mind as I watched him through the mirror taking the lug nuts off to change the tire. A loud roaring sounded behind us and I saw Luke shake his head then stand up to face the motorcycles that were suddenly surrounding us. They were everywhere, casing the truck in from all angles. I panicked when I noticed the red and gray vests that they were wearing.

They had come for us. I didn't know if it was him or me that they wanted, but they had us now. There was no way we could get out of this. Luke had sent Regg and Kev home, which left him alone and vulnerable; just as Red had said. I understood now why he needed the protection. I didn't know what their problem was with Luke, but judging by the way they glared at him, it was huge.

I was in the driver's seat with my face and hands plastered to the window. A man walked up to Luke and put his finger in his chest, Luke swung and connected with his left jaw. He was immediately grabbed by several others and pinned against the truck. I opened the door to get out. I wasn't sure what in the hell I was doing, but I would not let my man be beat to a pulp or killed without trying to intervene. I had no idea what these guys were capable of, but whatever punishment they expected Luke to endure, they would have to give me, too.

"Dallas, stay in the truck!" Luke bit out through clenched teeth. My eyes found his and I knew he meant what he said, but I couldn't leave him.

"Well, look who we have here!" the man said rubbing his jaw. I had seen him before. His eyes were cold and mean and the big scar on his face made him even more evil, if that were possible. He smiled, but there was absolutely no warmth in it. He turned, walking towards me and I heard Luke struggling with the other guys, trying to break free.

"Don't you fucking touch her!" he yelled at the man. There was no panic in Luke's voice, only malice. I knew that if he touched me or even got too close that Luke would try to keep him away from me. I quickly jumped in the truck and locked the door. The man stared at me with cold eyes, full of fury, as he stepped away and walked back in front of Luke.

Shit. I had to do something. I could call Regg, but he was too far away. I fumbled around in the truck to find my phone to call 9-1-1. I'm not sure why I opened the glove compartment. Maybe my instincts were telling me there was something in there that would save us. Maybe I had watched one too many actions movies. Whatever the reason, I reached over and opened it to find an 9mm hand gun resting on top of the truck manual.

I was smart with guns. I had carried one for years after my parents died, because my father had forced me to take classes on how to protect myself. There were about twelve bikers outside the truck and I had ten bullets in the clip. Chances were, these bikers were carrying also, but as I looked through the back glass at the men surrounding Luke, I knew that I had no choice. No one on the highway had bothered to stop. The few cars that we did see kept right on going, paying no attention to what was happening around them. Our only chance was this gun.

I could easily put the truck in drive and leave Luke to fend for himself, but I was not that kind of woman. I loved this man and I knew that if given the opportunity, he would give his life for me. I didn't know how things were going to play out when I stepped from the truck, but I sent up a quick prayer to God, asking that this turn out in my favor.

Holding a gun made me feel powerful. Even around all these grown men, who could have had twenty guns to my one, I felt untouchable. I had tough skin for a reason and now was a damn good time to use it. No one seemed to notice my presence until I flipped the safety and loaded one into the chamber of the gun. The sound was unmistakable and echoed around us.

Perfecting my stance and with confidence that I didn't know I had, I pointed the gun at the head of the man in front of Luke. He was about ten feet away from me and I knew I could put a bullet through his skull without missing.

"Let him go." I announced, my voice coming out strong and clear.

"You even know how to use that thing, sweetheart?" he asked me while raising his hands and nodding his head to the guys to let Luke go.

"Would you like me to show you?" I asked him, never breaking eye contact and managing to keep my voice from wavering.

"No, sugar, I don't," he said smiling at me. Once the guys let go of Luke, he produced a gun from the small of his back and walked backwards towards me, taking turns pointing it at different ones. By this time, everyone had their hands in the air.

"I'll see you soon, Frankie, but I think it's best if y'all leave right now," Luke said his voice low and commanding.

"You think you're the only motherfucker with a gun, Luke? Your Bonnie and Clyde show don't fucking scare me!"

Okay, now I was scared. I expected him to pull out a gun and kill us any minute. I couldn't breathe. My heart was pounding so hard, I figured they could hear it, and that panicked feeling had settled into my stomach. Somehow, I managed to keep my composure.

"You know me well, Frankie. If you or one of your boys even think about pulling a gun, I'll have a bullet in your fucking head and you know it. If I go down, you go down with me."

Frankie seemed to think this over. "Let's go," he suddenly announced to the other guys and I couldn't help jumping at the sound of his voice.

He gave me a smirk and then blew me a kiss. "I'll be seeing you real soon, sweetheart."

"Now!" Luke barked. Within seconds, the guys were back on their bikes and heading in the same direction that they came from.

Luke quickly put his gun away and carefully grabbed the one from me. He led me to the truck and I got in. It was like I was in some sort of a trance. *Did that really just fucking happen?*

He left the door open, but went to the back of the truck to finish changing the tire. I kept my eyes and ears open for the sound of motorcycles, but all was quiet, except for the passing of a handful of cars.

Luke changed the tire in what had to be record time and jumped in the driver's seat next to me. We were on the highway before he pulled his phone from his pocket and dialed someone. "Tiny. I need an escort. I'm on South 45, just outside of Tupelo. I need somebody, yesterday. Yeah, it's *Leaders of Hell*. They got me on the side of the highway, but I'm good. I don't think they'll be coming back, but just in case. I'll check in with ya later." Luke ended the call and waited anxiously, as did I.

Less that fifteen miles later, I heard the rumbling once again. Unknowingly, I grabbed onto Luke's leg and looked behind us, fearing for the worst.

"They're with me. We're good."

I immediately relaxed. Four motorcycles pulled ahead of us while four fell in behind. Already, I felt safer. I notices that the guys were not wearing the same cut that Luke wore. It was completely different. He must have noticed the confusion on my face.

"They are a support club. They help out when we need them. There is a local chapter in Monroe County, so I knew they wouldn't be long."

I nodded my head in agreement, but I couldn't find any words to say. Luke was visibly more relaxed, too. He reached over and took my hand into his. Just like him, there were times when I really just didn't want to talk. *This was one of them*.

I leaned forward and turned up the volume on the radio. I found a rock station and the music matched the mood. I let the shredding of an electric guitar help me relive what had just happened. I'm not sure if it was the rock music or the fact that I had handled that gun like a pro, but it made me feel like a complete and total bad-ass. I looked over at Luke and gave him a smirk. I was rewarded with his signature smirk. I heard him mutter, "Bonnie and Clyde." I smiled to myself. What a fucked up life we were living.

Chapter 21

Six rock songs later, Luke finally broke the silence. "You still reliving it?" he asked with no emotion in his voice. I nodded my head and smiled. I turned to face him in the truck, pulling my legs under me.

"I feel like I should be crying or scared right now, but in reality, I feel fucking awesome."

Luke laughed, "You ain't right. I bet you have re-enacted that scene ten times and each time you think of something a little more bad-ass that you could have done." He knew me too well. *It was actually a little freaky.* I had thought about what would have happened if shots had been fired. I envisioned myself moving like a ninja and me and Luke killing everyone, then riding off on the motorcycles. I day dreamed that we were like the people in the movie, The Matrix, and could dodge bullets by moving our bodies or holding our hands out so the bullets fell to the ground before they reached us.

I was such a pathetic loser, but I didn't care. It was better than curling up into the fetal position and crying myself to sleep. "Yeah, something like that," I said laughing.

"You did great, baby. Thank you," he said taking my hand and kissing my knuckles. "But, if you ever pull a stunt like that again, I'm going to spank you," he said seriously.

I smiled my big goofy grin. "Don't make promises you can't keep and don't rain on my parade. Admit it, I'm awesome," I said slicing my hands through the air like the karate kid.

"Does it not occur to you how bad that situation could have gone?" he said trying to hide his smile.

"Not really. I don't want to think about it," I responded shrugging, and I didn't. I knew these guys were bad and I had watched enough T.V. to know that they would retaliate, but we would cross that bridge when it got here.

My day dreams took over once again and I could see me and Luke at a standoff with these guys. This time I had some cool power that kept them from moving; freezing their limbs while Luke hypnotized them making them think they were puppies.

"Hey! Snap out of it, princess. This isn't the Wild West and it's not T.V. You seriously could have gotten hurt. You don't realize who these guys are."

"Yeah? Well, I'm aware that I could have gotten hurt, but I didn't and I wasn't going to just leave you out there to get jumped or whatever the hell it was that they had planned to do to you," I said getting defensive. *He should have stopped at "thank you."*

"They were not going to hurt me, Dallas. Maybe rough me up a little bit, but that would have been the worst of it," he said unconvincingly.

"Oh, really? Well, I think you are a liar. These men are mad with you about something and if it's enough to follow you- wait they tampered with your truck didn't they?" The realization hit me like a ton of bricks. I remembered the look on Luke's face when he came back to the truck. He knew what was going to happen. Luke stared straight ahead, not looking at me. "Tell me. You knew this was going to happen, didn't you?" I asked shocked.

"Of course I didn't know this was going to happen. Do you honestly think that I would intentionally put you in danger?" he asked completely taken aback by what I had said.

"No, I mean, you knew once you looked at the tire that someone had messed with it," I answered correcting the miscommunication.

"I had a feeling," he said, not looking at me once again. *Was he always this bad of a liar or was it just with me?* "Dallas, I told you that I would tell you everything, and I will, as soon as we are home and I can lock you in a room, so you can't run," he said exasperated.

Why was this suddenly my fault, and why was he afraid I would run? Memories of my past flooded me. There was a lot that Luke didn't know about me, either. If he were completely honest with me, it would only be fair for me to share my past with him. I didn't want that. I was poison. If Luke dug deep enough, he would find a lot of skeletons in my closet, then it would be him running, not me.

I had already assumed what was going on anyway. He was into something illegal, and was afraid to drag me into it. I got it. I'm sure something had gone wrong and these guys wanted to hurt him because of it. A lot of normal people would cut their losses and leave, but not me. Luke was the first real thing in my life, since I was sixteen. He made me feel alive and whole. I would not let anything come between us.

I didn't want to know his secrets. Well, I did, but I wanted him to tell me on his terms; not because he felt like he was forced to. One day, I would tell him everything. I would tell him about the kind of person that I really was, and it was not the person he met in a bar a month ago. Right now I wanted to keep my secrets buried inside of me, and the only way to do that, without feeling guilty, was for him to do the same thing.

"I don't want to know, Luke. We both have secrets and that's fine with me. When the time is right, you'll tell me, until then, all I want is us. I want to spend every minute that I can with you and when bullshit like this happens, we'll deal with it together."

The relief on his face was so tangible that I started to take back what I had said. *Was it that big of a deal for me to know?*

"You seem a little too relieved," I said eyeing him. He shook his head and smiled.

"Some secrets are not mine to tell, but to keep you, I would tell you everything."

"You have me. I am not going anywhere." And I wasn't. *I was his, as long as he would have me.*

Luke pulled me to him and once again, I snuggled into his side. "I sure do love you, Dallas Knox."

I smiled up at him smugly, "I know."

We pulled into a gas station before we hit the interstate and I smiled when I saw all of the motorcycles lined up outside in the parking lot. These were 'our guys' and it warmed my heart that they had come to meet us. I knew that they were really meeting Luke and could probably give a shit less about me, but it was nice to think about. We got out and I stretched my tired, sore limbs before following Luke to the pack of waiting bikers. Everyone greeted us with opened arms, like always. Smiles, nods of approval and shock crossed every face as Luke told the story of what had happened. They were proud of what I had done, but they were pissed that this had happened.

"It's been a long day for me and a tough week for Dallas, so we're gonna go home tonight, and we will hold church tomorrow to discuss the next steps," Luke said to all of them.

"A couple of the PROSPECTS and I will crash at the club house tonight. I don't feel comfortable leaving you alone right now." Tiny announced.

Luke nodded his head in agreement, "Thank you, brother."

More hugs were exchanged and goodbyes were passed between our club and the support club. It wasn't long before we were back in the truck and headed towards Hattiesburg. "Do y'all have a lot of support clubs?" I asked Luke, stifling a yawn.

"A few. This is a love-hate world we live in babe. We take care of the ones who love us. We watch out for them and they watch out for us. We take care of one another. It's a brotherhood. As for the ones who hate us, well, if they have a good reason to, then we try to come to an understanding, but some just hate us because of the power we have."

"And just how much power do you have?" I asked him curiously. *I mean, really. What could they do? Move mountains or some shit?* "Enough," he said smirking. "You sleepy?" I let out another ridiculously long yawn and nodded my head. I had gone from being poisoned to bed rest to a bitch with a gun who had warned off a bunch of bikers. *I was tired.*

"I bet you think that I sleep more than anyone you have ever met," I said trying to smile my adorably cute sleepy smile, although I was pretty sure that I looked like an idiot.

He smirked, "Nah, I'm just boring."

"You are a lot of things, Mr. Carmical, but boring is not one of them," I said curling up on the seat and resting my head on the window. Luke grabbed my feet and pulled them into his lap, forcing my head to lie down on the passenger seat. He took off my shoes and with one hand on the wheel, began massaging my feet through my socks. "That feels good," I mumbled.

He tuned the radio to a classic country station and turned up the volume. I fell asleep with the words from The Possums, "He Stopped Loving Her Today," in my ears and the skilled hands of Luke on my body.

Chapter 22

In every romance movie that I have ever seen, the woman always wakes from a nap well rested and looking strikingly beautiful. Well, this was certainly not a movie. I woke up when Luke shut the truck door, only to open another one and grab my bags out of the back seat to haul them in. I saw that he had my luggage from The Abbey and I was glad that he thought of everything. I sat up and a puddle of drool had formed on my forearm.

Thank God, Luke had walked inside and I had a minute to get myself together. I wiped my mouth on my shirt, trying to twist the wet spot on my sleeve so that it wasn't noticeable. Flipping down the mirror, I groaned as I saw the lines in my face that had formed from my wrinkled shirt. *Man, I look like shit*. I scrambled from the truck and made my way inside.

"Ooh baby, you look like shit," Tiny said meeting me at the door. He pulled me into his arms and I went willingly. *Something about him made me feel nurtured*. "I'm proud of you," he said leaning down and resting his head on top of mine. I nodded into his chest and he let me go, turning me toward the door and ushering me in. "Luke! I found this stray wandering around your garage." He yelled to Luke who was somewhere in the house.

"What?" Luke asked rounding the corner. His face was scrunched up in confusion. Tiny pointed at me and Luke softened. "That's no stray. She belongs here," he said coming to me and planting a kiss on my forehead.

"We'll be in the clubhouse, if you need us," Tiny said and headed out.

"My baby has had a rough day. What do you need? I am at your beck and call," Luke said holding my face in his hands.

"You have been at my beck and call since we met," I said my voice still thick with sleep. *I had only prayed for one damsel in distress moment. God was an over-achiever.*

"I like taking care of you. It makes me happy, happy, happy."

I smiled. *Luke watched way too much T.V.*

"How long do you want me to stay?" I asked looking up into his beautiful, smiling eyes.

"Forever," he answered shrugging as if it were obvious.

"I mean, I have to go home and get some things if I'm going to be here a while." He smiled.

"I'll take you home tomorrow. Right now, there is someone who is dying to see you."

He let go of me and opened the kitchen door. Neo came charging at me, sliding on the slick wooden floors. "Neo!" I said dropping to my knees so I could take him in my arms. His tail wagged and he licked me, squirming in my arms then tearing through the house showing his excitement. He rounded the kitchen and came back through the opposite side that connected from the living room and barreled into me once again. Neo had learned his way around here. The thought made me smile.

I rubbed his ears and head, then his stomach, as he flipped onto his back in front of me. I talked to him in that weird, high pitched voice people used when talking to a small child. Soon he became bored, and I was relieved. I didn't have the strength to play too much. Luke helped me off the floor then grabbed my hand and led me through the house to his bedroom.

"Bed? Bath? Shower? Couch? What do you want, baby?"

At first, I thought he was talking about where I wanted him to make love to me, but as he saw the glint in my eye; his demeanor changed.

"Oh no, I mean, do you want to go to bed or take a shower or just lay on the couch?" *I liked my idea better.* It was sweet of him to let me know that he was willing to wait while I recovered. I would probably have to beg for it, but right now, even though I trembled at the thought of him touching me; I really needed a shower.

"Shower," I said moving towards the bathroom. I looked in the large mirror that covered the wall behind the sink and sighed. *How did my body change so much in just three days?* It was only Saturday, yet it looked like I had been shut up in a dark hole for months. I was pale, thin and looked nothing like I did the last time I stood in front of his mirror. *Had that been almost a week ago?*

"Don't, baby. You look fine," Luke said coming up behind me and lifting my arms to remove my shirt. He carefully undressed me as I watched, unmoving, in the mirror. Every time an article of clothing left my body, he kissed where it had been. It was so intimate, but not in a sexual way. It was reassuring. I had never lacked confidence, yet when I was with him, I felt like I may not be enough. *Maybe it was because I had finally found someone who I cared for and I cared about what they thought.*

Once I was completely naked, Luke turned the shower on and walked up behind me placing his arms around my waist and resting his head on my shoulder; meeting my eyes in the mirror.

"I love you," Luke said, never taking his eyes from mine.

"I love you, too," I said, turning my face so I could kiss his cheek.

"How about I make us a picnic and we watch a movie on the couch?" he asked smiling. I knew that I would probably only make it through the previews, but just the thought of cuddling with him made the idea perfect.

"That would be great."

He straightened, kissing me on my head, and then left the bathroom. I rummaged through my bags, finding my toiletries, and stepped into the steaming shower.

Maybe I should have stayed another night in the hospital. I was so damn tired. This shit refused to go away. I felt like every ounce of energy I had was depleted. I must have used it on our near death experience. At least it went to good use and wasn't wasted on something like a shower. With a little effort and a lot of time, I emerged from the shower shaved and clean for what felt like the first time in eternity. I decided to pamper myself a little, even though I didn't feel like it. I knew that I needed it after spending a few days in the hospital. I put an exfoliating mask on my face, lotioned my body and dried and fixed my hair back to its former glory. I found a pair of ridiculously short pajama shorts and a matching tank top. *Maybe Luke wouldn't have any visitors inside tonight.*

When I walked into the living room, the scent of popcorn filled the air and I noticed movies scattered all over the couch. Luke was absent from the living room, but I found him digging through the cabinets when I came into the kitchen.

Luke was shirtless and wore only a pair of sexy pajama pants that had my mouth watering. The muscles in his back flexed as he reached into the top cabinet trying to find something that must have been shoved to the back.

"You need a chair or something?" I asked mesmerized by the way his body looked doing something as simple as grabbing something out of the cabinet. I tried to focus on anything but him. My panties were already wet at the thought of my nails running down his back as he drove into me.

"Nah, I got it. You have to hide shit around here or everyone..." He trailed off when he closed the cabinet door and his eyes found my body. They started at my face that was framed by my shiny brown hair, then to my hard nipples that poked out of the thin material of my top, onto my short shorts and down my smooth legs to my bare feet.

"Damn, baby. You trying to kill me?" he asked, finding my face with his eyes once again.

I bit my lip and shook my head, praying it would be enough to convince him that I wasn't that sick. I could tell he was struggling. He didn't want to be too forward or make me feel like all he wanted was sex, but I could tell by the burning look in his eyes that he wanted me just as much as I wanted him.

I walked to him and wrapped my arms around his neck. The stretching movement caused my shorts to rise and made the cheeks of my barely covered ass tingle from the air in the room. Luke placed his hands on my waist, a safe area, and shook his head at me. "This is not what I had in mind, baby. I just want to take care of you," Luke said in a low voice.

"Then take care of me. Please, baby. I need this. I need you," I begged, looking up at him desperately. He groaned in defeat as his lips found mine. I wasted no time invading his mouth with my tongue. I had missed this. Damn, he tasted good. Luke reached around me and slid his hands under my shorts. He groaned when he found the bare flesh hanging out of the bottom of my panties and squeezed tighter, lifting me and wrapping my legs around him.

My hands continued to roam his face and shoulders while my tongue caressed his as he carried me into the bedroom and gently laid me down and climbed on top of me.

"Make love to me, Luke," I breathed, tilting my head back to let him kiss my throat and neck.

He raised my shirt and found my hard nipples and took them into his mouth in turn. I moaned loudly as he gently sucked each one, while kneading his hands into my thighs and waist, then up my stomach and finally into my hair.

"You drive me crazy," he said taking my mouth over with his. I lifted myself up off the bed, trying to find something of his I could grind into. I needed that connection or I would explode. His hand found the elastic band on my shorts and was instantly inside, rubbing me softly through my panties.

"Fuck, you are so wet." He sat up on his knees in between my legs and looked down on me. My stomach arched off the bed with my deep breathing. I was completely breathless and it had absolutely nothing to do with what happened to me three days ago, but had everything to do with the man looking down at me. Everything about Luke turned me on; the tattoos that ran down his perfectly sculpted arms, the abs that were so cut you could count each once, the strong chest that rose and fell with every breath he took. But these were nothing compared to the eyes that were looking so deep into mine, I felt like he could read my mind. I could see all the way to his soul through his eyes. I could measure the depth of his love for me; endless as the ocean.

The look on his face was full of need and compassion. He looked at me like this each time that he made love to me, and each time it made me feel more important to him than the last. I knew this was going to be amazing. I knew, just by the look in his eyes that he was going to prove how much he loved me and how sorry he was that he couldn't be there for me; by making love to me in the way that only he could.

Luke seemed to remember what he was doing and slid my shorts down my legs taking my panties with them. I was left in nothing but my tank top, lying on the bed beneath him. He leaned down over me, pressing his length against my opening. My breath caught in my throat in anticipation of what was to come.

"I would move heaven and earth for you, Dallas. I will spend the rest of my days making you happy. I have loved before, but never like this."

He rested his weight on his arms and leaned down so that his forehead was touching mine and we were nose to nose. I closed my eyes and inhaled the scent of him.

"I need you, Dallas," he whispered to me. My heart clenched at the desperation in his tone.

"Please," I begged, although I had no idea what I was begging for- for him to be inside me, for him to keep wooing me with his words, for him to never leave? He kissed me as he slowly inched inside my tight walls. I felt myself expand to accommodate him and once again, I felt whole.

He moved inside of me slowly, taking care not to hurt me or make me uncomfortable. *This is what I loved about this man.* He was always so thoughtful. I knew that he cherished me just by the way that he touched me.

Soon, he was buried deep inside me and my body rocked against his. The passion and love shared between us was like nothing that I had ever witnessed. I would be for this man whatever he needed and him for me. My nails dug into the skin of his back and his answering growl only made me dig deeper. He pumped into me over and over, bringing me to an orgasm that had my whole body convulsing. I moaned loudly into his mouth and when he felt me open completely; he drove harder, saying my name as he collapsed on top of me.

Completely sated and never more comfortable, I laid lifeless on the bed as Luke dressed me, then carried me into the living room and laid down on the couch with me on top of him.

"Comfortable?" he asked. I slid my body in front of his and he flipped on his side and pulled my back to his chest. I laid my head on his arm and snuggled into him, giving him absolutely no room; he didn't seem to mind.

"What do you want to watch?" he asked, placing a kiss on the side of my head.

"A comedy," I said yawning.

"Still tired?"

"Uh-huh," my eyelids were becoming heavy. I waited for a smart-ass remark that never came. Luke pulled a blanket from the back of the couch and draped it over us. He slid his hand under my shirt and splayed it across my stomach like he had done so many times before. I found a little more room between us and pushed closer. He chuckled in my ear. I closed my eyes and although I was tired, I couldn't fall asleep. I listened throughout the movie as Luke's breathing slowed and within an hour, he was sleeping soundly.

I finished the movie, wide awake and even watched the credits. I was becoming restless. I didn't want to do anything, but I was tired of just laying here and my eyes were beginning to hurt from watching the T.V. at a side angle.

I slid from the couch, careful not to disturb Luke, and wandered into the kitchen. The cold popcorn was still on the bar. I grabbed the jug of milk out of the refrigerator and headed down the hall to the Harley Room. The large bike was centered in the room, as always, and I walked around surveying everything about it. Just like a child in a toy aisle at Wal-Mart, the urge to climb on it was just too much. I sat the milk down on the tool box and slid on the seat, praying it wouldn't turn over.

Before long, noises that resembled a sport bike, definitely not a Harley, were coming from my mouth. My mind took a trip back in time to when I was a child and my cousin, Mikey, and I would race imaginary cars under my grandmother's carport. I wondered where Mikey was now. *I should definitely give him a call.*

I decided that I had played enough and slid off the motorcycle, grabbing my jug of milk and taking a huge gulp. I leaned up against the tool box, thoughts of Luke fucking me on the bike, wearing nothing but his vest, running through my head. I felt something move and noticed that the tool box had wheels on it. Curious, I looked down and saw a seam in the floor that wasn't visible until the box moved. I couldn't help it. I moved the tool box a few inches further and found a latch to what I guessed was a trap door. What if he had bodies down there? Or maybe he ran a sex slave operation. I bet it housed millions of dollars' worth of cash and cocaine, along with guns. I could picture Mexican women, dressed in nothing but lingerie, wearing face masks while cutting the dope for him.

I knelt down running my hand back and forth across the latch. *This was wrong. I shouldn't do this. I was invading Luke's privacy.* I made a split decision that whatever was under there would stay unknown to me, as I quickly pulled the tool box back and grabbed my milk. I turned to get the hell out of there and ran right into Luke, who was standing in the doorway.

His arms were stretched above his head and he was hanging onto the door frame, looking like he was posing for the cover of GQ magazine. His face had that damn smirk on it and he was slightly amused. I was red with embarrassment. He had caught me snooping. *Fuck, Dallas!*

"Hey baby!" I said my voice coming out too high pitched, a sure sign of guilt.

"Find something?" he asked eyeing me warily. *Shit. What was I gonna say? I could lie... yes, I would lie.*

"I dropped my, um-" *Fuck it.* "Yes. I did. I was leaning up against the tool box looking at the motorcycle, and it moved and I found your secret hiding place," I said hanging my head in shame like a scolded child.

"Secret hiding place?" he asked biting his lip to hide his smile.

"Yeah, but I didn't look. I swear," I said trying to convey my innocence. *How old was I, twelve?*

"I know. I have been watching you for some time." *Oh shit.* "I went to grab some milk and it seems that it was missing."

I handed him the jug quickly and he took it, raising an eyebrow. "I live alone, so I always drink out of the jug. Sorry. Sometimes, I forget how to act." *Why was I acting like this? Because you just made an ass of yourself, you idiot.*

He stood there staring at me, his face in an amused smile. He put the jug to his lips and took a big swallow.

"It tastes better now, anyway," he said replacing the cap and reaching for my hand. "Do you want to see what's inside?" he asked leading me to the trap door.

"No." *Yes.*

He pushed the tool box out of the way and knelt down on one knee in front of the latch. "You sure? I can put your little curious mind at ease."

I shook my head at him. *Shit, this was humiliating. Why not just scream at me, give me a punishment fuck, then let me be on my way?* He turned the latch and pulled the door open. I peeked inside and half expected to hear loud music and see smoke boiling out of the top, but instead I saw the top of a hot water heater. I was actually a little disappointed that it wasn't some underground drug operation. The disappointment must have been evident on my face.

"Surprised, are we?" Luke asked laughing. I just stood there speechless. *A hot water heater. A fucking hot water heater.* "When I built the house, I decided to add this room at the last minute, so I had to put this thing somewhere, and I told the builders that helped me to just figure something out. I took one day off, one day, and I come back to find that they couldn't find anywhere in the plans to put it and make it look right, so they put it here."

"I thought you were running an underground sex slave trade," I said- *out loud*.

He threw his head back, laughing. "No, baby. The only person that I want to make a sex slave out of is you." He walked up to me and kissed me on my head. "Let's grab some supper, and then I want to show you something, if you are up to it."

"I would love that," I said still reeling from my embarrassment.

"Well, come on, nosey rosy," he said laughing and pulling me into the kitchen. *Asshole*.

"What are we eating?" I asked trying to change the subject and hoping I could do something to make him forget what just happened.

"My specialty!" Luke said excitedly.

Hmm, his specialty. I was thinking something on the grill-a steak or some kind of chicken or maybe even a smoked tender-loin. "Sounds delicious! What is it?" I asked enthusiastically. I really didn't care, but I was so anxious to move on to something other than my previous escapade, that I would have agreed to anything.

"Ham sandwiches with potato chips," he said laughing.

I didn't have an appetite any more. I just wanted to crawl in a hole and die, but I forced a smile and decided to try and choke down a sandwich. Luke was in a really good mood and I wondered what had made him so happy. "You sure are in a good mood," I said taking a seat at the bar and digging into my sandwich.

"I'm just happy that you're here," he said smiling and taking a seat next to me. I knew there was something else, but I figured it was some kind of inside joke and I wasn't too interested anyway.

"I'm happy, too." I leaned over and gave him a peck on his cheek and was rewarded with his gorgeous smile and a heart flutter.

We continued to make small talk, mostly about his business, and I was surprised to find out that he owned The Country Tavern. "Some of my security guys were out of town for a bachelor party, so I brought the club in to help out."

"Is that why you were in your truck?" I asked, wondering why I had not thought of that before.

"Yeah, I wore my cut because just the image it gives makes people think twice before they do something stupid," he said standing and clearing the bar of my plate and his. *That made sense. Had he seen me in there before the incident with the cowboy?* I wanted to ask, but it sounded stupid in my head, so I kept my mouth shut.

"So, what did you want to show me?" I asked standing and walking around the bar so that I could be in his arms. I thought he would hug me, but instead, he lifted me onto the counter so we were face to face.

"Do you like to stargaze?" he asked kissing my nose, my cheek, and my neck. My breathing became shallow and my insides tightened.

"Yes." I could barely speak. It had only been a matter of hours, yet I wanted to feel him inside me again.

"Good, because I have something I want to show you."

Lifting me into his arms, Luke carried me out the front door and across the driveway. My first thought was that we were going to lie down in the driveway, but he continued on and into the woods. The trail started out narrow, but widened the further we walked. I wasn't sure how far we had gone. He couldn't have been walking more than two minutes when suddenly, we were in a clearing.

What I recognized as a shooting house sat in the middle of a pipeline clearing. Luke sat me down and held his finger up to me in a *hold on* gesture. Then, he opened the door and went inside, leaving me to fend for myself against wild animals.

I was starting to get a little nervous, but in less than a minute he was standing at the door holding his hand out to me.

"This is where I hunt when deer season is in, but any other time, it serves as a great thinking spot when I'm struggling with something. Whether it is with the club or my family or my job, I can always come here and clear my head."

Luke the redneck, another personality to add to his many.

Inside the small shooting house lay an air mattress that took up most of the floor space. Windows were cut out on the side, but had been covered with plastic to keep the insects out. I watched Luke as he climbed onto a chair, undoing several latches and pushing the roof back to reveal the sky. I jumped at the sound of the metal roof hitting the building.

"I made a door out of the roof. Pretty cool, huh?" Luke asked smiling at me. I laughed and nodded my head in agreement.

"Yes, pretty cool." I didn't really think so until Luke pulled me down onto the air mattress beside him, and I looked up at the sky above me. Thousands of stars littered the black, velvety sky and the moon shone bright giving me a full view of everything around me.

"Wow," I said gaping with my mouth open.

"The only problem is you don't get to see *all* of the stars. Your view is limited because of the walls," Luke said from beside me.

"I think it's great. You know Lindsey has this in a bedroom."

"A door for a roof?" Luke asked turning his head towards me.

"No, I mean she has this lighting system above her bed. You look up and there are hundreds of stars on her ceiling," I said, still in awe of the view I had. Lindsey's room was great, but this was amazing.

"You like it?" Luke asked rolling on his side and propping his head up on his elbow.

"What?"

"The stars at Lindsey's."

I turned to look at Luke and saw him smiling like he had some big secret. "Yes," I said cautiously.

"I'll put that in my bedroom if you want." He sure was being cheesy tonight.

"I like this better," I said honestly.

Luke rolled back over on his back and we laid there for what seemed like hours looking up at the stars. My eyes were getting heavy, but I wasn't ready for this night to end.

"Tell me more about the club," I said breaking the silence.

"What do you want to know?" Luke asked not looking at me.

I wasn't sure what I really wanted to know, but as of now, I didn't really know anything, yet I had been in the middle of it ever since I had met Luke. "Why do people do it? I mean, I know why you did it, but why does anyone want to go through that?"

He turned his head and raised an eyebrow at me. "Go through what?" he asked curiously.

"The prospecting thingy." Relief flooded his face as soon as the words left my mouth. If I didn't know any better, I would assume that he thought I knew something that I shouldn't.

"Thingy?" he asked laughing.

"You know what I mean," I answered a little embarrassed. *I never spoke like that and now that I had, I felt like an idiot.* He must have felt the heat from my cheeks radiating around me and took mercy on me.

"Everyone wants to be a part of something, to belong to a group or a society or an organization. Our club is no harder to get into than the

Hattiesburg Country Club," he said smirking. "The difference between us and a country club, though, is we don't want you to try and be something you're not. If you belong in this world then you know it. You can feel it in your heart. If you don't, well, you just don't." He was now staring at me as if it was me that he was talking about and not a prospect.

"And how does someone know if they don't belong?" I asked almost in a whisper. I couldn't take my eyes off of Luke's. It was as if I was in a trance. Luke rolled over on top of me, snaking his legs through mine and bringing his arms up next to my face.

"They can feel it." Luke broke eye contact with me and started planting feather like kisses all over my face. "Every time they come around, every nerve in their body screams to them that this isn't right." I tilted my head back so he had access to my neck. "They feel like an outsider. They often ask themselves 'why did I get myself into this?'" His knee was now between my legs rubbing softly.

"Well, how do they get out when they realize they don't belong?" I asked breathless.

"They leave before they know too much," Luke was now looking at me. His expression was impassive; his breathing heavy and his knee had come to a complete stop. I knew Luke was warning me. I knew he was hoping to scare me into rethinking what I was getting into.

The problem was- I did belong. I could feel it in my heart. It was not just my love for him that kept me here. *There was something else.* I couldn't quite put my finger on it, but whatever it was had me convinced that I would give my life for any of them. I had never felt more a part of something than I did when I was with them.

"I'm not going anywhere. I love you, Luke, and I love the club and everyone in it. I belong here," I said searching his eyes for some sort of clue as to what he was thinking.

"There is a lot you don't know, things I can't tell you because it's not my story to tell. I'm not a good person, Dallas. I work very hard to separate the two lifestyles that I live. Dragging you into the middle of this is really going to complicate things. There are a lot of people who don't like me and to get to me they could go through you. That's why I have never really had anyone in my life like you. I just don't want to take that chance, but on the other hand; I can't let you go," he exclaimed frustrated.

It seemed that Luke was fighting an internal battle and was losing. He climbed off of me, but pulled me to him once he was beside me again.

"Luke, I'm a big girl. I have dealt with a lot of shit in my life. I can assure you that I can handle anything you throw at me. I already told you that I don't want to know what's going on and besides, I'm in love," I said with a reassuring smile.

"Well, that makes two of us, darlin'." Luke's kisses are powerful, better than anything I have ever felt. But this kiss was different. It was passionate, but firm. It felt like a kiss of warning, but also reassurance. There was nothing out here but us and the stars. I felt small in his arms, but like I could face anything with him at my side. He was my protector, my rock, my best friend, *my Luke*.

"It's getting late," Luke said pulling away from me.

I didn't want to sleep. I didn't want to go back to the house. I could stay with him in this shooting house forever, just the two of us. He stood up with ease and held his hands out to me. I let him pull me to my feet and he planted a swift kiss to my cheek before letting me go so he could close his "roof door."

We walked back to the house hand in hand, him lifting me across the gravel road. A million things were going on in my head, but my biggest question was if everyone knew who Luke was, then why did society accept him? He seemed to be a hit at the engagement party, and even the Mayor had spoken fondly of him and said he owed him a favor.

I didn't want to upset Luke anymore with my questions. It seemed like he was having a hard enough time convincing himself that it was okay to keep me in his life. I would ask Red sometime this week when Luke was not around.

As we walked up the driveway, I could hear music coming from the clubhouse. It seemed that Tiny and the others were having a pretty good time in there, but I was certain that somewhere there was someone sober; watching to make ensure Luke was protected.

"You tired?" Luke asked me, once we were inside.

"Yes, very," I answered not realizing until that moment how true those words were. I didn't think I could make it to the bed. Fatigue seemed to have taken over and I walked like a zombie until I was curled under the covers in the bed. I couldn't remember closing my eyes.

Chapter 23

For the next several days, Luke and I lived our lives like a normal couple. We ate junk food, watched movies, played with Neo, took showers, but the one thing that was lacking was the sex. It seemed like ever since that night under the stars, Luke was afraid to touch me.

He kept me busy during the day, making sure not to make any moves that would lead me to thinking he wanted something more. It couldn't be because I was sick, since we had made love the first night that I was home. I also noticed that he had been on his phone a lot, and when someone called, he left the room. I kept telling myself that I wouldn't push him. I was sure that something was going on that was keeping his mind occupied and if he wasn't touching me, then he had a good reason.

By Friday, I had cabin fever. I was going to go crazy if I didn't get the hell out of the house. Luke had been shady all morning and I had decided that after lunch, I was going to seduce him whether he wanted it or not.

While Luke was out at the clubhouse with Tiny, who had still not left, I decided to put makeup on for the first time in over a week. I applied some mascara, blush and lip gloss to my pale skin. This weekend, we would be spending a day at my house so I could lay out by the pool. Luke didn't know that yet, but I was sure that I could persuade him. I put on the red dress that he had brought for me and I had yet to wear. I let my long, straight hair down; relieving it from the ponytail it had been in for days. My legs were shaved, my face was pretty and my dress was short. There was absolutely no way I was going to let Luke deny me.

I walked into the kitchen to find him leaning on the counter with his head in his hands. *Something was wrong.* "Hey baby, everything okay?" I asked, walking over to him. He lifted his head and smiled, but I could see the worry in his eyes.

"Yeah, baby. I'm good. Look at you," Luke said gesturing with his hand at me. "You look gorgeous. Although, I'm gonna miss the sight of you in my t-shirts and shorts," he said. He pulled me to him and buried his face in my neck. I wrapped my arms around his neck and pulled myself up, wrapping my legs around him. He readjusted his grip, but still kept his face buried in my neck. *This was not working out like I thought it would.*

"Dallas, we need to talk," he said never looking up.

Oh shit. He called me Dallas, not 'babe' or 'baby' or 'darlin'-just Dallas. I couldn't answer him. I tried to unwrap my legs from around him, but he tightened his grip on my thighs and held me in place.

"I have to leave town for a few days. I should be back by Monday, Tuesday at the latest. I know I told you I would be here, but I've been putting it off and I have to go."

I breathed an audible sigh of relief and smiled. I managed to pull my head back and his face away from my neck so I could look at him.

"That's fine, baby. You have been great, but I'm good. I promise. I was actually thinking about inviting the ladies over to my place for a pool party. This is probably the last week that we can swim before the weather gets cold." That was the thing about Mississippi, the weather was always unpredictable. It was the middle of October, yet it felt like June.

"I am undeserving of you," Luke said right before crushing his mouth to mine. His tongue ran over my lips begging for permission and I opened my mouth inviting him in. His kiss was hard and deep. His fingers dug into my thighs then moved to my ass, kneading it. I needed this so bad. It had been days, and I didn't think that I would ever get enough to make up for it. I was expecting him to carry me into the bedroom, but instead he sat me on the counter, pushing the day's mail to the floor and laying me on my back. With two hands, he grabbed the middle of my dress and ripped it, splitting it down the middle. I gasped in surprise and delight. *Shit, he could turn me on.*

"I'll buy you another one," was all he said before his mouth was on my stomach, kissing his way up to my breasts. His greedy hands already had my bra off and thrown to the floor by the time he made it to my nipples. He sucked hard causing my back to arch off the counter in pleasure. This was rough, and exactly what I needed. His thumbs hooked into the thin lace of my panties and shredded them. He added them to the discarded clothes on the floor, which now consisted of his shirt and my bra. My dress still lay underneath me, open in the front as if I were wearing a bath robe.

Luke's mouth found my aching center and with just as much aggressiveness as his kisses, his tongue invaded me. I screamed, and writhed and came with pure ecstasy and pleasure. I was still coming down from my orgasm when he grabbed me under my arms, lifting me from the counter and pulled me to the floor, leaving my dress. I needed him inside me. "Please, Luke," I moaned. *It had been too long.*

"Please, what, Dallas? Tell me what you want."

I take back what I said earlier. I loved hearing him call me by my *name.* "I want you to fuck me," I said breathlessly. His mouth was unrelenting; kissing everything on me and all I could do was moan and throw my head back. The kitchen floor was hard, but at that moment, I was floating on air.

"How do you want it, baby?" Luke asked in my favorite raspy voice.

"I don't care, Luke. Just give it to me." He pulled away from me and sat back on his knees between my legs.

"Touch yourself," he demanded. I let my hands drift to my breasts, rolling my nipples between my thumb and fingers, pulling on them hard. I ran my hands down my stomach then over my lips, down to my entrance. I inserted a finger and it felt so good that I closed my eyes and opened my mouth, throwing my head back again. The thrill of touching myself in front of him nearly had me coming apart.

"Fuck, you are so hot, and all mine."

I opened my eyes to see him looking down at me. He was so sexy sitting there with his fists clenched like he was trying to hold back from touching me. His arms were flexed and his muscles bulged, showing several veins running down his arms, weaving in between his tattoos.

He grabbed my hand and pulled me up so that I was face to face with him. He took the finger that was inside me only moments ago and placed it in his mouth, sucking my juices off of my own hand. I quivered with excitement. Everything he did turned me on, and he just kept getting sexier. Too soon, he pulled my finger from his mouth and kissed the tip of it before standing gracefully in front of me.

"Undress me." I instantly dropped to my knees in front of him. He stood over me with his thumbs in the pockets of his jeans looking down at me on the floor at his feet. I took a moment to look at him, memorizing every curve of his arms, every ripple of his abs, and every line of his tattoos. He was the epitome of male perfection.

I looked directly in front of me. My position made me eye level with his crotch. *Oh my.* When I pulled his pants and underwear down, he sprang free and I was greeted by his impressive length. It looked like it had grown since I had seen it last. I could feel my thighs moistened from the wetness of my center. I took him in my hand, rubbing the soft satiny skin back and forth between my fist. I leaned forward, circling my tongue around the head and almost came apart when a moan escaped his lips. I looked up to see his head leaning back while his hand grabbed the back of my head and encouraged me to go deeper. I pulled him into my mouth, sucking until he reached the back of my throat.

I remembered doing this exact same thing to him, in this exact same position, only weeks ago, but this time he was letting me do it on my own. I was about to remove my hand and let him guide me as he had done before, when he pulled out of my mouth and pulled my hair, wanting me to stand. *Shit, this was hot.* He took my hand once I was on my feet and led me to the living room.

Before I knew what was happening, I was thrown over the couch and he was at my entrance. "I have wanted you so bad these past few days," he whispered behind me, his voice was soft and smooth once again. His fingers ran the length of my back while my ass was arched up in front of him. He trailed a finger down my ass and when it got *there,* he pushed with just the tiniest amount of pressure. I scrambled to get up and away. I had done a lot of things in my life, but that was not one of them. First, it freaked me the hell out. Second, it just wasn't natural, and I forgot the third when his finger moved to my clit, rubbing small circles over it.

"Tell me whose this is, Dallas," he said stroking me.

"Yours," I answered through a moan. *Fuck, I loved it when he said that.* He slipped his finger inside of me and began moving it in and out with ease.

"Who does your body belong to, Dallas?"

"You," I managed to say again.

"All of it?" he asked smoothly.

"You, Luke. I belong to you, all of me," I said pushing back against his finger.

He could move just a little faster. He removed his finger and trailed it back up to the forbidden place on my body. His large hand was in the middle of my back keeping me pinned down so that I couldn't move. "Don't move, Dallas, or I will hurt you and I don't want to hurt you." His voice was like sugar to a diabetic or drugs to an addict. *I craved it.* He was hypnotizing me with his voice, and I would have let him fuck me in the ear had he asked.

His finger was slick with my juices but he never put it inside me, just applied pressure to the outside of me, which wasn't that bad, but still mortifying. I was sure that I must have fallen and hit my head because what he was doing actually felt good.

"Put your knees up on the arm of the couch," he said stepping back, away from me.

Shit. This would, for sure, fully expose me. If he hadn't approached me *there*, then I would have been fine with it.

"Now, Dallas," his dark voice demanded. With shaky arms, I leaned up and pulled my knees up so that they were on the arm of the couch and my ass was open for all to see. I buried my face in my hands, embarrassed but totally turned on. "Baby, you have nothing to be ashamed of. You are beautiful. Everything about you is beautiful and to know that there is somewhere that only I have touched you, does something to me. I want to own every inch of you, baby, and I will, but I don't want you to ever feel ashamed or embarrassed about yourself. You're perfect." His words were sincere, but they did absolutely nothing to reassure me.

I wasn't embarrassed of my body. I wasn't ashamed of how I looked; it was just the thought of him wanting to touch me there that had my stomach in knots. I wanted to just say *"my ass is off limits"* but for some reason, I couldn't. Maybe that's what was bothering me. I think I actually wanted this.

Luke grabbed my hips and pulled me back towards him. I turned my face to kiss him as he reached around and grabbed my breasts in his hands, rolling my nipples between his fingers just as I had done. He pulled me off the arm of the couch, and with my back still to him, leaned me over once more and eased inside of me. He moved slowly, waiting for me to become accustomed to him once again, and when I began pushing against him, he picked up speed. He was thrusting in and out of me and all I could do was beg for more.

"Fuck me harder, Luke," I cried.

"Fuck, baby," he responded pushing into me harder and faster. Both of his hands were on my hips as he slammed into me, over and over. I came again and again as he pounded into me. My body was limp, lying across the couch, but I managed to turn my head so that he could hear my pleas.

"Please, don't stop. It feels so good. Please, Luke." He placed his hands on each side of my ass, spreading me open as he ground into me harder. I didn't think it could get any better, but the feeling intensified. He placed his thumb where his finger had been earlier and applied pressure and I came once again. As I did, he slipped a finger inside me, and the feeling was like nothing I had ever experienced. I screamed loudly, my climax coursing through my body. I felt Luke still inside of me as he leaned over and rained kisses down my back. His arms were beside him supporting his weight and he stayed like that, kissing me across my neck and back until his breathing returned to normal.

"You still alive, baby?" Luke asked from behind me. I grunted in response. I didn't think my mouth could form words. Luke laughed. "Shower?" I nodded my head in agreement. "You want me to carry you?" he asked still laughing. Once again, I nodded. He scooped me into his arms and carried my lifeless body into the bathroom.

"When are you leaving?" I asked once we were in the shower and the hot water had somewhat pulled me from fully sated state.

"In the morning. You'll be able to reach me on my phone if you need anything," he said, back in the mood he was in prior to our sexual escapade.

"Can I ask where you're going?" I asked cautiously. I didn't want to push him, but it would be nice to know. I was hoping he would tell me of his own free will, but it didn't look like that was going to happen.

"A chapter from another state has come into our territory. I have some issues with them from years back, and we are going to get a handle on the situation before it gets out of hand." He said the words as if he were reading from a book. He continued to wash his hair with his back to me.

"Are they the red and gray people?" When his body stilled, I had my answer. He turned around and smiled at me.

"Want me to wash your hair?" With that, I knew the subject was closed.

I decided that since Luke would be leaving in the morning, I would spend the rest of the day with him and go home Saturday. I had called Red and invited her and the others to come over. I'm not sure if they were coming because they wanted to or because Luke told them to, but they would be there around noon tomorrow nonetheless.

Red had called all of them for me and assured me that they were all excited about coming. I knew she would lie for them, but I didn't care. I was hoping that this gathering would get me the information that I needed. I had also called Lindsey, who claimed to be ecstatic about seeing me, as if I didn't talk to her every day.

She was doing a great job running the place and I had already notified Maria, in payroll, of her salary increase, which was probably why she was being so nice.

"So, what do you want to do today?" Luke asked during lunch, which consisted of a bowl of canned soup and a peanut butter and jelly sandwich. *He seriously needed some groceries.*

"I would really like to go for a ride, just to get out of the house for a while," I said, slurping up my last bit of soup. I would have to hit the gym hard next week. I had gained back the weight that I had lost and then some.

"On the bike?" Luke asked turning to me.

"Yes, on the bike. I have some jeans in my luggage that I have completely ignored since I have been here."

"You sure you feel up to it?" he asked eyeing me warily. *How hard could it be to sit and ride?*

"Positive. I need some sunshine," I said giving him my winning smile.

"Well, how can I say no to that face?" he said leaning over and kissing my head. "Go get dressed and I'll get this," he said clearing the dishes from the counter.

I hurried to the bedroom to dig out my suitcase that Luke had buried in the closet. Maybe he would take me to the beach or something. I could already feel the sand beneath my toes. I would bring my bikini along just in case. Chances are though, some girl's lingering eyes will cause me to go crazy and I'll have to make Luke put his clothes back on to keep me from slapping someone. I found my suitcase at the back of Luke's closet, on top of some boxes.

Beside my suitcase, I found a small cardboard box with my name written on it. *This must be the paperwork that I brought with me to Tupelo.* I'm not sure why I opened the box. I had already convinced myself that the contents were nothing more than a bunch of file folders, but I opened it anyway. What I found inside, changed mine and Luke's relationship completely.

"Dallas." I heard Luke call from the other room. It sounded as if he was calling to me from across the yard instead of from the kitchen. I sat on the floor of the closet in a daze, holding up photos of me over the past several months; photos that had been taken long before I had met Luke. One of me leaving my job, playing with Neo in the front yard, meeting a client at a restaurant; there were hundreds of them.

Other than the photos, there was the code to get in my gate at home, my birth date, social security number, names of my family members, phone numbers, and two keys-one to my car and one to my home. I never heard Luke walk into the room, but I could sense that he was behind me.

"What are you doing?" he asked angrily. I jerked my head around in shock and met his face. His sinister look took me even more by surprise. *Was he seriously mad at me for finding this?*

"What am *I* doing? Well, it looks like I'm taking a trip down memory lane. Please, tell me this is an amnesia box that I gave you permission to put together while I was out of it," I said venomously.

"It's none of your business. I don't appreciate you snooping through my house."

"None of my business?! Are you fucking kidding me? The photos are of me! This is my personal information!" I screamed. My body was shaking with rage. Luke was about to see why I was so hated. I was on my feet and in his face before he could speak. "Why the fuck do you have this?" I yelled at him through gritted teeth.

"Why are you going through my shit?" he yelled back. *Why was he so pissed about me finding it*? It was me who had the right to be angry.

"It's my shit!" I screamed back at him. "Now tell me what you are doing with it!"

"I'm not telling you a fucking thing. I trusted you to stay in my house and you do this? I would never invade your privacy like that, Dallas," he said trying to regain his composure and failing miserably.

"What the fuck are you talking about? I damn sure didn't go digging for it! It practically fell into my lap!" I was confused. He had placed my suitcase right next to it. I figured he wanted me to find it, and if he didn't, maybe he should have been a little more careful.

"You're a fucking liar," he said to me, sounding like he was trying to convince himself more than he was me. I stumbled back at his comment like he had slapped me.

"I can't believe that you just said that," I said in a barely audible voice.

"Get out of my house," he said with a coldness in his voice that I had never heard. I stood there with my heart broken into a million pieces. I didn't care about why he had the photos. I didn't care that the history of my life was scattered all over the floor of his closet. All that mattered to me in that moment was the fact that he no longer wanted me. I wanted to beg him to forgive me. I wanted to tell him that I was not lying and to please, believe me. My heart might have been broken beyond repair, but my pride was still intact.

I knew this was the end for us. I knew that things would never go back to the way they were. Luke had shown his true colors and what had started out as a one night stand between us, had turned into a nightmare. I would leave and he would not see me cry.

I grabbed my suitcase from the floor, leaving the box behind. I didn't even want to look at it. I made it to the kitchen, still hoping for him to call my name, but he never did. Grabbing my keys and my cell phone off of the counter, I walked out of his house and shut the door behind me. *I was losing the greatest thing that I had ever had.*

Chapter 24

I was on the highway before the first tear fell, and then like a tsunami, they overtook me, soaking my shirt and blurring my vision. The sobs were so strong that I could barely breathe. I was confused and hurt and I had no idea what the fuck was going on. I screamed at the windshield and banged my fist on the steering wheel, but nothing seemed to help. He had kicked me out of his house and out of his life, yet he held a box full of information about me that was gathered long before we were together. *Why did he have it? What could he possibly gain by having it?*

My phone rang, interrupting my thoughts. It was Red. I answered immediately, planning to cuss her out for lying to me, but instead I sobbed in her ear.

"Dallas, just calm down and tell me what happened," she said soothingly. I felt a little better, just at the sound of her voice. *How did she do that?*

"D-did you talk to L-Luke?" I stammered between sobs.

"Yes, all he said was that he found you going through his stuff and told you to leave."

"I-I didn't go through his s-stuff, Red. I swear! I w-was just looking for my suitcase and th-there was a box sitting beside it with my name on it. I thought it w-was my paperwork that I took t-to Tupelo." *What the hell was Luke hiding that he was so worried about me finding anyway?*

"So, you didn't go downstairs?" she asked surprised.

"What? No, I didn't even know he had a downstairs," I answered. *So Luke did have a secret room.*

"Okay, honey, just calm down, this is all just a misunderstanding, that's all." *Okay, now, I was mad.*

"A misunderstanding? He had pictures of me, Red! And he had my personal information, like my fucking social security number! If anyone deserves to be angry, it's me!"

"So, you still don't know, do you?" Red asked, but I could tell the question was not meant to be spoken out loud.

"Know what? Red, I swear to God, I will beat your fucking brains in if you don't tell me what the fuck is going on, right now!" I screamed. "If he wants to keep his club secrets then that's fine, but I'll be damned if he keeps shit about me, from me."

"Dallas, I'm not at liberty to tell you anything. Mostly because I don't know the whole story, but

I promise that I will tell Luke to call you," she said defeated.

Luke was going to jump her ass for letting it slip. *Oh well, serves her right for being an accomplice.*

"I don't need you to do anything for me. I can talk to Luke on my own." I hung up before she had a chance to respond. *Fuck her. I didn't need her any more than she needed me.* I dialed Luke's number and silently hoped it would go to voicemail, but of course, he picked up on the second ring.

"Dallas," he said calmly, too calmly.

"Why do you have those pictures of me?" I asked trying to keep myself calm.

"You were not supposed to find those, but since you did, I will tell you- as soon as I get back on Tuesday," he answered stiffly.

"Oh no, you are going to tell me now. I'm not waiting until Tuesday. According to Red, I should have already known."

"Yes, you should have. I was planning to tell you. I just couldn't find the right time. I was going to tell you on Tuesday and show them to you myself, but you beat me to it," he said smoothly. His tone was impassive and I envisioned him sitting on the couch wearing a face that matched it.

"Why did you do this to me?" I choked out. I didn't want him to hear me upset, but I couldn't help it. I needed to know why the only man that I had ever loved chose to kill me inside.

"I never meant for it to go this far." I could hear the emotion seeping into his voice, although he tried to contain it. "I have to go, Dallas," he said clearing his throat. "I'll see you on Tuesday and I'll bring Neo and the things you left with me. I'm sorry things turned out this way."

I wanted to scream at him. I wanted to run my car off the road so that he would come to my rescue. God had given me damsel-in-distress moments ever since I met him, yet when I really needed one, it wasn't there. Luke had saved me numerous times. He had saved me from cowboys and motorcycle gangs and DUI's. But above all, he had saved me from myself. I would thank him one day for what he had done for me, but right now, I just wanted to hate him.

I needed a drink-a strong one. I stopped at Our Place-a small bar that served liquor just off of the highway. I knew I looked a wreck, but I didn't care. I walked inside with my face red and blotchy from my endless crying, wearing nothing but Luke's basketball shorts, a black t-shirt and my flip flops.

The bar was almost empty, which wasn't unusual for seven o'clock on a Friday night. I ordered a shot of Jack from the bartender and threw it back, letting the liquor burn my throat and distract me from the ache in my chest. I motioned for the bartender to keep them coming and before long, the pain was dulled and replaced with a buzz that had me lightheaded.

The jukebox played an endless stream of country music, reminding me of the heartache that had summoned me here. When the tips of my fingers were numb and my speech slurred, I decided it was time to head home. I left the bartender a fat tip to silence the "Do you want me to call you a cab" speech, and stumbled to my car. I sat in the driver's seat looking numbly at the windshield. A movement to my left caught my eye. A motorcycle sat in the shadows of the vacant parking lot next to me. I knew it was probably one of Luke's PROSPECTS and the thought sickened me.

It was almost nine when I pulled out of the parking lot, and I knew that I had drunk too much, but all I wanted was to go home. I tuned to a rock station on the radio and increased the volume to drown out the voice of Luke in my head.

By the grace of God and cold air blasting from the air conditioner, I managed to make it home in one piece. Not seeing Neo when I pulled up, reminded me of Luke. Walking into the library reminded me of Luke and the first time he kissed me. My kitchen and counter and the stool on the end where he sat reminded me of Luke. My bedroom, where I had danced for him, my shower, my radio- everything reminded me of Luke.

I crawled into my bed and shut my eyes trying to think of brown cows and light bread and England; anything to get my mind off of him. But, when I thought of cows, I thought of milk and the gallon we had drank from when he caught me in his Harley room. When I thought of light bread, I thought of the peanut butter and jelly sandwiches that we had shared only hours ago, and when I thought of England, I thought of English which is the language that Luke spoke his lies with. Nothing worked. He was everywhere. At some point, with the help of a bottle of Jack, I managed to doze into a restless slumber.

Chapter 25

Two o'clock. That's what the red lights on the alarm clock next to my bed read when I sat up. Something had woke me; a noise, a loud noise. One I was familiar with, but had no desire to hear, yet my heart skipped a beat at the sound of it. More than one. There were many. I could hear them under my carport, the sound of the loud pipes echoing across the house. I looked back over at my alarm. One minute after two.

At one minute after two, I was making my way to the library to open the carport door and jump into Luke's arms. Two minutes after two. My microwave flashed green numbers that told me either I walked really slow, or my clocks were different. I wanted to document this. I wanted to have it stored in my brain for my grandchildren to know the exact time their grandfather and I reunited with apologies and explanations. Two minutes after two. The large clock that hung on the wall read two minutes after two and the second hand was only at six. Thirty seconds of time remained. I had thirty seconds to make a memory that would be etched in my brain for years to come. I would never get to have that memory.

When the door burst open, it was not Luke whose arms I would run into. It was the arms of the man who had watched me, the man who I had pulled a gun on, the man who wanted to take Luke's life for reasons that I didn't know -- the man with the scar in the red and gray cut.

"Well, look what we have here." The words that left his mouth were menacing, although he wore a smile on his face. Three large men walked in behind him. Each of them wore the same expression-hate. My feet were frozen to the floor of the library. *Maybe I was dreaming. Maybe this wasn't really happening.* "You remember me, don't you, Dallas?" I couldn't speak. I couldn't breathe. I tried to nod my head, but it would not move. "Well, I remember you. Take a good look at me. You are going to remember this face for the rest of your life, although, I'm not sure how long that's going to be."

His words went in one ear and out the other; although they did register and I took his advice. He stood about six feet tall. He had a stocky build with no hair on his face or his head. I didn't remember him being bald the last time that had I seen him. The large scar that ran down his face drew the attention away from everything else. I could tell that at one time, he was a very good looking man. He looked to be in his forties and was covered in tattoos that went from his neck to his fingers, and everywhere in between that wasn't covered in leather.

"You like my scar?" he asked amused. I quickly diverted my eyes to something other than his face. "Oh no, don't look away now. This scar is important to you. Do you know why, Dallas? Because the day that I got it, your fate was sealed."

The evil in his voice was unlike anything I had ever heard. It was full of hate, yet I had never done anything to this man that I could remember. "Get her outside," he said so low that I almost didn't understand him until I was grabbed by my arms and drug out the door.

My adrenaline kicked in and I suddenly remembered how to move. My body thrashed. I kicked and screamed and tried to bite anything that came in contact with me. I managed to get a piece of flesh from someone's arm and I bit down, hard.

"You bitch!" he yelled, letting go of my arm to check his wound. *I could taste the blood and saltiness of his skin on my tongue*. When he let me go, I was so shocked that I had actually hurt him that I froze. He grabbed my arm once again and back handed me with so much force that I fell sideways causing the guy on my left to catch me before I hit the ground. I felt blood trickling down my nose and into my mouth. I could already feel the swelling of my right cheek. My eyes watered as the realization of what was happening set in. *They were going to kill me.*

I put up as much of a fight as I could manage as they dragged me to the barn and flipped on the bright fluorescent light that hung from the ceiling.

"Tie her up," the guy with the scar ordered, throwing a length of rope at them. I struggled harder this time. I screamed for them to stop, but my words fell on deaf ears. I screamed for Luke and the answering response was, "He can't help you now." Another harsh blow landed on the right side of my face, then everything went dark.

Cold water stunned me back into consciousness. I was gasping from the shock of it when I noticed that I was hanging by my arms from the rafters in the barn.

"Wake up, sleeping beauty. I have a story to tell you. I don't like to be interrupted, so Crazy here is going to shut you up with a little something called duct tape." He threw his head back and laughed at his humorless joke.

This man was the one who should be named Crazy. Crazy stepped in front of me and pulled a piece of tape from the roll and placed it over my mouth. I thought that he would tear it off, but instead he wrapped it all the way around my head-twice. I screamed through the tape. I kept saying Luke's name over and over. No one could make out what I was saying, but I couldn't stop screaming for him. My right eye was now swollen shut and the one good nostril I had, limited my breathing, making my chest ache from the lack of oxygen.

"Shut up!" The man with the scar yelled at me. I immediately silenced my incoherent screams at his demand. "There, that's better," he said sweetly. "By the way, my name is Frankie the Cutter. I know you think that I got my name from this scar, but the truth is that I get enjoyment out of cutting people," he said laughing once again.

He must have been on drugs of some sort, because only people in an insane asylum acted like this.

"You sure are pretty, Dallas. I bet you have a smoking hot body. It's hot in here. How about we relieve you of some of your clothes?" He stepped closer and my screams began again. "Hey, hey, hey. No need to get upset. It's not like you're bashful, are you? I promise you, the more you scream the harder you are going to make it on yourself."

His voice was so sickeningly sweet that I would have vomited had my mouth not been taped shut. My throat burned from screaming, but I couldn't stop. I was scared and panicked and my natural reaction was to scream. It was the only defense that I had left. Frankie placed his hands over his ears and began stomping his feet on the ground. "Shut up! Shut up! Shut up!"

Crazy walked up to me and pulled a knife out of his pocket and stuck it to my throat. I stopped screaming, scared to move an inch in fear that he would cut me. "The man said shut up, so I suggest you keep that shit down," he whispered to me like he didn't want Frankie to hear. He slid the knife away from my throat, but before he could put it away; Frankie walked up behind him.

"Cut her clothes off for me, please," he whispered in Crazy's ear loud enough for me to hear. He was back to being calm and sweet, but his eyes were still full of hate. My screams went silent, but I couldn't help but whimper as he shred my clothes from me, leaving me hanging naked in front of them. Tears fell down my cheeks as I looked into the eyes of my intruders. *They were sick-all of them. If they wanted to kill me, why not just get it over with?*

"That's better. Thank you, Crazy. Now, back to my story." He said walking in wide circles in front of me with his hands behind his back. "You are a hard woman to catch. Luke did a very good job of protecting you. Did you know that Luke had been hired to protect you?" he asked, stopping to look at me for an answer. *I stared blankly back at him. Protect me? What did he mean?*

He sighed loudly and walked behind me. I jumped at the feel of his rough hands running down my back. I tried to squirm away from him, but I had nowhere to go. My wrists were already chaffed from the rope and my legs hung in the air giving me no leverage. His hand ran down to my ass, and I screamed when he placed it between my legs. I heard the snap of a knife opening and looked over to see Crazy holding it up and shaking his head. I stopped screaming, but couldn't suppress the whimper as he shoved two fingers inside me roughly.

"When I ask you for an answer, I expect one. Do you understand, bitch?" I nodded my head vigorously as he pulled his fingers from inside me. He walked back around to face me, sucking his fingers, and I had to swallow back the bile that rose in my throat. "Did you know that Luke was hired to protect you?" I shook my head letting him know that I was not informed of that. "Well, he was. He knew I was going to get to you. I tried everything, but you are a hard bitch to catch," he said waving his finger at me. "I tried seducing you with a good looking man, of course he had a little too much to drink and fucked it up, but hey, I tried. You know that's why Luke took you home with him? He found out that I had hired someone and knew if he didn't take you with him that I would eventually get my hands on you that night."

My head was spinning. I didn't want to hear this, but I did. "Then, I said, you know what? Fuck it. I'll just go get that bitch from her job, but no. You already had plans with Luke that night. I figured that I could tag along and see if I could start a scene and lure you away from the crowd, but you surprised me, Dallas! You fought for those stupid cunts that you didn't even know!" He stopped talking and walked up to me. I could feel his hot breath on my chest. He looked up at me with a menacing stare.

"I tried to poison you. Hell, I even paid someone to trash your place, hoping you would come up to Tupelo. But, you know what really pissed me off, Dallas? What really got under my skin?" He looked at me as if expecting an answer. *Not wanting his hands on me again, I shook my head.* "You accused my brother of touching you." My eyes widened at his words. *How did he know that I had accused anybody of that?* "Dennis!" he snapped causing me to jump.

Dennis appeared in front of me. He seemed to be coming down off of whatever it was Frankie was on. His face looked like it had recently been pummeled. The bruising had turned to yellow and purple and his nose was crooked from what I suspected was a break. "See, I sent 'ole Dennis here to get some information from Luke's house. I knew where it was, but I couldn't risk going myself. Dennis found the hidden room and retrieved the information that I requested," he said smiling at Dennis like a proud papa. "But you," he said turning his evil face to me once again, "fucked that up for us when you started talking in your sleep. 'I love you, Luke,'" he said mimicking me. "Fucking idiot. So, what did Dennis do? Well, I'll tell you what he did! He freaked the fuck out!" he said laughing. "You scared the shit out of him, so he tossed the box in the closet and left, but not before breaking a window in the clubhouse to throw Luke off what we were *actually* looking for."

That was why Luke thought that I had found the box. He didn't know why they were there. He thought they were after him.

"Oh, you figuring shit out now, ain't ya?" he asked looking at me. I started to nod, but he cut in. "But you told 'ole Lukey boy that Dennis here touched you, so while you were in Tupelo fighting off what you thought was the flu, Luke was beating the shit out of Dennis! Isn't that fucking crazy?!" he asked grabbing his head and spinning around. "So, since Dennis was accused of it, I figured he might as well do it."

I started shaking my head and whimpering. I knew better than to scream, but I contemplated doing it just so Crazy would cut my throat and put me out of my misery.

"Go ahead, Dennis. Feel those perky tits," he said reaching up and roughly caressing my breasts. I tried to writhe away from him, but it was no use.

From above them, I could see Dennis' excitement rising in his pants. "Don't worry about explaining it to us, man. We are all gonna get a turn. Take your time." *I couldn't take it. I would rather die than let these men touch me.*

I screamed as loud as my hoarse voice would let me. Even though my mouth was duct taped, the sound was enough to travel through and strike a nerve with Frankie.

"Cut the bitch's tongue out!" he screamed at Crazy who looked a little skeptical, but walked towards me, pulling his knife out of the holster. I screamed louder, pulling on the ropes that had cut into my wrists, but I felt no pain.

Out of my one good eye I could see the excitement in Frankie's face. Out of my one good nostril, I smelled the revolting scent of Dennis' breath. Out of my two ears, I could hear my screams and Frankie's laugh. I could hear Dennis' harsh breathing and the sound of Crazy's footsteps, but above all of that, I could hear the rumble of motorcycles.

The realization hit Crazy first. His face fell as his ears perked up, making sure that he had not been mistaken by the sound. He turned to

Frankie whose smile had turned into a grimace. Both men shared a silent moment between each other as they weighed their options.

"Another time, Dennis," Cutter snapped turning and heading for the door. He turned before he got there and gave a chivalrous bow. "Until we meet again, Miss Dallas." He ran out the door with Crazy and Dennis close behind him.

As the door swung open, I could see motorcycles speeding across the yard. When they stopped, I could hear Luke's voice barking orders. "Don't let them get away!" I started screaming and crying at the wonderful sound of my rescuer. My staccato screams sounded nothing like a scream due to the hoarseness of my throat, but I tried anyway.

Luke busted through the door that had swung shut and I cried harder at the sight of him. His face was contorted with worry, disgust, failure and pity, but the one emotion that outshone the others, was love. He ran towards me but even when he was right in front of me, I couldn't stop screaming.

"Shh, baby. I'm here. I'm here." His voice was so soothing and calm that it made me cry harder. He flipped open a pocket knife and rushed it towards my face, causing me to scream and move out of his grasp. I knew he wasn't going to hurt me, but the sight of the knife scared me. I wanted it nowhere near me.

Realization hit him and anger flooded his face before it changed to compassion. He held his hands up, as if trying to coax a wounded animal.

"I'm just going to cut the tape off of you, baby, and let your hands free, okay?" I nodded my head, still crying and whimpering. I looked up to see Regg coming through the door at full speed. When he saw me, he immediately lowered his eyes and slowed. I watched as he removed his cut, and then his t-shirt and walked up to Luke with it.

"Help me, Regg," Luke said with desperation.

"Cut her hands down first," Regg demanded.

Luke cut the ropes that were confining my hands and I fell into Regg's waiting arms. I could feel the blood begin to circulate through my body. My hands had turned purple and were swollen. Luke threw the knife to the floor and carefully grabbed me from Regg's arms. My head lulled back onto his arm and he readjusted, trying to make me more comfortable. I had absolutely no strength left to move.

Regg retrieved the knife and came back over to us. "Alright, Dallas, I'm gonna cut this tape from around your mouth first, and then we will get it out of your hair, but it's tight so I need you to hold really still." I tried to nod my head, but instead I blinked my one good eye.

Regg slipped the tip of the knife under the tape and with one quick movement, pulled it from my mouth. I thought as soon as the tape was off that I would want to suck in a deep breath, but I didn't have the strength to do it. Regg covered me as best as he could with his shirt, then Luke carried me across the yard and into the house. I didn't pick my head up to look and see if the others were still here, but all was quiet when we entered the house, so I assumed that they were not close by.

When we got to the kitchen, Luke sat me down on a barstool and asked for some scissors. *I could hear him talking. I wanted to answer him, but my mind would not function enough for me to tell him anything.* Regg began digging around in drawers while Luke looked at me with pain in his eyes.

"I'm gonna take care of you, baby. I think you're in shock right now, but you will get through it, okay?"

I continued to stare blankly at him. My tears had stopped and I felt like nothing but a blob of blood, guts, and bones. I had no feelings. *I was completely numb.* Regg must have located some scissors, because he and Luke were trying desperately to cut the tape away from my hair, salvaging as much as possible.

"I'm going to bathe her, Regg. Will you see if she has some hot tea or something?" Luke asked. His voice was pleading and fighting for control, but it was slipping.

"Sure thing, brother," Regg answered and began digging through the cabinets in search of tea.

I knew what was going on. I could see the events happening before me, but I couldn't react. It was like I was frozen. Luke scooped me up into his arms once again and took me to my room. He sat me on the bed and walked into the bathroom to begin running water. *I knew that he was only in the next room. I could see his shadow from my bed, but not having him touch me, filled me with panic. If I couldn't see him, then he couldn't see me. I needed him to be with me. He could leave if he chose, later, but not until I knew I was safe.*

Tears poured down my face and harsh sobs shook my body. I tried to call out to him but it came out as a squeak. "Luke! Luke!" He walked back in to see me shuddering, sobbing, and crying. *I wanted to stretch my arms out to him, but they were so sore that they wouldn't go past my waist.*

"I'm here, baby. I'm here. I won't leave you, I swear. Baby, I am so sorry that I wasn't here, but I'm here now and no one is going to touch you. I promise that I will kill anyone who comes within a hundred yards of you," Luke said his own eyes shining with unshed tears. "Come on, baby, let me get you cleaned up."

He picked me up and placed me in the hot water. *I didn't realize how dirty I was, until the water darkened with the dirt from my body. Mud and dirt caked my legs and feet. My fingernails were dirty and torn from clawing at their skin. My wrists were chaffed and bleeding in some spots, but what made me feel the dirtiest was where their hands had touched my body.*

I began to scrub my breasts with my hands, trying to erase the feel of their touch. Luke watched me intently. Understanding my movements, he leaned up and let the dirty water out. He adjusted the running water once again and yelled for Regg, causing me to jump. "What you need, man?" Regg asked from the door. He turned so his back was to us when he saw that I was in the tub.

"Can you grab me a big plastic cup?" "Yeah man, be right back." Luke turned back to me and swallowed loudly. "Baby, did they touch you?" he managed to choke out.

My answer was another sob and my head in my hands.

Luke gently pulled my head to his chest and held me while I cried. "It's okay, baby. It's okay," Luke soothed.

Regg walked back in and discreetly handed Luke a cup, then disappeared. Luke was on his knees beside me at the tub. He began rinsing my body while I kept my head on his chest. He gently pushed me off of him and gently bathed me. He wiped my face, being careful around my swollen eye and mouth, and then continued until I was clean. I noticed how he paused while bathing my most sensitive areas, but I never moved. I just stared like a zombie straight ahead.

Once I was clean, he dried me as much as possible in the tub, and then lifted me. My limp body was not helping him, but he managed to dry me completely. When he sat me on the bed and went to leave to find me some clothes, my hands gripped his shirt with just enough force to stop him.

"I'm just going to get you some clothes, baby. I'm not leaving."

I shook my head in response, not letting go of him. He nodded knowingly and picked me up like a child, wrapping my legs around his waist and my arms around his neck. I laid my head on his shoulder while he walked with me latched around him into my closet to get me some clothes.

"Will you sit here for me and let me dress you?" he asked as if he was talking to a small child.

I nodded in agreement and he sat me in the chair at my vanity table, then dressed me in some panties and a sleeveless satin nightgown that fell to just above my knees.

"You look so beautiful in satin, but I prefer you in my black t-shirts," he said smirking.

I wanted to smile at his comment, but I couldn't. Once I was dressed, he carried me out and place my on my bed. I kept a hold on his hand while he undressed. He wore shorts under his jeans and I wondered if it was because he dressed in a hurry. It was difficult for him to undress while holding one of my hands, but he never complained. He slid me over to the middle of the bed then crawled under the covers behind me, pulling my back to his stomach.

"I know this is a stupid question, baby, but are you okay? I mean, do I need to take you to a doctor or call someone?" I shook my head and closed my eyes. *I was safe. I was in Luke's arms and he would not let anyone hurt me. Regg was in my kitchen and he would not let anyone hurt Luke. The club was close and they would look out for one another and us. It would take some time, but everything would be okay.*

Before I fell asleep, I thanked God for everything he had given me. I asked him to forgive me for blaming him when my parents died, and for selfish reasons only, I prayed for Luke to never leave me.

I'm looking down and I see big red feet, a clown's feet. They are large and at the top of them sit leather chaps. I raise my face to see that the chaps have been painted blue, red and yellow; the colors of a clown.

The clown is dancing, moving his feet from side to side as if he is stepping on hot coals. He doesn't wear a shirt, only a vest-a leather vest with orange patches. Luke is dressed like a clown. I smile as I raise my eyes to meet his blues ones, but they are black and belong to a face that has a big scar across it. I scream.

"Shh, baby. It's just a dream. I'm here, Dallas, I'm here." Luke was rocking me, holding my sweaty body close to his and whispering reassurances in my ear. I turn over and sob into his chest. "I got you, baby. You are safe. No one is going to hurt you. I swear on my life. I love you, Dallas." *That's all I needed to hear.*

Chapter 26

I opened my eyes and found myself in my bed. Luke's arms snaked around me. *I'm not hanging from the rafters in the barn.* I couldn't see if it's daylight or not because my right eye is still swollen shut. I tried to swallow but my throat was on fire.

"Luke," I whisper. His eyes immediately flash open. They're still ocean blue, but are outlined in red and they're blood shot.

"You okay?" he asks, his voice full of sleep and concern. "Do you have something to drink?" I whisper to him hoarsely.

"I can get you something," he said moving to get up.

"Don't leave me," I said louder this time.

"Regg!" Luke called. Within seconds, Regg is at the door. He was freshly showered, dressed and looked like he has been up for hours.

"What ya need, brother?"

"Will you bring Dallas some ice water and orange juice, please?" Luke asked looking at me.

"Absolutely." Regg left and I turned my attention back to Luke.

"How you feeling this morning?" he asked moving my hair from my face and tucking it behind my ear.

"I'm scared, Luke," I admit. *I was scared of Frankie, Crazy and Dennis, but most of all; I was scared of Luke leaving me. Our whole relationship had been a lie. What if he didn't feel like he said he did?*

"I know, baby, but you're safe. We won't let anything happen to you." Regg came back carrying a tray with juice and water. I sat up in bed, then feeling exposed, I quickly covered myself. Regg was gracious enough not to comment, he just turned and left. Luke handed me the glass of water and I drained it without stopping.

"Juice?" he asked sitting up beside me. I nodded my head and he handed me the glass. I managed to get down about half of it down before handing it back to Luke. I scrambled out of bed and walked to the bathroom. I was about to make my way inside when I realized that there were cabinets in there that people could hide under. The shower curtain was closed and I couldn't see behind it. I started to breathe heavier. I placed my hands on the doorframe trying to steady myself, but before I could control it, I was hyperventilating. Luke was with me in an instant.

"Just breathe, baby," he said from behind me. He placed his hands on each side of my waist and held me until I regained my composure. "Come on," he said taking my hand and leading me into the bathroom. I never let go, even as I sat on the toilet to pee. He held my hand the entire time that I washed my face and brushed my teeth. I knew I was being a little over the top, but anytime he wasn't touching me, I panicked. I pulled him back to the bed and slid under the covers. He never hesitated as he laid down beside me and pulled me back to him, never letting go of my hand.

I wanted to talk. I wanted to get this out there and off of my chest, but I knew that I wasn't ready for it. But there was one thing that I *had* to know.

"Will you leave me?" I asked him. I was facing the wall so I couldn't see his face, but I knew he would tell me the truth.

"No, baby. I'm here forever, if you will have me. I love you. I have never lied about my feelings for you." I nodded my head, then closed my eyes letting sleep take me once again.

Chapter 27

When I woke, it was storming outside. The lightning and thunder were loud and competing with the sound of the hard rain hitting the metal roof. I glanced at the clock and saw that it was six-thirty in the evening, and my hand was empty. I turned over in bed to see the spot where Luke had laid was empty. I looked around the room and no one was there. *They were under the bed.*

I sat up and closed my eyes counting to ten and telling myself that I was overreacting. I could hear voices from the living room. They were mumbled, but audible. *Who was it? Our guys or the other guys?* I couldn't breathe. *It was happening again.* My chest constricted and all I could see was Frankie the Cutter dancing around me and placing his hands on me. My heart beat so hard that I was sure they could hear it in the other room. I decided the safest place at this point was under the covers. I dove back under the covers, pulling the blankets up over my head and tried to control my breathing.

"Dallas? Baby, you okay?" *It was Luke. He was in the room, but I was too scared to look.* "Hey," he said softly pulling the covers back from over my face. My body was shaking and I had broken out in a cold sweat. "Shit, baby, I'm sorry. I just went to the kitchen to grab something to drink. I'm here." He climbed in beside me and took my hand bringing it to his lips.

"Promise me you w-will take me with you next time," I demanded still shaking.

"I promise, baby. I won't leave your side," he said without hesitation. "You hungry?" My stomach growled on cue. *I was starving.*

"Yes."

"Well, come on and I'll feed you," he said smiling and piecing my heart back together.

"I need some clothes and the bathroom," I said looking at him trying to express my need for patience.

"Okay baby, whatever you need." He started to stand and I pulled his hand back. He looked at me expectantly; ready to jump at my every command.

"I'm not crazy, Luke," I said shamefully and not very convincingly. He pulled me onto his lap and softly ran his hand down the good side of my face.

"I know you're not crazy. You have every right to be upset right now. This will take time, but I'm here for you." He leaned forward and when his lips were an inch from mine, he paused looking into my eyes, searching for permission. I leaned into his kiss. Luke had kissed me many different ways. *I can always decipher what mood he's in when he does it.* This time, there was nothing but love. This man cared for me and I knew it. He would go to the ends of the Earth for me. I felt it in my heart.

He had a lot of explaining to do, and a lot of holes to fill in, but there was no doubt in my mind that he loved me.

"I love you, Dallas Knox. I will tell you everything, whenever you're ready." I smiled my best smile. *The one he loved. The one that he compared to Christmas morning.*

"Okay, but you have to feed me first."

I was dressed and ready to face the day. I had a lot weighing on my brain, but my plan was to take it one day, one story, and one step at a time. Luke held my hand, as promised, when we walked to the kitchen. I stopped in my tracks when I saw that my living room and kitchen were filled with people. Every club member and 'ol lady was there for me. They all stood and took turns hugging me and telling me that they loved me.

Even Lindsey was there. Maddie was sitting in the corner of the room. She didn't stand to hug me, but gave me a small smile. I knew she didn't want to be here. I smiled weakly back at her, then looked around the room at my family. These people loved me. They were willing to fight and put their lives on the line, just for me. I had stumbled through life thinking that the best things could be bought with money. I had put relationships, families, and friends on a back burner just to climb the ladder of success. I was a different person now. I had a family that loved me, a best friend that was irreplaceable, and a man who I would give my very own life for. I had prayed for a damsel-in-distress moment once. Little did I know, that one defining moment in my life, saved me from myself.

Saving Dallas-Making the Cut
Now available on Amazon

About the Author

Kim Jones is a writer with big dreams and a creative imagination. Her infatuation with the MC lifestyle inspired her to write a short story about a love affair between a prestigious young woman and a bad-ass biker. After falling in love with her characters, she turned the ten-thousand word short story into a novel. Juggling her full time job as a payroll clerk, her writing, and her role as ol'lady to her husband, Reggie, the novel was completed in March, 2013.

Kim resides in Collins, MS with her husband and two dogs. She plans to write two more books in the Saving Dallas series and release them in 2013.

https://twitter.com/authorkimjones
https://www.facebook.com/kimjonesbooks
www.kimjonesbooks.com

Acknowledgements

To my wonderful friends-Misty, Amy, Lindsey and Cassie, who read my book and convinced me it was good enough to sell. I never could have made it without yall. To my wonderful husband-I love you, baby! Thank you for being so supportive. I promise to cook more in the future. To my Twisted Family-your encouragement, knowledge, and support means more to me than you will ever know. To my MC friends and family-Your lifestyle has inspired me. Thank-you for your continued love and support. To my Jordan, Jones, and McQueen family and friends-thank-you for putting up with me. Without mama's fried chicken, daddy's promise of Easter baskets, Monkey's brutal honesty, Jay's great love stories, Kevin's reassurance, Jen's rich dreams, and Christian and Danny's patience for my continued tardiness; I would be lost. To Paul Kirkley and his hot body, and Carolyn Bolivar's photography-You are wonderful. To my readers, friends, colleagues, co-workers, and enemies...Thank-you Thank-you Thank you.

Made in the USA
Lexington, KY
09 October 2013